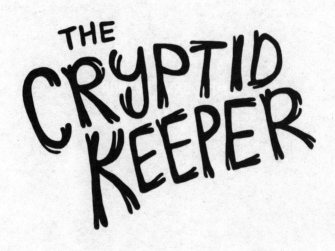

Lija Fisher

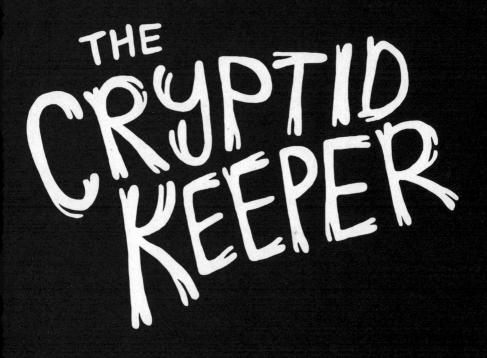

THE CRYPTID KEEPER

Farrar Straus Giroux
New York

Farrar Straus Giroux Books for Young Readers
An imprint of Macmillan Publishing Group, LLC
120 Broadway, New York, NY 10271

Copyright © 2019 by Lija Fisher
All rights reserved
Printed in the United States of America by
LSC Communications, Harrisonburg, Virginia
Designed by Aimee Fleck
First edition, 2019

1   3   5   7   9   10   8   6   4   2

mackids.com

Library of Congress Cataloging-in-Publication Data

Names: Fisher, Lija, author.
Title: The cryptid keeper / Lija Fisher.
Description: First edition. | New York : Farrar Straus Giroux, 2019. | Sequel
to: The cryptid catcher. | Summary: As thirteen-year-old Clivo Wren
continues to search for the immortal cryptid, he finds that not only is
the resistance getting more dangerous, so are the cryptids.
Identifiers: LCCN 2018028221 | ISBN 9780374305567 (hardcover)
Subjects: | CYAC: Animals, Mythical—Fiction. | Secret societies—Fiction. |
Adventure and adventurers—Fiction.
Classification: LCC PZ7.1.F5684 Cv 2019 | DDC [Fic]—dc23
LC record available at https://lccn.loc.gov/2018028221

Our books may be purchased in bulk for promotional, educational, or
business use. Please contact your local bookseller or the Macmillan Corporate
and Premium Sales Department at (800) 221-7945 ext. 5442 or by email at
MacmillanSpecialMarkets@macmillan.com.

To those who believe that when adventure knocks,
they don't just open the door.
They fling it wide open and say,
"Hold on, let me grab my sword."

1

Clivo Wren sat crouched in the dry yellow grass, a tranquilizer gun on his lap, peering through binoculars at the stream meandering through the boreal forest. A frigid breeze blew, and he wrapped his fur parka tighter around him. *Dang, it's freezing,* he thought. It was the beginning of summer, but apparently the warmth wouldn't hit northern Russia until much later. Why did every legendary creature he stalked have to live in the cold? There must be one by a beach somewhere that he could track in comfort from under a palm tree while drinking from coconuts.

Clivo gagged as he nibbled on some fish he'd caught and cooked the night before, then reminded himself to pack more food for his future quests. He'd been camping along the river for five days now, and his food had already run out, leaving him to survive on the plentiful trout from the river. He had considered snaring a hare for some variety, but had forgotten to bring anything to build a trap with, and he certainly didn't want to waste another of his tranquilizer darts. He'd already used one on a black bear who'd wandered near his tent two nights before, leaving him with just two darts. He would have hated to ruin this catch because he'd wasted all his darts on other wandering wildlife.

He pulled a notebook from his backpack and made a list of things he needed to improve his hunts in the future: More food, more darts, more beaches.

Clivo sighed and looked through his binoculars again at the dam of sticks and twigs blocking the river. It was the third one he'd built to bait his prey, and if he didn't find the creature soon, he knew he'd have to move to a different spot and build another one, which sounded like a miserable prospect. He was ready to go home and eat a hearty meal of something that didn't have scales. A hot bath didn't sound so bad, either, since he was freezing and beginning to stink like fish.

A loud crackle suddenly sounded from his ham radio and broke the stillness of the scene. "Dude! What's taking you so long?!"

Clivo scrambled for the radio in his pocket as other voices also shouted through it.

"Charles! Be quiet! We're not supposed to bother him unless it's an emergency!"

"But this is taking *forever*, Amelia! How hard can it be to find the Ugly Merman?"

"Dude, it's called the Vodyanoy. Use its proper Russian name and give it some respect!"

"Whatever, Adam. 'Ugly Merman' is so much cooler!"

"It so isn't!"

"Yes it is! No! Give me back the radio! I'm the one talking!"

Clivo finally managed to pull the radio out of his thick parka and spoke in a harsh whisper. "Do you guys mind being a little quieter?"

"Oh, hey, dude!" Charles replied chirpily. "How's the Arctic?"

"It's freezing! And I'm tired of chopping down pine trees to build dams with. You sure they're supposed to attract the Merman?" Clivo ran a gloved hand under his nose, which was dripping like a faucet.

"Pretty sure, Clivo." Now it was Stephanie's voice coming through the radio. "It hates anything that obstructs the flow of water. Satellite images show no dams along that stretch of river, whereas the rest of the river is covered with them."

"You sure you're in the right place, dude?" Adam piped in. "You do know how to read a compass, right?"

Clivo rolled his eyes. "Yeah, I know how to read a compass. I'm in the right spot, but you gave me, like, five miles of river to cover, so it took a little while."

"Hi, Clivo," Hernando's meek voice whispered through the radio.

"Well, hurry up, dude!" Charles whined. "I wanna see what the Ugly Merman really looks like!"

"It's called the Vodyanoy, man!" Adam yelled.

"Okay, guys, can you only contact me in case of emergencies, please? I'm kinda trying to stay hidden here," Clivo begged.

"Sorry, dude," Adam said.

"Dude, sorry," Charles agreed.

The radio thankfully went silent, and Clivo pocketed it. The Myth Blasters were an amazing team to work with, and they were always right on with their research on where exactly to find legendary creatures—cryptids—that shouldn't exist. But they were still new to the idea that cryptids actually *did* exist, as he was, so their excitement often got the best of them.

Clivo peered through the binoculars again and scanned the river. The sun was beginning to set, and soon it'd be time to return to his tent and build a fire. He was already dreading his evening meal of more cooked fish.

He tried not to be too hard on himself for coming totally unprepared, seeing as how it was only his fifth catch. Becoming an orphan and then discovering his dad was a cryptid catcher who was searching for the one special beast that could make humans immortal would have been a lot for any kid to handle. Finding out that his dad had secretly been training Clivo all his life to take over as the world's best catcher—which also included fighting off the bad guys—had almost sent him over the edge.

But Clivo eventually discovered that he was more than willing to face the dangers posed by the evil ones to find the immortal. After battling with two Luxembourgers who were dangerous but quite dumb, he knew he had to protect the world from the evil resistance, which sought to use the gift of eternal life for its own gain. He also wanted to protect the cryptids, which were beautiful, mysterious creatures that others sought to lock up in zoos or sell to science if they were ever found.

Clivo thought of Nessie, the Loch Ness Monster, and the Otterman—his first two catches. Neither had turned out to be the immortal, but he'd gotten to see them up close and even touch them, which had been like stepping into a wonderland. Nessie had been very sweet for a massive dinosaur that had been frozen for over sixty-five million years. The Otterman had seemed dangerous at first, with its razor-sharp teeth and claws, but ended up being rather polite and enjoyed eating chocolate much more than human flesh. The horrible thought of these majestic animals being experimented on in labs made Clivo's task of protecting them feel that much more pressing.

Clivo focused his thoughts back on the present and tried to think through the details in the crypto-research manual Adam had prepared for him on the Ugly Merman. The Vodyanoy was a water creature from Russia who'd been sighted since the 1800s. Local folklorists claimed it was a frog-faced naked man who enjoyed playing a game of cards while smoking a wooden pipe, and who occasionally partook in drowning the locals. But Adam's origin theory was that the Merman was actually a harmless Siberian salamander that had undergone a genetic mutation during a particularly strong solar flare and grown to humongous proportions.

Clivo had been relieved by the "harmless" part. Being chased by the Otterman had made him realize that he much preferred catching cryptids that didn't want to rip his face off.

He was just about to call it a night when a loud *crack* sounded. He raised his binoculars and instantly saw the source of the noise—a wart-covered frog the size of a baby elephant was wading in the river and powerfully tearing apart the dam.

One thing was for sure—the Ugly Merman sure was ugly.

"Wow, you really do hate dams, don't you?" Clivo whispered, excited that his time in the Arctic was finally coming to an end.

He grabbed his tranquilizer gun, figuring it should only take one dart to hit the creature since it was so round and bloated. He moved as silently as possible through the tall, dry grass, knowing that if he spooked the Merman it could disappear for days in the freezing-cold water.

When he was finally close enough, he raised his gun and took careful aim, feeling confident that he could easily hit his target. But just as his finger began pressing against the trigger, his radio crackled back to life, disturbing his focus.

"Charles! Give me the radio! Let him do his job!" Amelia yelled.

"I just want to ask him something!" Charles replied.

Clivo flicked his eyes back to the Ugly Merman, which had lifted its head and was staring directly at him, its frog-like face looking very angry.

Clivo fired.

The dart was on target, but suddenly a red tongue at least six feet long whipped out of the monster's mouth and knocked the dart harmlessly into the water.

"Come on!" Clivo mumbled.

His cover blown, he quickly stood up from his place of camouflage and fitted another dart into the gun just as a large log went flying past his head. "What the—?"

He looked up as the creature's enormous and extremely powerful tongue wrapped around a boulder and flung it with ease straight toward him. Clivo barely had enough time to duck and roll before the rock smashed into the ground right where he had just been standing.

"I thought you were supposed to be harmless!" Clivo yelled.

The creature kept attacking Clivo with a constant barrage of projectiles, croaking like a frog all the while. Clivo was so busy scurrying away from the logs and rocks flying at him that he didn't have time to raise his gun.

"All right, buddy, this is getting ridiculous!" Clivo complained as a fish whacked him right in the forehead.

He gripped his gun and rolled down the hill just as the Ugly Merman wrapped its tongue around another rock. Clivo sprang to one knee and fired.

The dart made a smacking sound as it hit the giant frog right in its blubbery belly. The creature let out a mournful croak, its short limbs pawing at the air, before slipping into unconsciousness with its gigantic tongue splayed out on the ground.

Clivo waited a good few minutes before approaching the creature to make sure it was completely passed out. He was pretty sure the lasso-like tongue could easily pick him up and throw him halfway to the North Pole.

When he was certain he wasn't in any danger, he knelt by the creature and pressed the blood sampler to its skin, keeping his eyes on the tongue the whole time.

As the blood traveled up the sampler's chamber, Clivo admired the creature with fascination, as he always did with the cryptids he caught. It looked nothing like a merman, but it sure was unique. It had a bulbous, slimy green body with a broad, flat face and large, protruding eyes. It snored loudly, and its breath smelled like the inside of a sardine can that's been left out in the sun for a few hours.

There was really nothing beautiful about this creature, except for the fact that it was a two-hundred-year-old mysterious animal that was supposed to exist only in imagination and folklore. Clivo patted the slimy skin and smiled. He would do everything in his power to keep it safe from nefarious people who sought to capture and cage it.

The blood sampler finally beeped and Clivo blew air through his lips in disappointment.

NOT IMMORTAL.

Well, apparently this wasn't going to be his last catch after all.

He took a selfie with the creature to show to the Myth Blasters and gathered his things to leave. A hot shower sure was going to feel good.

To be sure some wayward fisherman didn't come across the beast while it was still unconscious, Clivo waited at a distance on the hill until the creature woke up and slid into the water. Then, as Clivo was about to leave, something in the distance caught his eye—a glint of light he hadn't seen before. He knew there was nothing in that direction except more expansive wilderness of yellow grass and pine trees, so who was out there?

It was too late in the day for someone to be out hunting— unless, Clivo realized with a shudder, he was the prey. There were evil groups out there who were not only after the immortal, but also after *him*. He was known as the best catcher in the world, thanks to his father's training and help from the Myth Blasters, and the bad guys were eager to know his secrets. So he stayed on his toes, always making sure he wasn't followed or tracked. He had no desire to be thrown into a dungeon and tortured for information.

Clivo quickly packed up his camp and made the long trek back to the small nearby village, constantly glancing behind him for some sign that he was being followed. His dad had been killed by a fellow cryptid catcher, though which one, Clivo didn't know.

But the one thing he knew for certain was that that person was coming for him next.

II

Two days, three countries, and four airports later,
Clivo finally hailed a taxi and arrived at his home in the
Rocky Mountains, outside of Old Colorado City. The snow
from winter had melted and the aspen trees were sprouting
green leaves that shimmered in the breeze. His cozy craftsman-
style home was tucked away in the pine trees. Curious sculp-
tures and mementos from his dad's world travels littered the
lawn, causing the taxi driver to lift an eyebrow in surprise at
the interesting scene.

Clivo entered the house and was instantly attacked by
Aunt Pearl's two long-haired cats.

"Okay, guys, that's enough, it's good to see you, too,"
Clivo said, trying to shake Julio Iglesias and Ricky Martin
off his leg.

"You back, sweetie?" Aunt Pearl called from the kitchen,
the sound of banging pots and pans echoing down the hall.

"Hi, Aunt Pearl," Clivo said, knocking on Bernie, the
suit of armor in the foyer, in a ritual he always did for good
luck. The inside of the house was also filled with treasures

from his dad's trips: a zebra's head hung on the wall (from which Aunt Pearl had hung a WELCOME sign), a didgeridoo stood in a corner, and a brass incense burner dangled from the ceiling on a chain. Clivo reminded himself to start collecting souvenirs from his trips, as well, to add to the museum-like feeling of the home.

Clivo entered the kitchen as Aunt Pearl pulled what smelled like peanut butter cookies from the oven. Pearl was tall and thin like a stork and had a beak-like nose, but ever since she had admitted to Clivo that she spent more time salsa dancing than at church, she had quit wearing her conservative drab clothes and fully embraced colorful tops and flowy skirts.

"Welcome home, sweetie. How was your thing?" Aunt Pearl asked, a bit of flour dotting her pointed nose. She kissed Clivo's dimpled cheek and ruffled his shaggy brown hair with her fingers.

"Oh, the math camp went really well. I learned all about the different kinds of triangles—you know, acute, obtuse, isosceles . . ."

"That's great, sweetie. Can you please hand me the spatula?" Aunt Pearl asked absentmindedly.

"It's in your hand, Aunt Pearl," Clivo pointed out.

"Huh? Oh! Silly me, I'd lose my head if it wasn't attached!" Aunt Pearl giggled.

Clivo had had to come up with believable reasons why he kept leaving for days at a time. His dad had used the cover story that he was an archaeologist traveling the world for digs, but obviously that reason wouldn't work for a kid. So he simply told Pearl he was attending various science and math camps, which she was pleased to hear about. Ever since Clivo had turned thirteen, she was terrified that he was going to start exhibiting horrible teenager traits, like lighting things on fire or stealing cars. But hearing that he was supposedly turning into a studious nerd made her very happy. Little did she know that his "camps" were trips around the world to find an immortal legendary creature.

"Were you okay with my friends while I was away?" Clivo asked, accepting a warm cookie from Aunt Pearl.

Aunt Pearl looked disconcerted. "Oh, they're all very nice, if a tad energetic. I was wary about having a house full of teenagers, but so far they haven't started an underground gambling ring in the basement—have they?"

Clivo laughed. "No, Aunt Pearl, they haven't. And I can't tell you again how much I appreciate you letting my science team stay here for the summer. We're really getting a lot done."

Aunt Pearl fiddled nervously with her fingers. "Oh, you're welcome, sweetie. They're all very nice, but again, they are rather *exuberant*. Perhaps the one with the big teeth should lay off the energy drinks?"

"I'll tell them to keep it down, Aunt Pearl," Clivo said, taking the plate of goodies that his aunt was offering. "Thank you for the cookies!"

"Tell the tall one they're gluten-free!" Aunt Pearl called after him.

Clivo walked down to the basement, where the Myth Blasters had set up their headquarters, and instantly heard the exuberance that Pearl had been talking about.

"Dude, how many times do I have to tell you that banshees don't exist? She's just a spirit from Irish mythology who screams a lot," Adam yelled, his gangly arms swooping through the air like a flamingo.

"I'm just saying that demons and fairies are cryptids, so maybe we need to expand our search into looking for some of those!" Charles yelled back, his curly hair puffier than usual and his buck teeth protruding from between his lips like an angry rabbit's.

"I'm not chasing after fairies!" Adam retorted, his voice rising even more and his thick-framed glasses bouncing on his nose. "Demons, maybe, 'cause they're super manly, but even in that case, I don't think Clivo wants to go after something that'll stab him with a fiery pitchfork!"

"Hey, guys," Clivo said, entering the room and putting down the plate of cookies.

"HEY!" a chorus of five happy voices said in unison.

Clivo winced at the loud shouts.

"Welcome back, dude!" Charles said, hurrying over. "Kinda took you a while this time. You losing your touch or something?"

"Be nice, Charles," Stephanie said, giving Clivo a big

hug, her face blushing its usual shade of pink. Her blond hair was tucked into a ponytail, and a stray wisp tickled Clivo's nose.

"Oh, do we hug now? Is this a thing?" Amelia asked, lifting her round body from a chair to embrace Clivo, her sparkling nose ring standing out against her dark skin. "Oooo, too tight."

"I'm just going to fist-bump you, dude," Adam said, his bony arm reaching out to give Clivo a fist bump.

"I'd like a hug, please," Hernando said quietly. Clivo leaned over to give the short boy a squeeze.

The Myth Blasters lived in Portland, Maine, but at the end of the school year they had all decided that being in the same place for the summer would make it easier to do their cryptid research. It was safer, too. With the evil resistance trying to find Clivo and the immortal, he felt better having the Blasters close by in his secluded mountain home.

After the Blasters had gotten permission from their parents to attend a special "math and science camp in the mountains" for the summer, they'd all arrived on Clivo's doorstep, much to Pearl's concern. On one hand, she was excited that Clivo had nerdy friends to keep him out of trouble, but on the other, she was wary about having so many teenagers in the house because every book she'd read said that the only thing teenagers did was create mischief.

Upon arrival, the Blasters had set up the basement so they could keep up their cryptid research and continue narrowing down which one might be the immortal. After their handiwork, the basement looked like mission control for a group dedicated to finding mythological creatures. Laptops sat on desks, maps covered the walls, and shelves filled with hundreds of books on legends and folklore were crammed into each corner. Tapestries hung from the ceilings, and white Christmas lights blanketed the room in a cozy glow. The only thing missing compared to their previous headquarters was the vast array of candles and lanterns used to light the space. It was the one thing Clivo nixed because an old wooden house surrounded by forest was not a place to play with fire. Instead, he'd bought some fake candles that cast an orange light upon the spooky figurines of cryptids that dotted the space.

Clivo had bought all of the equipment the Blasters asked for with his Diamond Card, down to the equipment Charles used to figure out if photographic evidence of supposed cryptids was fake or not. Clivo normally wasn't allowed to buy such extravagances with the card that had been given to him by his cranky old boss, Douglas Chancery. And Douglas didn't know about the Blasters yet, mainly because Clivo didn't want to give the old man more people to yell at. But Douglas was so impressed with Clivo's catching skills that he allowed Clivo to buy the equipment without question, provided that he promise not to get used to making such expenditures.

The one thing Clivo wasn't allowed to spend money on

was new clothes, which Douglas deemed to be a nonessential item, along with food. So Clivo still wore the ill-fitting ones from Palace of Pants that Pearl bought for him, which led to merciless teasing at school. But Clivo didn't care. Whatever extra money Douglas gave him he wanted to use to help the Blasters.

"So, how'd the catch go?" Stephanie asked when everyone was sitting around a large wooden table that was worn and weathered, like something King Arthur and his Knights of the Round Table would have used.

"Pretty good, except the Ugly Merman was anything but harmless," Clivo reported, scratching his face. "He had this long, disgusting tongue that kept throwing things at me."

Charles clenched his fists with joy. "A weaponized tongue is so awesome!"

Adam grabbed a cookie. "That's weird," he said. "Maybe the cryptids are living so long that they're adapting better protection mechanisms." He eyed the cookie suspiciously. "Are these gluten-free?"

Clivo nodded. "Aunt Pearl is well aware of your dietary restrictions."

"Awesome, gluten makes me bloat," Adam replied, taking a giant bite out of the treat.

"It sounds like you need to be super careful going forward, Clivo," Amelia said, bringing the conversation back on track. "Adam's right; as old as some of these creatures are, who knows how their bodies have adapted."

"Don't worry, I'll be more on my toes from now on," Clivo said, grabbing another cookie. He was still happy to be eating anything that was not fish. "Speaking of which, any idea where my next catch will be?"

"Let's take a look at the map," Adam said, bounding over to a piece of brown parchment paper tacked on the wall like an old pirate treasure map. Pins marked where either Clivo or his dad had found cryptids. Adam grabbed another pin and stuck it in the northwestern part of Russia where Clivo had just found the Ugly Merman. "So," Adam continued, "your dad taught you four foreign languages—Russian, Hindustani, Japanese, and Arabic. We assume those are the places where he wanted you to look for the immortal. You just caught the Merman in Russia. Over Christmas break you found the Japanese Thunder Beast—"

"That guy was awesome," Charles said.

"Having a flying wolf heading straight toward me was actually a bit less than awesome," Clivo corrected.

Charles waved his hand dismissively. "You can take it, dude."

Adam cleared his throat. "As I was *saying*, over spring break you caught the Barmanu, the Bigfoot-like dude in Pakistan, where you spoke Hindustani. So the only language we haven't covered is Arabic."

Amelia tapped her fingers on the table. "I'm still figuring out exactly what region your dialect is from, and once we figure that out we'll locate the nearest cryptid. It shouldn't be more than a few days."

"That's fine," Clivo said, stretching his arms over his head and yawning. "I could use a few days of soaking in a hot bath, anyway."

"And if the next catch isn't the immortal, then we're out of clues," Stephanie said. "We've been doing our best to research which other cryptid it might be, but we haven't come up with much."

"But don't worry, we're on it," Amelia said encouragingly.

"On it," Hernando agreed quietly.

Clivo stifled another yawn. "I don't know whose job is harder, you guys finding the cryptids or me catching them."

Charles snorted. "Dude, we make magic outta nothing."

"You definitely do." Clivo stood up. "If it's okay with you guys, I'm going to shower and go to bed. I still smell like a beached whale."

Charles wrinkled his nose. "I was wondering where that smell was coming from. I thought Adam was trying a new cologne."

"Same as always," Adam said, proudly sniffing his shirt.

"Good night, team," Clivo said.

Clivo dragged his backpack and tired body upstairs to his bedroom, shooing the cats out of the room with a gentle nudge of his foot. He needed a good night's rest without being smothered by furballs.

After a long, hot shower that he could have stayed in forever, he printed out his selfie with the Ugly Merman and grabbed a photo album from its secret hiding place in the back of his closet. He flipped through the photos of his dad's cryptid catches, a smile always on his face and a legendary creature propped up at his feet. Clivo paused on the family photo, the one with him as a baby cradled in his mom's arms and a gunni, a wombat-like creature with antlers, held in his father's. He traced his finger across the photo and let the familiar ache of grief settle in his chest. He had lost his mom to cancer and his dad to a murderous fellow catcher, and Clivo missed them every day. They were the good guys—some of the few— and they had left him the legacy of finding the immortal, a legacy he intended to fulfill.

Clivo flipped a few more pages to his own photos, bright with fresh colors. The look on his face with Nessie always made him laugh—he looked so surprised and shocked to have actually found his first cryptid. He appeared absolutely terrified in the photo with the Otterman, who had chased after him. But with every photo, with each passing catch, Clivo could see that he looked more and more confident.

Clivo turned to a fresh page and secured the Ugly Merman photo to it. He definitely looked rattled from the unexpected battle with the creature's mutant power tongue. But something else in the photo caught his eye, as well. In the background, near a desolate hill, was the light he swore he had seen the evening of his catch. Why was it bothering him so much? Something wasn't sitting right; he just wasn't sure what it was.

A while later, a timid knock sounded on his door, and he opened it to find Stephanie holding a cup full of a steaming liquid. "Sorry to bother you. I thought you'd like some warm milk with cinnamon."

"Oh, thanks, Stephanie. After a week in the Arctic, I still haven't completely thawed out." Clivo gratefully accepted the cup. He took a sip and noticed that Stephanie just stood there, looking uncertain. "What is it? Are you and Amelia okay in your room? Are you comfortable enough? Do you need more blankets or something?"

Stephanie shook her head. "Our room is fine, even though we can hear Charles snoring through the walls. And the boys are okay in their bunk beds next door, despite Adam's complaining about the non-hypoallergenic pillows." She giggled for a moment, but then her face turned serious. "We didn't want to bother you with this 'cause it's probably nothing, but there's something weird going on."

Clivo laughed. "Weirder than finding a merman with an attack tongue?"

Stephanie smiled, but she pulled at a stray piece of hair nervously. Clivo stopped laughing. "Sorry, I didn't mean to make a joke. What's going on?"

Stephanie glanced down the stairs, probably to make sure Pearl wasn't eavesdropping, and slipped inside the room, shutting the door behind her. Clivo pulled out the desk chair for Stephanie to sit on and turned to find her looking through the photo album. She noticed him watching her. "Sorry," she said quickly. "I didn't mean to pry."

"No, it's fine, I should have showed this to you guys a while ago, since you helped my dad find some of the cryptids."

Stephanie continued to flip through the pages, her eyes slowly taking in each creature. "They're incredible, aren't they? Such amazing beings."

"They are," Clivo agreed. "I know we're eager to find the immortal, but discovering these guys along the way has been really special, too."

Stephanie stared in awe at the photo of the blue tiger. "I wish I could see one of them in person. Just once."

Clivo knew the feeling. It really was incredible seeing a legendary creature for the first time. But he didn't want to make her feel like she was missing out on much, so he simply said, "Trust me, when the Barmanu is trying to eat your head, seeing it in photos seems like a much nicer experience."

Stephanie smiled and delicately closed the photo album. "Anyway, like I was saying, it's probably nothing, but for a while now I've noticed something bizarre going on in the crypto chat rooms."

"What do you mean?" Clivo asked, taking a seat on his bed.

Stephanie shifted on the chair and folded her legs beneath

her. "Fellow cryptozoologists always share information about cryptid sightings. They're not all accurate, of course, but most of the time there's a shred of truth to them. As soon as I found out your dad had caught the chupacabras, it struck me that I hadn't heard of any sightings of the creature for a while. So I dug around and couldn't find sightings for other creatures that either you or your dad caught, starting from around when they were caught."

"Which ones?" Clivo asked.

Stephanie's blue eyes flashed with worry. "All of them. All except Nessie, I should say. She's still happily in the loch. But it's like the others just . . . disappeared."

Clivo's chest tightened. He put down the warm milk and leaned forward. "Do you guys have any theories about what's going on?"

Stephanie shook her head. "We really don't know. We're hoping that the creatures just get spooked and go into hiding after their encounters with you. But the Myth Blasters are data people, and the data are showing us that after a cryptid is caught, it's never heard from again."

Clivo exhaled sharply and ran his hand through his shaggy wet hair. "So, what do we do? I know we want to find the immortal, but we also want to protect the other cryptids. What if something I'm doing is somehow hurting them?"

"I know," Stephanie said, frustration furrowing her brow. "We'll keep monitoring to see if some chatter about sightings comes back. Again, it could be nothing. In the meantime, just be alert on your catches. If you see something out of the ordinary, just, I don't know, pay attention."

Clivo thought of the weird light in the distance and the feeling that he was being watched. But there was nothing Stephanie could do about it, and he didn't want to worry her more than necessary. "Thanks, Stephanie. I'm glad you told me. Let's hope it's nothing."

Stephanie stood up to go. She slowly opened the door to see if Pearl was peeping around the corner. "Just be careful out there, Clivo. I'm not sure what's going on, but it gives me goose bumps."

III

The next day was Friday, the night he usually had dinner with his best friend Jerry and Jerry's parents. After Clivo lost his dad, the Coopers had let him move in for a bit while Aunt Pearl was away on an Acapulco salsa-dancing adventure. Spending time with a family in a cozy home, despite the constant pranks that Jerry pulled, had made Clivo feel less alone in the world.

"So how's that math and science camp you've got going on there, son?" Mr. Cooper asked as he scooped up a heaping mound of mashed potatoes. Mr. Cooper was a standard dad, with a paunchy belly and a rumpled white collared shirt that stood out brightly against his dark skin. The only thing un-standard about him was that he was head of the SETL Institute, an organization dedicated to the Search for Extraterrestrial Life in the galaxy.

"Oh, it's going really great, Mr. Cooper. The other kids are super smart, so I'm learning a lot." Clivo dished up some mac and cheese and felt a rush of relief. He'd missed a lot of dinners lately because he was so busy with the Blasters, and he was happy that the Coopers were over their healthy-diet phase and back to eating regular stuff instead of boiled cabbage and raw nuts and berries.

Mrs. Cooper, a turnip-shaped woman who was so pale it looked like she had lived in a cave her whole life, pinched Clivo's dimpled cheek. "Oh, it's nice to hear that you're doing so well, honey. Teenagers can really go off the rails sometimes."

Clivo laughed. "Yeah, Pearl is just waiting for me to start stealing cars or something."

Mr. Cooper cleared his throat and looked meaningfully at Jerry, who raised his eyebrows in mock shock. "I didn't *steal* your car, Dad, I simply tried to *hot-wire* it should I need it in case of an emergency. And I couldn't figure it out anyway, so no harm, no foul."

Jerry had inherited his father's dark skin, but not his father's love of science. Jerry preferred sports, though he kept getting kicked off every team he joined because of his practical jokes. He had already been booted from the summer flag football league for putting itching powder in everybody's jerseys, which had led to his team losing their first game because nobody could stop itching and scratching. Jerry managed to return two punts for touchdowns because nobody else on his team could quit wriggling long enough to run or catch the ball, so he considered the game a victory.

"You ruined the electrical system so the radio only plays country music, Jerry. *Country*," Mr. Cooper pointed out.

Mrs. Cooper shook her head. "You know that twangy music puts your father in a foul mood."

Clivo stifled a laugh. It was always nice spending time with the Coopers, even though they did bicker a bit, because he always felt so welcome in their home. Even Hercules, the droopy-eyed basset hound, was happy to see him, as evidenced by the dog resting his snoring snout right on Clivo's foot. "So, Jerry, since football isn't happening this summer, are you working in your dad's lab again?"

Jerry misbehaved so much that during the school year his dad had finally gotten him a job at the SETL Institute to keep him out of trouble. Jerry had initially claimed it wasn't that cool working there, until he finally fessed up that the institute had indeed found aliens, they'd just kept the information super classified (information that Jerry stole, of course).

It was nice having a best friend who also knew important international secrets.

"I guess," Jerry said, going in for an extra hamburger.

Mrs. Cooper swatted his fork away. "Eat your vegetables first!"

"I'm a growing man, Ma! I need to eat flesh! And who broils broccoli? It's all burnt and crispy and disgusting!"

Mr. Cooper eyed Jerry. "Apologize to your mother, Jerry."

Jerry gave his mom a kiss on the cheek. "Sorry, Ma. Thanks for dinner."

Mrs. Cooper rubbed her son's head. "You are the light of my life. Now eat your broiled broccoli or I'll stuff it in your mouth myself."

"Anyway, getting back to your question, son," Mr. Cooper said to Clivo, and then sighed, adjusting his incredibly large glasses on his face. "Yes, Jerry is back working with me at SETL."

"Yeah, it's cool," Jerry said, wincing as he crunched on the burnt broccoli. "Dad's giving me more responsibility this year besides making him coffee."

"Yeah? What are you doing?" Clivo asked, sneaking his broccoli to Hercules, who had snorted himself awake.

"I get to . . . Wait, can I share this part, Dad? It's not top secret?"

Clivo almost laughed. Even if it *was* top secret, Jerry would share it with him later, anyway.

"Jerry, you know I don't share top secret information with you, so go ahead," Mr. Cooper responded.

Jerry winked at Clivo. Jerry knew plenty of top secret things, mainly because he kept stealing the password to his father's work computer. "Anyway, we have this new machine that analyzes bits of asteroids for living microbes and stuff. You know, to see if there's smaller life besides big green alien people, or whatever aliens look like, floating around out there. I get to label and tag the asteroid samples before the lab tech gets them."

"Just don't contaminate them again!" Mr. Cooper said.

"You were handling the samples with those greasy hands after eating french fries! Wear the gloves! If there were any living microbes on that sample, you probably killed them all, that's for sure."

Clivo paused, his fork over his plate, as a thought came to him. "How do you contaminate something?"

Jerry sighed. "I'm *learning* that anytime you introduce something foreign to a sample, you contaminate it."

"Like with french fries!" Mr. Cooper said. "Before your goof was discovered, half our team was thinking there was a burger joint floating around in space."

Clivo put his fork down, a question forming in his head. Something was happening to the cryptids after he caught them. Was *he* somehow contaminating them? If he was injuring the cryptids, he'd never forgive himself.

"Mr. Cooper, can this machine tell if you're hurting a sample by contaminating it?"

"Oh sure, sure." Mr. Cooper wiped his chin with a napkin. "The machine can tell if life is present, and it can also tell if something that's been introduced to it kills it. Like with *french fries!*"

Jerry threw down his napkin in frustration. "I get it, Pa! I'll wear the gloves! Point received and understood!"

Clivo continued with his line of questioning. "And, let's say you had a drop of, oh, say, blood. Could this machine tell if something contaminates the blood and causes real harm?"

Mr. Cooper pushed his glasses higher up on his nose.

"Well, with blood you really just need an electron microscope to see its cells. These are very interesting questions, son. What is your science group working on up there? You're not hiding a vampire up in the mountains, now, are you?" Mr. Cooper slapped his hand on his knee and let out a guffaw.

Clivo joined him in the laugh. "No, sir. No vampires. Just maybe a contamination problem."

Jerry looked at him with a questioning expression and stood up. "Okay, parents, we're going to retreat to my man cave for a bit before Dad drives Clivo home."

Clivo and Jerry took their plates into the kitchen and then headed upstairs to Jerry's room, with the dog padding after them. Clivo put his hand on the door to open it and was immediately hit by an electric shock.

"Whoa!" Clivo exclaimed, jumping back and shaking his stinging hand.

"Jerry! I told you to dismantle that torture device!" Mrs. Cooper yelled from downstairs.

"Clivo was my last victim, Ma! I promise!" Jerry replied.

Jerry pulled a string that was hanging from the top of the door and safely turned the knob.

"What was *that*?" Clivo asked, still shaking his hand.

Jerry had a wide grin on his face. "You haven't been here in a while, so you haven't seen my improvements. Ma has started snooping through my stuff, so I've set a few booby traps to let her know a man is entitled to some personal space."

"Remind me to never get on your bad side." Clivo gingerly took a seat on the desk chair after first making sure he wasn't going to sit on anything that was going to electrocute his rear end.

Jerry flopped onto his bed, Hercules cradled comfortably in his arms. "So what's this contamination thing you were talking about? Bring me up-to-date with everything."

Clivo scratched his head. "The Myth Blasters have discovered that all the cryptids my dad and I caught have disappeared. I'm just figuring out possible scenarios for what's going on."

Jerry rubbed Hercules's belly. "But aren't the cryptids, you know, *disappeared* already?"

"They're hidden creatures, for sure, but there's still sightings of them. But out of all the cryptids my dad and I have found, only Nessie has been seen since. I hope it's nothing, but I don't have a very good feeling about it." Clivo stood up. "Speaking of which, I should probably get back."

Jerry rolled a snoring Hercules onto the bed and stood up, too. "You just sat down, but okay." Jerry spoke the next part quickly, probably because Clivo was rushing toward the door. "But before you go, I was kinda thinking . . ."

Clivo stopped at the door. "Yeah?"

Jerry stuck his hands in his pockets and looked bashful, which was *not* a common look for him. "Well, I was kinda thinking that maybe I could come up and, you know, help you guys. You're always so busy now with everything, I hardly get to see you."

Clivo pouted his lips and said in baby talk, "Aw, do you miss having me around?"

Jerry punched him on the arm. "Shut up, Wrenmaster! I'm just saying that if you're going to be off saving the world, you're gonna need more than just nerds on your team. And yes, I'm man enough to admit that I miss hanging out. There, you happy?"

Clivo rubbed his arm where Jerry had playfully hit him. He was going to be black and blue from the visit if he didn't get out of there soon. Still, he thought about what Jerry had just said and realized that he really had been ignoring his friend. Sure, he had been involved in important stuff, but what was the point of saving the world if he didn't preserve the friendships that were in it?

Clivo sighed. "I'm sorry, Coops. I know I haven't been around a lot. My mind has just been elsewhere. I'd really like for you to be a part of the team, I just don't really know what you could do."

A flash of hurt crossed Jerry's face. "No, no, I get it. I'm not the smart guy and I can't speak five languages. I can run a football, but that's about it."

Clivo had never seen his confident friend look so disconcerted. Jerry was obviously struggling with where he fit into Clivo's new life with the Blasters. Clivo suddenly remembered something Stephanie had told him the previous fall: *There are many different ways to be smart.*

Clivo looked around the room, wondering how Jerry could possibly fit in with the team. He rubbed his fingers together, still stinging from the electric shock, and a thought struck him. A smile spread across his face as he thought more about it. It was perfect and used all of Jerry's skills. "Actually, now that the Myth Blasters' headquarters is in the house, we could probably use some more security." Jerry lifted his eyes to Clivo's, seeming interested. "I mean, my dad kept the house off the grid so nobody could find us there, but still. It wouldn't hurt to have a few booby traps around."

Jerry's face lit up with excitement. "Booby traps! Oh man, you know I'm the best at booby traps! I will make your house so safe that not even Houdini could break into it!"

Clivo held up his hands before his friend could get ahead of himself. "Okay, but you have to promise to let Pearl and the Blasters know where the traps are. Aunt Pearl can't get suspicious, and the Blasters need to be focusing on finding the immortal, not getting electrocuted."

Jerry's face squinted in disappointment. "That makes it less fun, but okay. I'll keep a master map of all the traps." He bashfully shoved his hands into his pockets again. "Thanks, man. Thanks for bringing me on board. I was worried I had lost you to nerdville."

"Hey, we're the original team, right? We'll always be Wrenmaster and Coops," Clivo assured him.

Jerry smiled, his grin stretching across his face. "Till the end of time, man. Till the end of time."

Mr. Cooper dropped Clivo off at home, and Clivo ran downstairs to the Blasters, who were hard at work, as always.

"Charles, I'm not sending Clivo after the Yeti unless you have some shred of evidence that it might be the immortal," Amelia was saying. "It's too dangerous."

"And too AWESOME!" Charles countered. "How can it *not* be the immortal? It's so wicked!"

"Hey, guys," Clivo said, entering the dimly lit room.

"Hey!" Adam said, kicking his gangly legs off his desk. "How was dinner with what's-his-name?"

"Jerry? It was really good. I actually thought of something regarding the missing cryptids." Clivo had decided he would wait to tell them about Jerry's new role. They had agreed not to add anybody new to their team, but they knew Jerry from when he gave them secret access to a SETL satellite, so hopefully they wouldn't get their undies in a bunch over it. They might make Jerry go through some kind of initiation, but Clivo would worry about that later.

"What did you discover, Clivo?" Stephanie asked, turning away from her computer, where it looked like she had hacked into a satellite and was steering it over a massive sandy desert.

"I was thinking about what every cryptid had in common, apart from being caught by me or my dad," Clivo began.

"They're totally awesome, that's what," Charles said. Amelia shot him a glare to tell him to be quiet. "Sorry, continue."

Clivo spoke slowly, trying to arrange his thoughts. "It's possible that they've all gone into hiding because we scared them. Or—and I really hope this isn't it—what if the tranquilizer I used on them is somehow contaminating them, making them sick? Or worse?"

Amelia twirled her nose ring between her fingers. "It's a solid theory. We know so little about the physiology of the creatures that who knows what could happen when a foreign substance is introduced. Now we just need to prove or disprove it. Any chance you have some cryptid blood lying around here?"

Clivo held up the blood sampler that had been crammed into his backpack since his trip to Russia. "Would a bit of Ugly Merman blood do?"

"Nice!" Amelia said, taking the sampler from Clivo. "Charles, does your magnifier have enough power to see red blood cells?"

Charles went to his workstation, where he pulled out a large microscope. "Not a problem. Just give the doctor a minute, then I'll be ready for the patient."

Charles exchanged a lens in the device for another and

put a glass slide underneath it. He pulled a bright red sweatband from a drawer and put it around his head to pull his frizzy hair away from his eyes. After a few rolls of his neck, he peered through the microscope at the slide. He held out his hand, like a doctor asking for a surgical instrument. "Blood, please."

Amelia rolled her eyes, but unwrapped a sterile eyedropper and extracted a bit of blood from the sampler.

Charles placed the drop on the glass slide and adjusted a few knobs. "Oh, yeah, this baby is kicking. Lots of squirming thingies moving around. Next patient."

Amelia unwrapped another dropper and this time filled it with some liquid from a tranquilizer dart. "Not too much," she said, carefully passing the dropper to Charles. "We don't want to drown it."

"I got it, I got it," Charles said, bringing the eyedropper close to the blood.

"Hang on!" Adam suddenly shouted. Charles paused, his hand above the blood.

Adam ran to a closet, where he pulled out several pairs of goggles. "For all we know, this baby could explode once that tranquilizer touches it."

Everyone put on the goggles, and Hernando casually stepped to the back of the room and hid behind a chair.

Charles continued with his task, though his hand had begun to tremble, and delicately placed a tiny bit of the amber liquid onto the red dot of blood.

Clivo peered over Charles's shoulder as the colors swirled together, but no explosion happened. The liquids blended and melted into each other, the colors mixing together like ink. He was worried the colors would all of a sudden go black or begin smoking, providing proof that he had somehow poisoned the cryptids, and maybe even killed them. But eventually the mixture stopped its movement and became a single still dot on the glass slide.

Charles lifted his head from the instrument and wiped his forehead. "Everything's fine, dude, the red blood cells are still squirming around. You haven't done anything to hurt the creatures."

Clivo exhaled in relief. "Good. Thanks for doing that, guys. I didn't want to tranquilize another cryptid until I knew for sure it wasn't injuring them."

"And perfect timing, too," Amelia said, holding up some pages from a printer. "We've identified your next catch."

"Already?" Clivo asked, amazed. He'd been hoping to have a few more days of rest. "Please tell me it's somewhere warm."

Stephanie pointed to her computer screen, which showed a satellite image of what looked to be pyramids sticking up from a vast desert. "Yep, you could definitely say that."

IV

The next day, Clivo was on a plane waiting to take off for Cairo, Egypt. Actually, it was a plane bound for JFK International Airport in New York City, where he would transfer to a flight to Amsterdam, where he would then catch a flight to the land of the pharaohs. The itinerary alone made him tired, but he was sitting comfortably in first class, sipping from a glass of orange juice. Douglas, his boss, had made him fly coach at first, but now that Clivo had proven himself to be a good cryptid catcher, Douglas had grudgingly allowed him to upgrade his travel, for which Clivo was very grateful. Catching cryptids was hard enough, but being wedged in coach for fourteen hours made the whole experience even more challenging.

Speaking of Douglas, Clivo's satellite phone suddenly rang, its loud torpedo warning shattering the peace of the cabin. Clivo fumbled for the phone and spoke quietly into it. "Hi, Mr. Chancery. Nice to hear from you, as always."

"Where are you headed now?" Douglas growled. Clivo

could just picture the cranky old man with his red, bulbous nose and flyaway mane of gray hair.

"Oh, I'm just about to take off for Cairo," Clivo replied. He knew Douglas tracked all of his expenditures on the Diamond Card he used, so he wasn't surprised that Douglas knew he had bought a plane ticket.

"I hope this is for business, not pleasure," Douglas said, sounding like he was munching on a very crisp potato chip.

"Yeah, right, I'm going all the way to Egypt to work on my tan," Clivo replied.

"Don't get smart with me, kid. Just because you've caught a few cryptids doesn't mean you've lost the potential to be a pain in my rear," Douglas said, crunching away.

Clivo had to smile. Douglas was definitely a grump, but Clivo had come to appreciate his sour quirks. And Douglas was one of the good guys whom Clivo's father had worked with as well. "Is there a reason you're calling, Mr. Chancery?"

Douglas went into a coughing fit, as if he had inhaled a piece of chip. When he could finally speak, his voice was raspy. "I just wanted to make sure you had enough tranquilizer darts. You're running pell-mell all over the place and you must be getting low on supplies."

Clivo thought of the five cryptids he had used darts on, as well as the bear, and also the one they'd used to research if he was contaminating the cryptids. But he didn't want to mention the last two to Douglas, who'd probably accuse him of being wasteful. He also didn't want to mention the fact that the cryptids he'd caught were somehow disappearing. Douglas wanted the creatures protected as much as Clivo did, and he probably wouldn't react well to such news. "Um, I could definitely use some for my next catch. Thanks, Mr. Chancery."

"Fair enough. I'll drop some off when you're back home. Oh, and quit taking taxis every time you come home. I'm not some limousine service. Buy a bike and build some stamina, would you?"

"Should I flap my arms and fly across the ocean or can I still buy airplane tickets?" Clivo asked with a sigh.

"Ha! I should make you swim, but I'm feeling generous. Good luck, kid, and remember . . ."

"Don't mess it up," Clivo said, completing the sentence he knew all too well.

Douglas let out a raspy laugh. "You're not so bad, kid, you know that?"

Clivo was about to respond when he realized Douglas had already hung up.

The plane took off and Clivo settled into his seat, pulling out his printout of the latest crypto-research notes from the Blasters.

Salawa Crypto-Research

Okay, dude (Adam here), this was kind of a rush job since Arabic is spoken in, like, a million countries, and narrowing down which one has the dialect your father trained you in and then narrowing down which cryptids live there and which one *might* be the immortal took FOREVER. Anyway, here we are with the Salawa.

The Salawa is super cool because it's one of the oldest cryptids out there. It's been around since 3100 B.C. That's a long time for a dude to be roaming.

The creature was part of ancient Egyptian mythology as the spirit animal of Seth, who was the god of destruction and chaos. The god of chaos was Seth? What a terrible name. Why not Ace, Blaze, or Argento? Whatever.

Anyway, the Salawa has mainly been sighted near the town of Naqada, where tons of awesome tombs were built that now lie in rubble. Local lore suggests that the Salawa runs around protecting these tombs, some of which were built in honor of Seth. Does the god Seth reside in one of these tombs? Who knows—once we find the immortal, we'll turn our attention to the existence of gods, but we kinda have a lot on our plate right now as we deal with SAVING THE WORLD.

What Is the Salawa?

The Salawa, according to legend and sightings, is a dog-shaped creature with square ears and a long snout. Nothing too crazy about that. The thing to watch out for might be its stiff tail, which ends in a sharp, pointed fork. This dude has been around a long time, so it might have adapted some wicked protection mechanism we don't know about. I'd recommend staying away from the tail.

Another Thing to Worry About

Hey, Clivo, Amelia here. We have reports of a group of people in the region who call themselves the Wasi ("Guardian" in Arabic) and protect the Salawa. Word in the chat rooms is that if anyone comes searching for the cryptid, they are quickly shown the door in a not so very nice manner. The Wasi protect the creature because they still believe it's the spirit animal of Seth and that anyone who hurts it will unleash Seth's wrath in destruction and chaos. So watch out for them. And look out for the forked tail. Other than that, you should be fine.

Clivo shut the summary and rubbed his forehead. Just when he'd been hoping for a nice, easy catch, he now had to worry about a desert duel with a god of destruction and chaos. Perfect.

He signaled the flight attendant for a refill of OJ. He was suddenly feeling a little parched.

After almost twenty-four hours of travel and transferring planes twice, Clivo finally landed in Cairo. The first thing that hit him was the *heat*. The air was so hot and humid it felt like someone was holding a washcloth soaked in boiling water over his face.

As a valued Diamond Cardholder, he was normally escorted through the airport by a bodyguard, since most Diamond Cardholders were super-wealthy VIPs at risk of getting kidnapped. But now that Clivo knew that people *were* on his trail, he had asked not to be accompanied during his travels. He had heard too many stories of people getting kidnapped *by* their bodyguards to trust anyone.

After navigating through the crowded airport, he

booked himself a flight on a small jet plane and flew the remaining one and a half hours to Naqada. He had gotten plenty of sleep on the plane ride south from Amsterdam, so he felt awake enough to stare out the window at the foreign landscape as it passed below him. The plane flew along the Nile River that sparkled in the blazing sun, the scorched desert stretching off into the distance. Ancient pyramids and other crumbling antiquities dotted the sandy terrain. Clivo felt like he was traveling back to where civilization began, and it was mesmerizing.

The plane landed and Clivo grabbed his backpack and found a taxi. He was grateful he could speak basic phrases in Arabic, because he'd have had no idea how to get around otherwise. His driver took him past villages that dotted the flat terrain along the dirt road, their small brick buildings bright with walls painted all sorts of colors. After about half an hour, the taxi driver dropped him off at a small hotel the color of the desert sand, its rounded roofs and arched door-ways making it look like a small palace.

Clivo showered and put on the loose-fitting, ankle-length robe known as a djellaba he had bought at the Cairo airport, which felt cooler against his skin in the hot air than his regular clothes did. He always tried to dress as the locals did on his quests because he wanted to blend in as much as possible, though there was nothing he could do about his pale skin, which stood out against the darker faces around him.

It was late in the day and he was beginning to feel the effects of jet lag, but he wanted to eat a good meal before turning in for the night. There was only so much airplane food his belly could stand before he needed to eat something that wasn't served in tinfoil.

He wandered through the small village and found an outdoor café where people in garb similar to what he was wearing were sitting and drinking tea. He ordered some delicious lentils and oven-fried cheese that he wolfed down while glancing around to get a sense of his surroundings. On his previous catches he had been mainly concerned with where to find the cryptid. Now, ever since his catch in Russia, he was more aware of the people nearby who might be trying to find *him*.

As he shoveled the food into his mouth, he suddenly got a chill down his spine, like someone was watching him. He glanced up and saw three men leaning against a low-slung mud-colored building, all of them dressed in the same loose garb. But these men also wore black turbans with a hieroglyph on the front that looked like a dog with square ears. Clivo swallowed as he recognized the symbol of the god Seth from the Blasters' synopsis, and his nerves really kicked into high gear after noticing that all of the men's eyes were trained on him. He guessed they were Wasi, protectors of the Salawa.

Here we go, Clivo thought.

The strangers approached his table. One of them, a

handsome man with shoulder-length curly black hair and dark eyes, pulled out the chair across from Clivo and sat down. The two larger men stood behind him with scowls on their faces.

"*Marhabaan*," the man greeted him.

"*Marhabaan*," Clivo replied.

The man smiled. "Why don't we use English? Your American accent is terrible. As is your outfit."

Clivo sat back in his chair. So much for blending in with the locals. "What's wrong with my clothes?"

"Your dress is local. Your shoes are not," the man said, pointing to Clivo's tennis shoes.

Clivo winced. It had never occurred to him to buy different shoes. "Can't blame a kid for trying to respect the local customs."

The man leaned forward, his fingers casually running along the wrought iron table. "I won't interrupt your dinner for long. I don't know what an American child is doing in the middle of the desert—"

"I'm actually a teenager, which technically isn't a child anymore," Clivo said before he could stop himself. He was so nervous one sneaker-clad foot was tapping like crazy underneath the table.

The man raised his eyebrows, as if he was surprised to have been interrupted. "Fine. I don't know what an American *teenager* is doing in the middle of the desert, but—"

"My dad is an archaeologist, and he's working at the

Sheikh Abd el-Qurna dig site. I'm just along for the ride." Clivo spewed out the cover story he had memorized on the plane ride over.

The man sat back in exasperation. "Can you just let me finish my dire warning without interrupting me?"

The two bodyguards in the background huddled in closer, and Clivo noticed the glint of swords tucked into their robes. But he also noticed something else. On a chain around each man's neck, there dangled a small glass vial which contained a dark red liquid that looked like blood.

"Sure. Sorry, continue with your dire warning."

The man leaned forward again, a shadow falling over his dark eyes. He also wore a vial of red liquid around his neck. He caught Clivo looking at it and discreetly tucked it into his robe. "This place and the things in it are not to be trifled with. I warn you, don't anger the gods, for their vengeance is swift and merciless. For five thousand years we have protected this place and the things in it, and so we shall for five thousand more."

There was a long pause until one of the bodyguards cleared his throat and nudged the seated leader with his elbow, as if there was more to the dire warning.

"Huh? Oh yes. Leave tomorrow and forget this place. Leave its mysteries. If you don't, you have welcomed *our* wrath, and it will not be gentle."

Clivo waited a moment to make sure the man's dire warning was finished. Then he leaned forward, steadying his voice as much as possible. "I promise you, I am not here to anger any gods. I respect your land and everything in it. But I can't leave until my dad is done with his dig."

The man stared at Clivo, as if reading him. "Is it common for every American teenager to travel with *these*?" The inquisitor reached into his robe and laid Clivo's two remaining tranquilizer darts on the table.

Clivo's eyes went wide and his stomach froze. "You robbed me?"

The man smiled at him, revealing a gold-capped incisor. He pulled out another item and waved it in Clivo's face— Clivo's passport, which he'd left in his room along with his backpack. The man casually flipped through it. "Egypt does not take too kindly to foreigners stealing their *antiquities*, Clivo Wren. I could throw this away and have you put in jail, where you would have plenty of time to think about your transgressions."

Clivo's foot increased its nervous tapping. Languishing in an Egyptian prison was not what he'd had in mind for the summer. It not only seemed very unpleasant, but he also was the last good guy left searching for the immortal. If he was stuck in prison, the bad guys would surely find it and all would be lost.

He leaned forward and spoke softly yet with determination. "I am not here to steal anything. I'm here on an important mission to save the world. Trust me, let me do what I need to do or we will all be in trouble."

The man and his goons laughed. "And what do you think is more dangerous than angering the god of destruction and chaos, Clivo Wren? The last time the Salawa was threatened, a flood that lasted three days swept through this region, nearly wiping it from the map. Nothing is worse than an angry god!"

Except a group of power-hungry humans who want to become immortal and enslave the world, Clivo thought.

But he didn't say anything. He couldn't reveal to these men the truth about the immortal. If the Salawa was determined to be the ultimate, they'd probably just worship and protect it more. It'd be a full-out war.

Clivo groaned to himself. Why couldn't the immortal just be a cryptid nobody cared about? Like a giant sloth that emitted noxious gases instead of a spirit animal that protected a holy being?

The man's face relaxed and he slid the passport across the table. "You have been booked on the first flight out tomorrow morning at six, and your passport number has been given to the authorities. Say goodbye to Egypt, my friend, for you will never be allowed to return again."

Clivo grabbed his passport and breathed a sigh of relief, which lasted just a moment until he realized that if he wasn't allowed back in the country, it meant that he *had* to figure out if the Salawa was the immortal—tonight. Without any tranquilizer darts.

The man nodded and slowly stood up. He leaned over

and spoke quietly into Clivo's ear. "Some things are not meant to be found."

Yeah, I hear that a lot, Clivo thought as the man walked away, his two minions shooting Clivo parting glares.

Clivo quickly paid for his meal and ran back to his hotel. He flung open the splintered door and discovered his room in shambles.

"No, no, no," Clivo moaned.

His backpack was flung open and his clothes were strewn around the room. He frantically dug through the pack, but his tranquilizer gun was gone, as well as the blood sampler. He threw the bag across the room in frustration. He doubted there was a hardware store in the middle of the desert that sold tranquilizer guns and darts. And even if he did find the Salawa, there was no way for him to check its blood to see if it was the immortal.

Clivo paced the room angrily before pulling himself together and glancing at the clock on his bedside table. It was six P.M. He had twelve hours to find a dangerous and mysterious creature and catch it, with no gun, no darts, and no way to confirm if it was the creature he'd been looking for, before being banned from the country forever.

He groaned and dropped his head into his hands. This was the last clue the Blasters had to go on. There was no way he could leave without confirming if the Salawa was the immortal or not. What would be the point of catching other cryptids if this one was their last, best chance at discovering the immortal? He *had* to find it.

Or did he? Clivo thought of the necklaces hanging around the Wasis' necks. The vials had sure looked like they were filled with blood. Was it possible that they had somehow gathered some Salawa blood?

Clivo noticed a pair of his boots scattered on the floor. He ran to them and was overjoyed to find the ham radio he had stashed in one of them to keep it safe during the flight. At least something was going right. He still had his satellite phone on him, but Douglas would probably just yell at him for messing up the mission.

He grabbed the radio and called the Blasters.

"Hey, it's Clivo, is anyone around?"

The radio was silent for a moment and then a quiet voice spoke. "Hello, Hernando speaking."

"Hey, Hernando! I have a quick question for you," Clivo said, a plan forming in his mind. A very risky plan.

"Should I get the others?" Hernando asked uncertainly. "They're still eating breakfast."

"No, unless you can't answer my question for me," Clivo said quickly, shoving the back of a chair under the doorknob to his room so nobody could burst in and threaten him more.

"I will do my best," Hernando replied meekly.

"I think I just ran into three Wasi, and they all had vials

of some kind of liquid around their necks. Any chance it's blood from the Salawa?"

Clivo heard a quick shuffling of papers, then Hernando's quiet voice spoke again. "According to our research, the Wasi are indeed known for carrying Salawa blood around their necks. Years ago, a group of hunters shot and injured the Salawa. The Wasi fought them off and healed the Salawa. But they took some of its blood that had spilled on the ground and promised to always wear it around their necks as a vow to never let any harm befall the Salawa again."

"Okay, thanks, Hernando, that's what I needed to know," Clivo said, glancing at the clock again. Time was ticking.

There was a long pause, and Hernando spoke even more quietly. "Clivo, please be careful. The hunters who hurt the Salawa were *killed* by the Wasi. They don't like people messing with their cryptid."

"Don't worry, Hernando. I'm not going after the cryptid, I'm going after the Wasi. I need one of those necklaces."

Hernando let out a yelp. "Clivo, no! It's too dangerous!"

Clivo ran his hand through his hair in frustration. "I don't really have a choice, Hernando. They've already stolen my tranquilizer gun and blood sampler. I'm running out of options."

"You could come home?" Hernando offered meekly.

Clivo exhaled heavily. "Is that what you really want me to do, Hernando? When we could be this close to the immortal?"

Clivo could almost hear Hernando fretting on the other end of the radio. "I'm not good at encouraging people to run into danger, captain."

"Well, I could sure use some encouragement right about now," Clivo said, not even sure how he was going to implement his plan.

There was a long pause at the other end of the line. Finally, Hernando cleared his throat and spoke. "In my family, my dad always taught me that as long as you try, you've succeeded. You don't need to win, you just need to give it your best shot, and by doing that, you've already won."

"Thanks, Hernando," Clivo said, getting ready to sign off.

"Wait, I'm not done yet," Hernando said quickly.

"Oh, okay. Sorry, go ahead."

Hernando's voice got a little stronger. "But thinking that way isn't really going to work here. You can't just try, Clivo, you need to *win*. You need that vial of blood and you're not going to leave that desert until you've got it, because we are counting on you. The world is counting on you. Accept nothing less than success. You've got this."

Clivo blinked. "Wow, Hernando. That was really good."

"Really?" Hernando said, his voice returning to its usual timidity. "That took a lot out of me."

"Well, I appreciate it. I gotta go, I have some Wasi to catch."

"Go get 'em, captain."

V

Clivo was about to load up his backpack with the supplies he needed for the night, but then he realized he didn't have any. He felt naked—he was so used to having a bag filled with his catching supplies, including the tranquilizer gun, that to be going out with just his bare hands felt dangerous, to say the least. He tried not to think about the fact that this was his first time trying to catch a person rather than a cryptid—a person who carried a long sword, to boot. But Clivo thought about Hernando's words—he had to do this. There was no other option.

Clivo stuffed his belongings back into his backpack and left it by the door, figuring that if all went well he'd be making a quick getaway to the airport. The only things he took with him were his wallet and passport, phone to call Douglas, and radio to contact the Blasters in case he didn't have time to make it back to the hotel. If he had to leave behind his old Palace of Pants clothes, it wouldn't be the biggest tragedy.

He looked at himself in the hallway mirror, at his dimpled face and mess of brown hair, then looked down at the

Tibetan Buddhist bracelet he always wore as a reminder of his father. He still had so many questions—about how his father had gotten started in all this, why he'd never shared any of it with Clivo—but above all, he missed his dad and just wished he were around so Clivo could tell him everything, especially how nervous he was. But he had to admit, Hernando had done a pretty good job of firing him up.

"All right, Wren," he said out loud to his reflection. "Let's go catch some people."

Clivo snuck out the bathroom window and climbed over a stucco wall in the courtyard. He crept around the building and saw what he had been hoping for. The two large goons from earlier were perched on little stools across from the hotel, playing some kind of card game, their eyes occasionally spying on the entrance to the hotel, probably to make sure Clivo didn't sneak out.

The first part of Clivo's plan was complete: Find a Wasi. As for the second part of his plan, well, he had no second part. As of that moment, he was winging it.

He surveyed the scene in front of him the way his dad had taught him to while on what Clivo now knew were training expeditions in the mountains. The wide street was bathed in the orange of the setting sun, and indoor lights from the nearby houses were clicking on in anticipation of night. Two-level brick buildings with narrow alleyways between them extended along the street. Merchants with carts filled with fruits, vegetables, and other wares were slowly packing up their things for the evening. Before long, the street would be deserted.

If Clivo had been catching a cryptid, at this point he would have used his tranquilizer gun. But he didn't have a gun, and even if he did, he was sure he couldn't shoot a person. That just felt weird, even if it was only to render them unconscious. So what were his options? He needed one of the necklaces dangling from the goons' necks, so he simply needed to remove it from a large guy who had a sharp sword and a desire to kill him. Piece of cake.

Clivo examined the scene again and noticed there was an empty fruit cart wedged at the top of the alley, right behind the two muscular men. If Clivo could reach out from behind the cart, rip off a necklace, and escape the way he'd come, he'd be able to make a clean getaway since there was no way the men could maneuver their hulking bodies around the cart.

It was as good a plan as any, and Clivo decided to go for it. He crossed the street behind some people strolling along and made his way around the buildings and down the alley until he was crouched underneath the wagon behind the men.

He listened as the men chatted in Arabic about the little things in life, like how their kids and wives were doing and how their favorite tennis star did terribly in the last match. Clivo found it odd that two men wearing sharp swords were talking calmly about the events of the day, but what did he expect them to be talking about? The latest torture devices they had just purchased?

Clivo positioned himself so he could reach through the spokes of the wheel and reach one of the men without the other seeing him. Not that that mattered—the second he pulled off the necklace, they'd both be onto him.

As they talked and laughed in their deep voices, Clivo stretched out his arm, his fingers delicately reaching for the gold chain that shone against the closest man's dark skin. He kept his breathing quiet, but the exertion of stretching his arm to its full length was taxing.

The man he was reaching for suddenly leaned back with a laugh and Clivo caught his finger around the chain. The man reached for his neck as his partner swung his eyes to Clivo, whose face was pressed against the side of the cart.

Clivo smiled sheepishly. "Any chance you'd consider *not* chasing after me?" The man, who had a nicely trimmed beard, scowled and pulled out his very sharp-looking sword. "Yeah, I didn't think so," Clivo said.

Clivo ripped the necklace off the man's neck, pocketing the vial of blood safely in his robe's pocket before scurrying backward under the wagon and taking off running down the alleyway.

As he sprinted toward the other end of the alley, another Wasi stepped from behind the corner and blocked it. Clivo recognized him as the leader he had spoken to earlier. The man smiled his gold-toothed smile and slowly pulled his sword from its scabbard, the whisper of the steel sliding out of its sheath echoing up the alley.

Clivo skidded to a stop and glanced behind him, where the two goons had already pushed aside the wagon and were preparing to run toward him. Clivo's quick assessment of the situation made it very obvious that the only way to go was *up*.

He grabbed onto a nearby windowsill and launched himself up the side of the building, its crumbling mud bricks giving him plenty of hand- and footholds as he climbed. When he reached a second-story window, he accidentally knocked over a clay pot on the sill, and it landed on the head of one of the bearded goons below him, knocking him over so his turbaned head struck the pavement, the two blows together putting him out cold.

"I'm really sorry! I actually didn't mean to do that!" Clivo shouted down in apology.

The remaining goon, who had a fabulous set of bushy black eyebrows, glared at Clivo. The man ran back to the wagon, jumped on top of it, and started climbing to the roof. Clivo had two options: drop back down into the waiting arms of the Wasi leader, or continue on his way to the roof. He chose the roof.

Clivo vaulted onto the flat surface and took off running. His tennis shoes scraped against the loose dried mud, and he heard the thumps of sandal-clad footsteps giving chase behind him.

Up ahead, Clivo saw the next alleyway approaching. He didn't have time to consider if he could make it across, so he gathered his long robe away from his feet, sprinted as fast as he could, and jumped with all his strength over the gap, his arms flailing like the wings of a baby bird trying to take flight.

He barely made it to the other side, and landed promptly on his belly. The bushy-browed goon behind him picked up speed and leaped as well, but Clivo could instantly tell that the larger man wasn't going to make it.

Sure enough, the man's fingertips caught the edge of the roof and quickly slid off. A crash of pottery sounded a second later.

Clivo ran to the edge of the roof and looked down, relieved to see the man dazed but relatively uninjured in the middle of a pile of shattered pots and vases. An older woman was yelling angrily and hitting the man with a broom.

"Two down, one to go," Clivo panted as he turned and once again began running.

He jumped over one more alleyway, just to be sure the last Wasi wouldn't be able to keep pace with him on the ground, and finally climbed down into a deserted street. As soon as his feet touched the dirt, he turned and came face-to-face with the lead Wasi.

"Seriously?" Clivo moaned.

"Give me what you stole," the man said, holding out his hand.

"What is *with* you people? It's a little vial of blood! Can't a kid have a souvenir?"

"I won't ask again. The necklace, NOW!"

"I'm not giving it to you, so let's just cut to the fighting part, OKAY?" Clivo's heart was racing and he was dripping with sweat in the humid night air. He wasn't sure how well he would do fighting in the djellaba he was wearing, but realized he'd better figure it out, because the situation was about to explode.

The man hesitated for just a moment, then raised his sword and took a fighting stance. "It won't be the first time I've shed blood to protect the guardian of Seth—*oof*!"

Before the man could even finish his sentence, Clivo punched him in the stomach and threw him to the ground. The Wasi squirmed on the dusty street, struggling to catch his breath and untangle himself from his robe, which had gotten wrapped around his legs. It gave Clivo just the few seconds he needed to escape.

As he turned to run, he saw from the corner of his eye that the Wasi was clambering to his feet. Clivo took off like a sprinter and ran through alleyways, zigzagging as fast as he could among the buildings, listening for footsteps behind him. It was now fully dark and he ran without care, doing his best to shake the guy he knew would be coming after him.

Clivo had no idea where he was going. He just knew he had to get as far away from the village as possible, and going back to the hotel was definitely no longer an option. He was glad he had had enough foresight to carry his wallet and passport, phone, and radio with him; his clothes and boots would just have to be left behind. The only thing that mattered was the cryptid blood tucked safely in his pocket. If the Salawa turned out to be the immortal, Douglas could come back and deal with it. The most important thing was to identify if it was or not.

Clivo had been running for so long that it took him a moment to realize that the buildings around him had turned into ruins, and there wasn't any light coming from the crumbling structures. He ducked behind what was left of a sandy wall, his breath coming in gasps. He listened, waiting to hear if anyone was running up behind him.

When all was quiet, Clivo pushed himself away from the wall and glanced around, amazed by what he saw. He had run straight into the ruins of some ancient Egyptian city. What had been homes were now crumbling walls of brick, the roofs long since dissolved leaving the rooms open to the sky. He wandered through the sandy ruins, amazed that what he was touching might be thousands of years old.

He turned down a wide road, the surface rutted as if from chariot wheels, and passed what looked to be part of a pyramid. A hieroglyph that was carved into the sloped wall looked almost exactly like the symbol on the Wasis' turbans. Was this pyramid meant to be an offering to the god Seth?

Clivo spun around as he heard a scratch on the hard

sand, but nothing was behind him. The full moon was bright and cast shadows between the buildings, offering plenty of hiding places for whatever beast wandered this forgotten place. There, over to his left, a shadow suddenly moved. But it wasn't the shadow of a man—it was too short and wide.

Clivo's heart froze. Was it the Salawa? He didn't have a tranquilizer gun or any other means of protecting himself, and if the creature had developed any kind of crazy adaptive weapon mechanisms, Clivo would be powerless against it.

He had just dropped to his hands and knees and peered around the corner of the pyramid when a sharp blade appeared directly below his chin.

A familiar voice sounded next to him. "As I believe you Americans say . . . *gotcha*!"

Clivo stood up and faced the man he'd been running from—and the man's curved blade, glinting in the moonlight. He needed to buy himself some time, so he said the first thing that popped into his head. "What's your name?"

"Why does that matter?" the man sneered.

"I feel like since you have a sword against my throat, it's only proper that I know your name," Clivo said, trying to lift his chin away from the sharp edge.

This seemed to throw the man off-guard. *Good*, Clivo thought. Clivo had learned in jujitsu class that winning was all about who had the power, and power was a very easy thing to shift.

"My name is Tim," Tim finally said.

"Tim?" Clivo balked, the name catching *him* off-guard.

"It's a very common Egyptian name," Tim snarled. "What kind of a name is Clivo? It sounds like a vegetable."

"Um, that would be chives, which is an herb," Clivo corrected him. The conversation was making him relax, which was good. He needed to be relaxed for what he was planning next. "So, listen, Tim. It may seem like you have all the advantage here, with the sword and all, but I'm going to warn you once, and only once, that the best thing you can do for yourself is let me go. If you do, I promise I will head straight to the airport and never return."

"That sounds like—how do you say?—a fair deal," Tim replied. He held out his hand. "The blood, please. Then you are free to go."

Clivo tilted his head. "You see, Tim, that wasn't part of the deal." Clivo was keeping his voice calm, but really he was panicking inside. He had no idea how good Tim was at fighting, and it was always dangerous to enter a fight with an unproven foe.

Tim brought his face close to Clivo's, his breath smelling like tea and spices. "Why do you need the blood? Everyone who comes here is searching for the creature, but you are content to leave with only its blood. Why?"

"Before I answer, may I ask why so many people want to find the Salawa?" Besides buying more time so he could prepare himself, Clivo was genuinely curious. He knew why he was searching for the cryptid—to find the immortal—but why were others so intent upon finding the legendary beast?

Tim stepped back, but kept the sword trained on Clivo. Tim's voice became soft and reverent. "There is an old Latin saying: 'I believe because it is incredible.' Humans used to believe in myths and gods because they gave us hope in a world that nobody understood. Now everybody understands everything. With a few strokes on a keyboard, all the world's knowledge is at our fingertips. There is no mystery. So people come here, desperate to find something that can't be found on their little computer devices. They need to believe that there is still something out there that needs to be discovered. Some new frontier to conquer. Some mystery." Tim took a deep breath. "But what they don't realize is that myth *does* exist in this world, and meddling with it is more dangerous than they could ever imagine. Some things are not meant to be found, but if they are, they could destroy us all."

Clivo spoke honestly and fervently. "I agree with you, Tim. And I promise you that I want nothing more than to keep the Salawa a secret. I *know* it exists, but I have to take some of its blood to protect us, to protect *you*. We're on the same team, I promise you."

Tim tipped his head at what Clivo was saying. "So then I ask you again, why do you need its blood?"

Clivo paused. He wanted nothing more than to tell Tim everything. He seemed to be a man of great honor who might not use the gift of immortality for evil. But how could Clivo be sure? He wavered for a moment before remembering a promise he had made to the Blasters—"Trust no one."

"I'm sorry, Tim, I can't tell you that," Clivo sighed, realizing their moment of truce was about to come to an end. "All I can say is that I'm not leaving here without the blood."

Tim smiled, almost in understanding. "We all must do what we believe to be right. It's a shame to have to defeat you, Clivo Wren, for I believe we could have been allies. But defeat you, nonetheless, I will."

Just as Clivo had tensed his body for the battle, a movement sounded to his left.

He and Tim swung their heads around, and Clivo gasped as the Salawa poked its head around the corner.

Clivo felt what he always felt when he saw a cryptid for the first time—complete awe. The creature looked like a wiry red-furred dog with a long snout and square ears. Its black eyes, holding some kind of intelligent understanding, stared not at him, but at Tim.

"*Adhab*!" Tim shouted.

The Salawa must have understood the word "Go," because it slunk back behind the corner.

Shaking himself out of his shock, Clivo took the opportunity offered by the distraction. The cryptid had not only appeared, but also understood Tim's command. The Wasi could actually communicate with the mysterious beast.

He lunged at Tim, quickly grabbing the sword and

throwing it into the sand. Clivo had been trained in a lot of things, but sword fighting was not one of them, and he had no desire to become a shish kebab on Tim's blade.

A short scuffle ensued. Tim was strong, but without his sword he was no match for Clivo's jujitsu training.

Clivo pushed Tim back and picked up the sword, holding it at arm's length before the man's face. "Please believe me when I say that I'm doing this for both of us."

Tim nodded in defeat, a look of sadness crossing his face. "And for both of us, I hope you understand the consequences of the path you are choosing."

Clivo led Tim to a pillar and tied him to it by the sleeves of his flowing robe. When he was sure Tim couldn't escape, he said, "I'm sorry, but I have to leave you here. I'm sure this place will be crawling with tourists in the morning and you'll be rescued."

"I will," Tim said, seemingly almost in reassurance.

"And I trust that I don't need to be worried that the Salawa will attack you?"

Tim laughed in surprise. "Attack me? No. We live in harmony with the mysteries around us. Unlike the rest of the world, which seeks to destroy them. I have nothing to fear."

Clivo laid the sword delicately at the man's feet, wishing he could say more. "What I'm doing is honorable. I hope you understand that."

The Wasi looked at him with wisdom that seemed to

stretch back thousands of years. "Then you must prove it. Not to me, but to yourself."

Clivo was about to back away, but he had one more question. He pulled the vial of blood from his robe and held it in front of him. "Can you just please tell me: is this really the blood of the Salawa? If you can promise me it is, I will promise you that I will stop people from coming here to seek the creature. Not every person, but a lot of them. But I need you to work with me on this."

Tim's eyes flashed in anger. "We come from different worlds. I believe that 'working together' is an impossibility."

Clivo gritted his teeth in frustration. He had to know if the blood was really from the Salawa or he'd have to find a way to return. It was true, they were from different worlds, but couldn't they find a way to work together if their goals were the same?

A memory suddenly flashed through his mind, one that he had almost forgotten. "My mom, before she died, used to shake an ancient Egyptian rattle over me, to protect me from the god of storms."

Tim's eyes looked at him curiously.

Clivo went on. "I know what it means to need protection from things we don't understand, and if you can promise me that this is really the blood of the Salawa, I promise to protect your people from others who want to anger the god of chaos."

Tim considered the request. Finally, he nodded. "On my life, it is the blood of the beast. I have trusted you, now please make good on your promise."

Clivo nodded. He had learned that that's how trust went. You gave it to someone and hoped they honored it in return. It was one of the things that couldn't be proven in the Myth Blasters' lab, because there was no formula for it. Trust was given on faith. And Clivo trusted Tim and the agreement they had made, and he swore to keep up his end of the bargain.

"One last thing," Tim said.

"Yes?" said Clivo.

"Your accent. It's actually quite good. You had an excellent teacher."

"Thank you," Clivo said. "He was the best."

He gave a parting wave and ran off quickly, worried that Tim would somehow order the Salawa to give chase. But nothing followed him. Clivo checked behind him every few steps, but he was alone. Perhaps Tim didn't want to send the creature after someone who obviously knew how to fight, or maybe he simply trusted the agreement they had made.

Clivo paused at the top of a ridge and glanced behind him.

In the moonlight he saw Tim, still tied to the pillar. But he saw something else, too. A doglike creature with square ears, a forked tail sticking up straight, crept toward Tim.

Clivo readied himself to run down and protect Tim should the cryptid attack.

Instead, the creature sniffed Tim and settled to the ground, as if to watch over the Wasi for the night.

Clivo shook his head in disbelief, with everything he knew about the world and its mysteries shifting in his mind. Apparently it was still possible to live in harmony with the cryptids, to live in a world where the creatures didn't have to disappear to remain safe.

Clivo pulled the satellite phone from his robe to call Douglas for help, but then thought better of it and pulled the radio out instead.

"Hey, guys, anyone around?"

The speaker crackled to life with Charles's exuberant voice. "Dude? What's taking so long? You taking a tourist trip on a camel or something?"

Clivo smiled, the world suddenly returning to normal. "I'm good. But I need you to get me out of here immediately."

Clivo heard frantic tapping on a keyboard. "No problem, dude. Operation Exit Egypt under way."

VI

Two days later, after hiking back into Naqada, taking an overnight train to Cairo and several planes back to Colorado, riding a bus, and then walking up the dirt road, Clivo was finally home. He arrived with no luggage and was still wearing the loose-fitting robe, which was stained with sand and sweat.

Clivo hobbled toward the front door, his legs aching from both sitting and walking, and cursed Douglas for his new no-taxis-at-home rule. It was early in the morning, the sun just peeking over the tall pine trees. The forest was cool and smelled like fresh morning dew, which was a welcome relief from the oppressive heat of the desert.

After the panic of the other day, Clivo was finally able to relax and not worry that someone was about to attack him.

But just as he reached the front porch, Jerry came running out of the house, his arms flailing wildly.

"Don't take another step! Freeze! Freeze!"

Clivo froze, all the relaxed muscles in his body suddenly seizing tight.

Jerry ran down the steps and brushed a few leaves from a spot on the ground, revealing what looked like a lasso. Clivo relaxed again, as much as he could anyway, because since becoming a cryptid catcher, he'd felt like he might never be able to fully relax again.

"Jerry, it's not a snake, it's just a rope. And what are you doing here? It's, like, eight in the morning."

"Just a rope? I hardly think so," Jerry said. "This is phase one of my booby-trap plan! Remember, you said I could come over and secure your home with my skills?"

"Oh, yeah, sorry. I've been kinda busy and totally forgot," Clivo replied, already regretting his decision to let Jerry rig up his house with traps.

Adam bounded out the front door, pointing an accusing finger at Jerry. "Clivo, this dude isn't part of the team! He just came storming in here like he owned the joint!"

"I am part of the team! Clivo said so!" Jerry spat back.

Adam's voice rose several pitches. "How is that possible? You haven't even gone through an initiation yet!"

Clivo rubbed his hands over his face, his exhaustion threatening to overtake him. "Guys, can we please deal with this later? There's more important stuff to talk about right now."

"Fine, dude, but this issue needs to be dealt with in a timely manner," Adam warned.

They entered the house and the two cats instantly sprang up, their claws clinging to Clivo's robe as if he were a scratching post. He was too tired to even brush them off, so he waddled toward the kitchen with the creatures swinging from his clothes, following the delightful smell of waffles coming through the doorway. He poked his head in and discovered a disaster. A frazzled-looking Pearl was at the sink washing a mound of dirty dishes, a bit of waffle batter dangling from her hair.

Pearl looked up, relief crossing her face when she saw Clivo, but it was quickly replaced by a look of confusion when she noticed what he was wearing. She scooped off one cat with each arm and deposited them on the floor, then gave Clivo a big hug. "Hi, sweetie, I didn't realize you were going to Zanzibar for the science fair."

Clivo kissed her on the cheek and behaved as if everything was normal. "The airline lost my luggage and this was all I could buy at the airport."

"Oh, that makes sense. Well, your friend Jeff came by this morning," Pearl said, looking a bit concerned. "He was fiddling in the yard and told me to use the back door only."

"Oh, Jerry?" Clivo corrected, picking up some dishes from the kitchen table and bringing them to the sink. "I'm sorry, I forgot to tell you that he's going to be doing some, um, experiments outside. I hope that's okay?"

"Oh, sure," Pearl said, though she sounded uncertain. "Are there going to be any more teenagers showing up? I hate to be a nag, but I haven't been able to get out dancing much, what with all the cooking and cleaning and washing and such."

Clivo rubbed his hands over his face again. He had been so concerned with finding the immortal that he had forgotten about how everything might be affecting Pearl. "I'm sorry, Aunt Pearl. No, there's no more teenagers coming. And please don't do all these dishes, the other kids need to help."

Pearl breathed a sigh of relief and wiped her hands with a towel. "Oh, you are such a good little rascal." She kissed his cheek, taking a moment to sniff him—he knew he must smell horrible—and pranced off, the cats padding behind her. "I can just make it to a dancing class if I leave right now!"

"Remember to use the back door!" Clivo called after her.

Clivo took the stairs to the basement, where the noise of everyone yelling was causing a cacophony of epic proportions.

"Adam, he doesn't have to do one of your dumb initiations!" Amelia yelled. "Just let him be!"

"Yeah, I don't have to prove anything to you! Wrenmaster and I go way back, so if anything, *you're* the intruder around here!" Jerry said, poking a finger in Adam's chest.

Adam rubbed his bony sternum. "It's part of the code, dude! Nobody's part of the team until we initiate them!"

"It is part of the code," Hernando agreed apologetically.

"Even Clivo went through an initiation," Charles added. "Everyone has to prove that they're worthy."

Jerry laughed. "Worthy? I'm more worthy than all you nerds put together!"

Adam laughed loudly in Jerry's face. "As IF!"

"Guys!" Clivo yelled. The room fell silent and everyone looked at him.

Adam pushed his bottle-sized glasses up his nose. "Nice djellaba, by the way. Looks comfortable. Would you mind if I borrowed it?"

Clivo ignored him. "Listen, Jerry stole secret satellite codes for us that could have gotten him sent to a military academy if he was caught. Can't we consider that an example of his worth?"

Charles stroked his chin in deep thought. "It does appear that he already went out on a limb for us."

Adam shook his head. "I still think he should do some kind of obstacle course or something."

Amelia rolled her eyes. "It's fine, Clivo. Jerry's your best friend, and that's good enough for me."

Stephanie gave Jerry a big hug. "Welcome to the team, Jerry. It's great seeing you again."

Jerry took Stephanie's hand and kissed the back of it like a gentleman. "Your kindness is only surpassed by your intelligence."

Charles made a vomiting sound. "Oh, give me a BREAK!"

Amelia turned to Clivo. "Now that *that's* settled, I believe you have *a lot* to tell us."

They all sat down at the table, a bit of jostling going on

over who sat where now that Jerry had joined the group. But everyone eventually settled in and Clivo told them everything that had happened in Egypt, with the Blasters hanging on his every word.

"So, all in all, I guess everything went pretty well," Clivo said, which was funny to say considering he had faced down three men with swords. "I got the blood sample, but I didn't have to bother the cryptid or anger the god of chaos, which was a bonus."

"The fact that the Wasi can communicate with the cryptid is super cool," Charles said. "I'd love to have a conversation with the Yeti. I bet that dude has got some *stories*!"

"It really is interesting," Stephanie added. "We've always looked at cryptids as being so separate from us and our world. I'd totally forgotten that they live right alongside us."

"Speaking of which," Clivo said, "I promised the Wasi that I would do my best to keep people away from the Salawa. Is there a way that you can spread word on the chat rooms that the Salawa is a hoax? I know it won't keep every person away from searching for it, but it might help."

Amelia wrote a note on a piece of paper. "No problem, I'll find a way to debunk the legend. A promise is a promise."

"And about the chat rooms," Clivo continued, "any reported sightings of the cryptids I've caught?"

Amelia looked at him and shook her head, her face dropping with concern.

"Enough chitchat. Let's see the blood!" Adam exclaimed eagerly.

Clivo pulled the vial out of his robe, and everyone looked at it in awe.

Amelia was the first to speak, her voice reverent. "So that could be the elixir of life right there."

"Do you really think it's possible that this one is it?" Clivo asked.

Stephanie's blue eyes watched the vial as it swung gently from the chain held by Clivo's fingers. "Right now it's just an educated guess based on the clues we have—the languages your father taught you and the fact that the cryptid has been around since the time of Nostradamus. That's really all we have to go on."

Clivo watched everyone's eyes following the swinging vial, as if they were being hypnotized. He quickly pocketed the blood, breaking the spell. "Douglas is going to be here shortly to drop off a new blood sampler as well as a tranquilizer gun and darts, though he was *not* happy about me losing all my supplies."

"Are you going to let him sit in while we sample the blood?" Amelia asked.

Clivo looked down at the table. "I'm actually not sure. I didn't tell him about the blood sample."

"Why not?" Stephanie asked, leaning her cheek on her palm. "Do you not trust him?"

Clivo shook his head. "No, I totally trust him. It's

just . . . I don't know. He's never told me exactly what he's going to do with the immortal. And none of us have ever discussed it together, either. I feel like we should know what we'll do before we're holding the most powerful thing known to man."

"Geez, that's a good point," Amelia said, chewing her bottom lip. "We had all decided to keep the immortal away from the bad guys, but we never really talked about what the good guys should do with it."

Charles slowly raised his hand. "If we need a test subject to see what immortality is like, I happily volunteer."

"Charles, don't be dumb," Amelia said, rolling her eyes.

"What?" Charles retorted. "I said, if we need a test subject!"

A car door slammed and Clivo looked out the basement window. "Okay! Douglas is here! Listen, guys, how about I just get the supplies and then we can figure out what to do?"

"Should we meet him?" Stephanie asked, standing up.

Clivo considered it. He didn't see what harm it would cause, but he didn't see what good it would do, either. Things had been running pretty smoothly with Douglas, so he thought maybe it was best to just keep things as they were.

"Let's keep you guys a secret for now. Douglas can get pretty feisty, so it's best if I do what I can to keep him calm."

The words were no sooner out of Clivo's mouth than he heard some kind of a snap and a yell of surprise followed by a string of loud curse words.

Everyone ran to the window and gasped at the sight of Douglas hanging upside down off the ground, dangling from a rope wrapped around his ankle.

Jerry shot his arm into the air. "Booby trap number one is a success, ladies and gentlemen!"

Clivo threw Jerry a side-eye and headed upstairs. "Stay here, everyone! This isn't going to be pretty."

Clivo ran upstairs, grateful that Pearl was already gone. Having an angry upside-down man in her yard would probably confirm her fears that teenagers were troublemakers.

He opened the front door and put on a cheery front. "Good morning, Mr. Chancery! I see you've triggered our security alarm!"

Douglas swung around until his bright red face was angled toward Clivo. His crazy gray hair stuck out in every direction. "If you don't get me down from here immediately, you twit, I'm tranquilizing you!"

"Of course, just let me see how I do that." Clivo followed the rope to some kind of pulley system and began to lower Douglas.

"Carefully!" Douglas bellowed.

Clivo slowly lowered Douglas, who rolled on the ground for a few seconds while getting his ankle free from the rope and then stood, his tweed jacket covered with leaves.

Clivo chuckled sheepishly. "Sorry about that, Mr. Chancery, just trying to keep the fortress safe."

Douglas glared at Clivo and mumbled a few choice words, but fortunately didn't go off on a tirade. He picked up a silver metal briefcase that had fallen to the ground and shoved it into Clivo's hands. "There's your supplies. Try not to lose them this time. And I included some more petty cash, but remember to give me receipts. You spent too much on food last time."

"Thanks, Mr. Chancery, I'll do my best."

Douglas took out a handkerchief and wiped his face. "And what happened in Egypt? It's not like you to fail on a mission. Are you losing your touch already?"

Clivo shifted the briefcase in his arms. "Um, I actually didn't fail, Mr. Chancery. I was able to get some cryptid blood without actually catching the cryptid."

Douglas stared at him. He seemed uncertain about what to say, which was a rarity for him. "And why would you do that? Your job is to tranquilize the cryptid, not just get its blood."

"Well, it was kind of my only option at the time, Mr. Chancery."

Douglas wiped his face with his handkerchief again, his face turning from red to purple in frustration, which confused Clivo. If he got the blood, what did it matter if he actually caught the cryptid or not?

"Listen, kid, don't start changing up the game on me. Don't get all fancy and creative with how you get the cryptid blood. Just do what your dad did—tranquilize the cryptid, check its blood. There, simple, two easy steps. Can your brain handle that?"

"Yes, Mr. Chancery, I can handle that," Clivo said, knowing it was usually best to just agree with the man.

Douglas looked Clivo up and down, as if seeing him for the first time, and let out a raspy laugh. "And what in the heck are you wearing? Is this some new style you kids are trying nowadays?"

Clivo's tension was released and he laughed along with the cranky man. "No, sir. I was trying to blend in with the Egyptian locals and haven't had time to shower yet."

Douglas laughed again and patted Clivo on the shoulder. "Whatever works, kid. Just be safe out there. And take a shower, you smell like a camel."

"I will, Mr. Chancery. Thank you. I'll let you know when I've completed my next catch." Clivo picked up Douglas's cane and helped the man hobble back to his fancy black car, waving as he drove down the driveway.

As Clivo walked back inside, he knew he should feel elated by how well that had gone, but something was bugging him. Something Douglas had said, or rather hadn't said.

Why hadn't Douglas wanted to stay to see if the Salawa was the immortal? He had seemed more concerned about the fact that Clivo didn't actually catch the cryptid—but the whole goal was to identify which one was the immortal. Wasn't it?

As Clivo walked back inside, his mind whirling with questions, he realized he needed to focus on the more important task at hand: checking the Salawa's blood.

"That didn't go so bad!" Jerry said with a wide grin when Clivo got back downstairs. "Dude took pretty well to being hog-tied!"

Clivo shot his friend another look, but didn't say anything.

He put the briefcase down on the table and opened it to find a new gun, ten darts, and a blood sampler. He put the blood sampler on the table and laid the vial of Salawa blood next to it. "Okay, guys, moment of truth. If this cryptid turns out to be the immortal, what do we do?"

Everyone looked at one another, as if waiting for someone else to speak first.

Finally, Amelia cleared her throat. "The proper way to approach a question is to consider all possible answers, regardless of whether you agree with them or not."

Stephanie nodded in agreement. "Only by seeing the full map can you properly choose which road to go down."

"Okay, then," Clivo said, spreading his hands on the table. "Let's talk about all the possible answers."

"The first one is obvious," Amelia began, folding her hands in front of her. "Let Douglas know and he'll handle it. He must have thought this through already."

"But we don't know what his plan is," Stephanie added.

"True," Amelia agreed.

"So," Clivo offered, "if we don't tell Douglas, and we handle it, what then?"

"We make ourselves immortal and don't tell anybody else," Charles said. Everyone stared at him. "What? You said *all* possibilities!"

Hernando raised his hand. "But wouldn't we want to make others immortal, too? I don't think I'd like to spend my life making friends only to see them die before me over and over again. It sounds sad."

"Yeah," Jerry said, "and I'd like an immortal girlfriend at some point, too. No offense, but you guys aren't the only people I'd want to spend eternity with."

"It's a good point," Amelia said. "If we wield the gift of immortality, who do we decide to bestow it upon?"

Charles interlaced his hands behind his head. "In a certain way, we'd become gods. People would kneel before us, begging us for the gift." Again everybody stared at him. He threw his hands up and yelled, "Do you want all the possibilities or not?"

Adam had remained oddly quiet during the conversation. When he spoke, his voice was uncharacteristically soft. *"Be careful when you fight the monsters, lest you become one."*

Amelia nodded solemnly. "Nietzsche."

"What's that?" Clivo asked.

"Who's that, you mean." Adam stood up and paced around the room, grabbing an apple and slowly chewing it, deep in thought. "A German philosopher from the 1800s. He basically said that even the strongest-willed humans will risk their lives for more power, and even enjoy wielding its cruelty over others."

Hernando shook his head. "I don't like being cruel to others."

"Adam is right," Stephanie said, her face blushing pink. "We're fighting people who want power. We have to be careful about taking that power for ourselves, or we're no better than them."

Amelia nodded, her voice solemn. "We would become the monsters."

"I don't like monsters very much," Hernando whispered.

Clivo thought about everything that had just been said. "Okay, so it sounds like in order to fight evil, we need to make sure we do the opposite of what evil would do. Which means that when we find the immortal, we keep it a secret and make sure nobody else ever discovers it."

Charles shifted in his chair. "Do we do that after we make ourselves immortal?"

Amelia slapped her hand on the table. "Charles! Let it go! We're not going to make ourselves immortal!"

"I demand a vote!" Charles whined.

"Charles is right," Clivo said. "We're a team. We all need to agree on this."

Amelia sat back in her chair. "Okay, all in favor, of keeping the gift of immortality a secret?"

Everyone raised their hands.

Stephanie added, "And *not* using it on ourselves?"

Everyone except Charles raised their hands.

Charles furrowed his brow. "Hang on, I'm thinking, I'm thinking." He silently ticked things off on his fingers and engaged in an obviously very heated discussion with himself. Finally, he reluctantly raised his hand and let out an exhausted sigh. "I just don't see how I could become immortal and not turn into a total jerk. But if I discover how, I reserve the right to change my vote."

Clivo grabbed the vial and the blood sampler. "Okay, team, looks like we have a plan. We find the immortal and keep it and the elixir of life a secret. From everybody."

Stephanie put a hand over his to stop him. "What about Douglas?"

After his conversation with Douglas, Clivo still had a nagging feeling that something wasn't right; he just wasn't sure what. "We need to make sure he agrees with this vote," Clivo said. "Until we're sure he does, we keep it a secret from him, too. Agreed?"

Everyone nodded.

Charles rubbed his hands together. "Looks like we're going rogue!"

Clivo uncorked the vial of blood and brought it toward

the sampler. He paused, wondering if he was ready for this. He glanced at his team, and when they all gave him nods of reassurance, he knew in that moment that, without a doubt, they'd all remain the good guys, even in the face of great power.

He delicately placed a drop of blood on the needle and waited as it traveled up the chamber, the screen blinking like a ticking time bomb.

The basement went eerily quiet. Nobody seemed to breathe as they kept their eyes locked on the sampler—except for Hernando, who had covered his face with his hands.

After an eternity, a beep sounded and two words flashed on the screen: NOT IMMORTAL.

Everyone exhaled loudly in relief and collapsed back in their chairs. Adam flapped his arms as if shaking off a spider. "Whoa, dude! That was intense!"

"I may need a nap," Hernando agreed.

Charles ran his fingers through his nest of curly hair. "Yeah, I'm definitely gonna have to prepare myself better emotionally next time."

Amelia spun her nose ring with her fingers in thought. "Focus, guys. All this means is that we have to go back to finding the immortal, except now we're all out of clues."

Clivo stood up, thoroughly exhausted from the events of the past three days. He felt like he needed to rest for a month before going on another catch. "I'll let you guys get to your research. If you need me, I'll be in the shower or in a catatonic sleep."

Clivo headed over to the stairs, but stopped at the first step. "Oh, and while you're working on saving the world, can you also please do your dishes?"

VII

Clivo took a hot shower, washing all the sand off of him, then lay in bed. It wasn't even noon, but the exhaustion of traveling around the world while in mortal danger with very little sleep had done him in.

He was sure he would immediately fall asleep, but too many things were rumbling through his mind. What had happened to the cryptids he'd caught? Who was the immortal? And why was Douglas so irritated that he hadn't actually caught the Salawa, even though he'd still gotten a sample of its blood?

Clivo thought back to his Ugly Merman catch and the feeling he'd had that someone was watching him, or was at least close by and knew what he was doing. He knew there was an evil resistance out there that was working hard to find the immortal, and even to find *him*.

But what if someone had already found him? And if he had been discovered, why hadn't the people captured him and tortured him for information? What if they were simply tracking him? But tracking him for what?

He sat bolt upright in bed and ran downstairs to the basement, where the Blasters were all hunched at their workstations either reading books or tapping away on their computers, once more diving into the hunt for the immortal. Jerry was in a corner, fiddling with some wires.

"Dude, I told you not to touch those!" Adam yelled to Jerry.

"Relax, man! Do you want a security system or not?" Jerry shot back.

"A rope swing is hardly a security system!" Adam retorted.

"Hey, guys," Clivo interrupted, his brain spinning. "Do you think it's possible that someone is stealing the cryptids I find?"

Six pairs of eyes shot up and looked at him. Amelia put her book down. "It's a possibility. But how? And why?"

"I don't know," Clivo said, wandering around the room in thought. "I know the Luxembourgers wanted to sell them to science or to a zoo. Maybe someone's been profiting off my catches?"

"Cryptidnapping?" Charles asked. "That's a cold thought, man."

Stephanie said the next part carefully. "Douglas is the only person, besides us, who knows about the cryptids you've caught."

Clivo had thought about that, too. "I know. But I can't imagine he'd do something like that. My father wanted the cryptids protected just like I do, and he never would have worked for Douglas if Douglas was harming them."

"Are you sure about that?" Adam asked, popping some grapes into his mouth.

"I am," Clivo replied almost defensively. "My dad was one of the good guys, and he wouldn't have trusted Douglas unless he was, too. Douglas yells and swears a lot, but he's one of us."

"So who might be taking them?" Stephanie asked.

"I don't know," Clivo said. "You guys are the problem solvers. How do we solve this?"

Amelia tapped her chin with her finger. "How long do you hang out after you've caught a cryptid?"

"Not long," Clivo replied. "I wait, at a distance, until the creature wakes up so I don't just leave it there unconscious. Then I go."

"So that's the one variable we have to change, the only one," Stephanie said, nodding at Amelia as if she understood where this was going. "We need to send you on another catch, one for a creature that is hopefully not dangerous to you and definitely not the immortal."

"But this time," Amelia continued, "you need to stick around and see if anyone comes and claims the cryptid."

Clivo thought about it. "That sounds like a good plan. I hate to take time away from looking for the immortal, but if the cryptids are being taken, we definitely need to put a stop to that."

"Like I said," Charles said with a wink, "we're going rogue."

"Give us a couple of hours," Stephanie said, cracking her knuckles. "We've discovered a lot of cryptids in our research. We'll find a harmless one for you."

Clivo was about to exit when Jerry pulled him aside. "Hey, man, why don't you let me come with you? You don't need to do all this by yourself. It wouldn't hurt to have a bit of muscle on your side."

"You wanna be my wingman?" Clivo asked, surprised that the idea had never occurred to him.

Jerry gave him a sly smile. "Always have been, always will be."

Clivo thought about it. It *would* be nice to have company on his world travels. And with the cryptids becoming more dangerous, it wouldn't hurt to have someone else by his side.

But what if something happened to Jerry? Sure, he was athletic and great at sports, but he wasn't trained in martial arts like Clivo was. Clivo had to protect the cryptids, but he also had to protect those around him. He couldn't risk Jerry's life just because he wanted some company.

"Thanks, Coops, but why don't you stay here?" Clivo said, coming up with a good reason so he wouldn't hurt his friend's feelings. "I really need you to fortify the headquarters, and I won't be able to keep you a secret from Douglas if he starts asking why I had to buy two plane tickets." He leaned in close and whispered, "Besides, these guys need your muscle more than I do."

He pointed toward Charles, who was exuberantly practicing some kind of sloppy karate moves in the middle of the room.

Charles saw them looking at him and held his arms out wide in challenge. "What? It stimulates my thinking mechanisms!"

Jerry turned back to Clivo, studying him closely. "All right, man. I see what you mean. Just be careful out there."

Several nights later, Clivo was lying in a bush in southern Germany, his tranquilizer gun at the ready. Right before leaving on this catch, he had spent a whole day alternating between sleeping, showering, and sleeping again. He could have used a few more days of rest, but he couldn't waste the time. He had to find out if someone was stealing the cryptids.

Now Clivo was on his third day of waiting patiently, despite his growing exhaustion, for the creature to arrive. He mentally went over the cryptid he was seeking—the Elwetritsch, a chicken-like creature with a long beak and antlers. Adam hadn't had time to write up its origin story, so the Blasters just told him the legend: the creature was a mixture of a chicken and a goblin. Because the Blasters hadn't been able to prove the existence of goblins, Adam had balked at endorsing the idea, saying that it was "awesome, but cheesy."

The Elwetritsch definitely wasn't the immortal, because it had only been sighted since the mid-1900s. Nostradamus, the French seer whose prophecy spoke of the immortal, had lived in the sixteenth century, so the immortal had to be at least that old. The cryptid Clivo was waiting for should also be relatively easy to catch and, hopefully, harmless . . . It was a chicken, after all.

Clivo hated the idea of using a cryptid as bait, but it was the only way to find out if someone was taking his catches.

He watched the glow of several blue lanterns placed in a clearing in front of him. Going on Elwetritsch hunts was a favorite tradition for the locals, although they used it more as a joke. The locals would place lanterns in the forest because the creature was supposed to be curious, then leave a watcher to wait for it while the others went to flush it out of the brush. But the "flushers" would just retreat back to the pub, leaving the watcher waiting for hours for a beast that never came.

However, there had been times when the Elwetritsch did appear, and it was always when a blue lantern was used, so Clivo had surrounded the clearing with nothing but a blue glow.

Clivo slapped a mosquito that had been nibbling on his neck. He hoped he didn't have to spend a week searching for the chicken—he'd be sucked dry by all the mosquitos. More than that, he didn't want to wait a whole week to figure out what was going on. The summer would be over before he knew it, the Blasters would return to their homes in Maine, and he'd go back to searching for the immortal on school breaks. Needless to say, it was a little tough to focus on his homework when he knew the world was in danger.

Clivo yawned, then shook his head to stay awake. His eyelids began to droop, so he shifted to a less comfortable position. Just as his head began to loll, a rustle sounded in the shrubbery right next to him. He turned his head to find the Elwetritsch standing right there, staring curiously at him.

It was indeed a chicken, with an abnormally long beak and a full set of antlers. Clivo had to stop himself from laughing. The creature definitely looked harmless and was actually kind of cute.

"Whatcha looking at, buddy?" Clivo asked.

The Elwetritsch hopped forward and pecked at Clivo's watch, which glowed with blue numbers. *Well, at least the Blasters were right about the creature liking the color blue*, Clivo thought.

Clivo slowly swung his gun around. He was too close to the creature to actually shoot it, but perhaps he could just gently prick the beast with the dart. He wanted to scare the creature as little as possible.

"Hey, friend, I'm sorry to have to do this to you, but I need your help." The chicken kept pecking at Clivo's watch, a little squeak coming from its throat. "And if someone takes you, I promise that I'll come and find you, okay? So just hang on. You may be going on a journey somewhere, but I'll have you back here in no time."

The chicken lifted its head, blinking its round eyes curiously.

Clivo lifted his gun, prepared to tranquilize the poor creature. "This may sting just a little bit, but then you'll just go to sleep."

Clivo brought the needle closer to the chicken and was just about to prick it when the beast went from being very cute to *very* aggressive. It rose up on its feet and spread its wings, flapping them with enormous speed and intensity. Feathers flew around Clivo's face, blinding him, as the chicken let out a squawk so shrill it pierced Clivo's eardrums.

Clivo recoiled away from the flapping monstrosity in front of him just as the Elwetritsch jumped forward and stabbed him with its sharp beak.

"Ow!" Clivo exclaimed, looking at his hand, where a droplet of blood was forming at the stab wound.

The cryptid lowered its wings and began running through the brush as fast as its little legs would carry it.

Clivo ignored the stinging of his hand and brought the gun up in one fluid motion, firing a dart that thankfully found its mark. The chicken fell over in an explosion of feathers.

"So much for you being harmless," Clivo said, then

groaned, shaking his hand, which was beginning to throb something terrible.

He ran up to the chicken to check its blood. Even though the Blasters were sure it wasn't the immortal, Stephanie had said he needed to do everything exactly the same as he did on every catch. The only thing that would change was that he would wait to see what happened after.

He checked the Elwetritsch's blood, and the sampler, sure enough, said the chicken wasn't the immortal. Then he took a selfie that he sent to Douglas.

His head was beginning to hurt and he was having a hard time thinking all of a sudden. Had he done everything the same? What else was he supposed to do? Oh yes, retreat a bit and wait.

Clivo trudged toward a small hill, where he would have a view of the part of the forest the chicken lay in. His legs felt heavy, and he was sweating more than he knew he should be in the cool night air. *What is wrong with me?* he wondered. *Am I getting sick?*

He made it to the top of the hill after what felt like forever and collapsed onto the ground, well hidden in the heavy undergrowth. He took out his binoculars and waited, though every time he looked through them he felt like he was going to be ill. The world shifted and blurred, and he was having a hard time focusing on the forest in front of him.

The next thing Clivo knew, he was flat on his back

completely unable to push himself upright. His limbs felt jellified and his tongue was like a cotton ball. He looked at his hand where the chicken had pecked him and saw an angry red welt that burned like it contained a hot coal. Had the chicken poisoned him? If so, it was probably a good idea to let someone know what had happened.

He pulled the phone from his backpack, his fingers feeling like they were twice their size. He fumbled with the buttons on the device, but couldn't remember how to operate it. Even if he could have, his fingers had all of a sudden become completely useless.

He collapsed onto his back as he went completely limp, and he stared at the stars that danced above him like fireflies on a string. His brain had gone foggy, and he couldn't remember where he was or why his hand hurt so much.

He didn't know how long he had been lying there—it could have been hours or days—when he heard a jangling, as if his mom were above him, shaking the ancient Egyptian rattle to protect him from the god of storms. The rattling got louder and more intense and he knew his mom was there, doing everything she should to protect him.

Clivo reached toward the stars. "Mom? Dad? Are you up there? I can't see you."

He swept his hand across the sky, reaching for the sound, wishing that his parents would appear and whisk him away from wherever he was. He knew he needed help, but he couldn't remember why. All he knew was that he felt totally alone and didn't understand what was going on.

"Mom? Dad? Where are you?"

The rattling got louder and Clivo was sure his mom was about to appear, her smiling face arriving to remind him that everything was going to be okay, that she had blessed him with protection and nothing could harm him. Clivo reached up to the sound that was now filling his ears as a bright light suddenly was flying above him, like an angel.

"I found you, Mom," Clivo said, tears streaming down his cheeks. "I finally found you."

Wind blasted across Clivo's face as a low-flying helicopter swept directly over his head. Bits of dirt hit him in the face like a slap and for a moment the grogginess drifted from his mind. Wasn't he supposed to be watching for something? he wondered.

He flopped onto his side, pushing through the fogginess of his brain, his body still feeling as heavy as a wet carpet. He picked up the binoculars and held them between his wrists because his fingers had completely stopped working.

He watched as the helicopter landed in a clearing. The door opened and a person jumped out, a gun in their hands. They disappeared into the shrubbery and returned a moment later holding an unconscious chicken, its antlers sticking out from under the crook of the person's arm.

Clivo's brain shifted into focus. The cryptid! He was

supposed to be watching for someone stealing it! He tried to get a good look at the person's face, but they had on a hat and a scarf that obscured most of their head.

The person gently put the cryptid in a cage attached to the top of one of the landing skids of the helicopter, climbed in, and flew away, the wind from the blades once again slapping Clivo in the face with dust and dirt.

"Shoot," he said, before slipping into complete unconsciousness.

VIII

Each time Clivo returned home, he felt the worse for
wear, and this time he felt the worst by far—his body still
wasn't working quite right after his confrontation with the
demon chicken, as he was now calling the Elwetritsch. He
had woken up cold and woozy hours after witnessing the
mysterious abduction of the cryptid in the German woods.
It had been a slow and painful trudge back to the nearest
village, and his long journey home had felt no easier or
quicker.

After riding in planes and on buses and ending with a
long walk up the mountain, he finally limped toward the
front porch, carefully watching his step so he wouldn't get
caught in Jerry's lasso of doom. He entered the house and
poked his head into the kitchen, where there was a loud
clanking of dishes and salsa music playing. Charles and Hernando were at the sink washing a large stack of dishes, frilly
aprons tied around their waists. Pearl was sitting at the kitchen
table, drinking some tea and tapping her feet in rhythm to
the music.

"So, anyway, Pearl, the thing about most teenage guys is that they don't have the intellectual capacity to deal with the physical changes that happen when turning from boys to men," Charles was saying over his shoulder as he scrubbed the dishes with soapy water. "But me and Hernando here are smart enough to ease into our manhood without totally freaking out."

"We're manly men," Hernando agreed, drying a dish with a checkered towel and gently putting it away.

Pearl put her hand to her mouth and giggled. "Well, it certainly has been much nicer having you boys around since you've started cleaning up after yourselves." Then Pearl noticed Clivo, and her face dropped. "Sweetie! You're home! Are you okay?"

Clivo gave her a reassuring smile. "I'm fine, Aunt Pearl. Just tired."

Clivo knew that if he looked as bad as he felt, he probably appeared to be a zombie. His arm suddenly shot out in a spasm and his hand hit the refrigerator. He grimaced in pain, but returned a smile to his face. "Glad to see the fridge is still working."

Charles and Hernando glanced at him with concern and began to quickly finish up their washing.

Pearl got up from her seat, walked to him, and took his face in her hands. "Sweetie, what are they doing to you at those math and science camps? You look horrible."

"I'm just tired, Aunt Pearl, but I'm fine." His leg suddenly jerked, accidentally kicking Julio Iglesias, who went running off with a hiss. "Sorry, kitty, I didn't see you there."

Charles pulled off his rubber kitchen gloves and hustled over to usher Clivo out of the room. "Yeah, buddy, I'm sure you're exhausted, but we just want to hear how the experiment went."

Hernando gave Pearl a little bow. "Thank you, as always, for a wonderful dinner, Miss Pearl."

Pearl smiled, but watched with worry as they led Clivo away. "No problem, boys. Maybe you should have Clivo do a bit less addition and subtraction; he looks like he's about to pass out."

Charles and Hernando helped Clivo down to the basement, where he collapsed into a chair at the table. He rubbed his hand, which was still red and swollen from the chicken bite.

"Oh my gosh, Clivo, what happened to you?" Stephanie asked, running over with the first-aid kit.

"The 'harmless chicken' poisoned me, that's what happened," Clivo said, wincing as Stephanie examined the bite.

"You were drugged by the chicken?" Charles asked with a guffaw. Amelia hit him in the arm. "Ow! What? That may be the most awesome thing I've ever heard!"

Adam came over and looked at the bite. "Sheesh. We might want to cut out a sample and see what we can decipher about the venom's properties."

Clivo shot Adam a look. "We're not cutting into my

hand, but thanks for the offer." His other arm shot out and knocked over the bowl of fruit. "Argh! Sorry! Just some left-over effects from the pecking."

Stephanie started applying a bandage to his wound. "Do you need some rest, or do you want to tell us what happened?"

"Believe me, I could sleep for the rest of the summer, but we don't have time," Clivo said, the memories of the previous night coming back to him—as much as he could remember, anyway. "A helicopter showed up and took the Elwetritsch. I was right, someone's been kidnapping the cryptids after I locate them."

"Who? Did you get a good look at them?" Amelia asked, sitting a good distance away from Clivo and his flapping arm.

"I'm surprised I saw them at all, with all the hallucinating I was doing," Clivo said. "All I could make out is that it was one person who jumped out of a helicopter. Sorry, guys, it's not much to go on."

"Any bit of information is helpful," Amelia said, scratching her eyebrow in thought.

Clivo clenched and unclenched his hand a few times once Stephanie was done bandaging it. "Anybody have any ideas why the cryptids would be taken?"

"None." Stephanie sighed and put away the first-aid kit. "There's no mention in the chat rooms about any catches, no acquisitions by zoos, no circuses that are suddenly touring with the chupacabra. Whoever is doing this is keeping it really quiet. But we'll keep looking."

"Okay," Clivo said, frustrated that he hadn't gotten a better look at who took the chicken. "Any chance you have a lead on who the immortal might be, at least?"

Stephanie blushed. "Not at all. It's not easy for us to admit when we're stuck. But . . . we're stuck."

Amelia drummed her fingers on the tabletop. "It might be time to consult the Oracles."

Adam flew into a rage. "No! No Oracles! We don't need those guys!"

"They're so obnoxious!" Charles agreed.

Clivo had no idea what was going on. "You guys have an oracle?"

Stephanie smiled. "Oracles. That's what we call them."

Charles collapsed into a chair. "That's what *you* call them."

Adam sneered. "*We* call them dumb."

"Who are these guys?" Clivo asked, intrigued. "Are they fellow cryptozoologists?"

"Not really," Stephanie said, tucking a wisp of hair behind her ear. "They're just encyclopedias of knowledge when it comes to myths. Like we've said before, very few stories are pure imagination; there's usually some kind of truth to them."

Amelia nodded. "So, when we get stuck, we usually

consult the Oracles. Just hearing their stories often gets us to see something differently, thus solving the problem."

Adam groaned. "Ugh! I *hate* them!"

Clivo leaned over to Amelia. "Why do Adam and Charles dislike them so much?"

Amelia rolled her eyes. "BBS."

"Bigger Brain Syndrome," Stephanie clarified. "When too many smart people are in the same room, they prefer to compete with each other instead of actually listening and learning something."

"I have nothing to learn from them!" Charles insisted.

"Yes you do, and you have," Amelia shot back. "Now quit being a baby! You know this is the right call!"

Charles stomped his foot and let out a pouting sound.

"So where are these guys? Can we Skype them?" Clivo asked.

"No, they do things old school," Amelia replied. "If we want to talk to them, we have to see them on the weekend at their shrine in Boston."

Adam moaned again. "They are so *obnoxious*!"

Clivo thought about how to get the Blasters to Boston without Douglas knowing. He was already worried about telling Douglas that someone was stealing the cryptids, so he didn't want to explain why he needed to fly six people across the country. Douglas still didn't know about the Blasters, and it just felt right to keep it that way.

But it occurred to Clivo that he did still have some of his petty cash. As long as he didn't use his Diamond Card, Douglas couldn't track where he was going.

"Okay, who wants to come with me to Boston?" Clivo asked.

Charles snorted. "All of us. We do everything as a team, dude."

Before dawn on Saturday morning, Clivo and the Blasters left the house quietly in darkness, walked down the dirt road, and took a bus to a small airport outside of Denver. Clivo stood in the dusty terminal and looked around until he found what he was looking for.

"Serge!" he said, waving.

An extremely muscular man wearing a nice suit that looked like it was about to burst at the seams turned around. "Mr. Wren!" The man had a high-pitched voice that was quite the opposite of what one would expect from such a large, bulked-up person. "I got your message! Is this your special cargo?"

"Yes, sir, these are my friends," Clivo said, shaking Serge's hand. Serge was the bodyguard for any Diamond Cardholders who flew out of the Denver area, and he had become a personal friend of Clivo's. Clivo had wished many times that Serge could protect him on his catches, because the man was so strong he could probably take the Yeti down with one hand. But, as close as he was to Serge, Clivo just couldn't trust him yet with information about the cryptids.

Serge shook everyone's hands. "Any friends of Mr. Wren's are friends of mine."

"I'm Adam. You are a man who obviously enjoys his protein," Adam said, looking up at Serge in awe.

Amelia winced as Serge went to take her hand, but then looked at him with surprise. "Amelia. You have a very gentle grip for being as strong as an ox."

After the introductions were finished, Clivo asked, "Serge, were you able to find someone who's willing to fly us out of here for cash?"

Serge checked his watch. "Oh, yes, he should be ready for you guys. Come on back, folks, let's get you settled."

With his VIPs following, Serge bypassed the airport security checkpoint with a wave at one of the guards, who nodded. Serge led them behind the empty Pangaea Air counter and opened a door that led into the bowels of the airport. They walked through a concrete hallway lit with fluorescent lights, passing a few workers in orange vests. The hall was filled with the whir of airplane engines, and the air smelled like gasoline.

Serge opened a heavy door to the outside, where a clunky cargo plane was already waiting with its twin propellers running.

"Oh no," Clivo mumbled to himself.

An old man dressed in a brown leather jacket like an English barnstormer came around the tail, his white scarf blowing in the breeze. "Hey, Clivo! Good to see you again!"

"Clivo, you remember Alex?" Serge said.

How could Clivo forget? Alex had flown him to Alaska the previous year to search for the Otterman, and it was a flight Clivo had been sure he wouldn't survive. Alex was supposed to be a great pilot, but you would never have known it by the haphazard way he zigged and zagged through the clouds.

"It's nice to see you again, Alex. These are my friends," Clivo said, already dreading the flight to Boston.

"How you kids doing? You all running away from home or something?" Alex let out a joyful cackle and slapped the plane, causing a screw to come loose and drop to the ground.

Charles looked at Clivo, his lips pulled back in fear until his buckteeth stuck out. "This is your plan? To fly across the country in that garbage heap?"

Clivo did his best to reassure him, even though he wasn't feeling so sure himself. "Don't worry, Alex is the best. He flew me to Alaska in an ice storm and we did just fine."

"Except for a few close calls!" Alex laughed. "Remember when I almost nosedived into that frozen lake? Woo-hee that was a doozy!"

Hernando swooned, and Clivo grabbed his arm to hold him up.

"Take care, ladies, see you soon," Serge said, gently helping Amelia and Stephanie into the plane.

Adam eyed Serge up and down as he boarded. "When I return, we're going to have a serious talk about your gym routine. I could use some pointers."

Serge slapped him on the back and laughed. "Anytime, Adam."

Adam winced at Serge's powerful touch and climbed in.

The plane took off into the cloudless skies, with Clivo settling into the front seat next to Alex, who had lowered his goggles and zipped up his leather jacket.

"Okeydokey. Boston, here we come." Alex reached out to plug some coordinates into a keypad. The second his finger touched the system a shower of sparks flew out, a few of them landing in Clivo's lap as he frantically brushed them away with his hand. "Whoa! Ha! Does that every time!"

Charles stuck his head between the two of them. "I'd just like to mention that our combined IQ is 810, so if this plane goes down, you're losing a whole generation of future geniuses, dude."

"Don't you worry, my friend! I once landed an airplane in Vietnam with its wings and wheels blown off. Ol' Bertha here will get us where we need to go!" Alex patted the throttle, which promptly came loose. "Oh boy, that's not good. Hand me some of that duct tape there, will you, Clivo?" Clivo quickly handed him a roll of duct tape from a seat pocket and Alex secured the device back in place. "There we go! Right as rain."

Everyone tightened their seat belts as Alex guided the plane into the clouds. As soon as they had reached cruising altitude, Alex stretched his arms behind his head and let out a good, long yawn. He glanced at Clivo. "So, you going to Boston to do some more monster hunting?"

Clivo laughed. Alex had suspected that Clivo was going to Alaska to search for legendary beasts, and the old man had cautioned him against revealing the world's mysteries. It was more important for people to believe in their myths and magic, he'd said. "Nope. As far as I know there aren't any mythological beasts in Boston."

Adam shouted from the back. "What are you talking about, dude? There's the Boston Bahumagosh!"

Clivo turned around and shot Adam a look to be quiet.

"You know, it's interesting," Alex began, scratching his scruffy chin. "Ever since you went to the Revelation Mountains, there's been no sightings of the Otterman. It's like he just disappeared."

"Yeah, I've heard the same thing," Clivo said, not looking at Alex.

Alex shook his head. "It changes people, not having their myths. Makes them feel like there's no mystery left, nothing more to uncover. We quit being pioneers and just float through life, waiting for something to believe in."

Hernando spoke quietly from the back. "We're pioneers, sir. We believe."

Alex turned, causing the plane to bank sharply to the right, and flashed Hernando a wrinkled smile. "That's good. You keep that sense of adventure, you hear me?"

"BIRDS!" Clivo shouted.

Alex whirled around and banked the plane sharply to the left to avoid a large flock of black birds that had been about to get chopped up by the propeller. Everyone screamed, but Alex let out a joyous cackle. "Oops! Sorry, fellas! Almost clipped your wings there!"

In the back of the plane, Charles began throwing up into an airsickness bag. Adam let out a sound of disgust. "Dude! Be a man!"

Amelia unbuckled her seat belt and crawled forward until she was next to Alex. "Sir, if someone was stealing creatures like the Otterman, what do you think they'd use them for?"

Clivo looked at her, shocked that she would ask such a pointed question of a stranger, but she nodded at Clivo that it was okay.

Alex took off his brown leather cap and scratched his head. "Well, we had a story about that exact same thing happening a few years ago."

"Really?" Clivo asked, shifting to face Alex. "What happened?"

Alex took off his goggles and wiped them with his scarf, the plane's nose slowly drifting downward. "We had this guy in Montana one time. Rob was his name. He was a real magic cookie. He was a homesteader, meaning he lived in a cabin with no electricity or running water, and only ate what he could hunt, grow, or trap. He was pretty harmless, always kept to himself, though he was never known to be the nicest of fellas."

"Can you pull the plane up, please?" Charles asked desperately from the back.

"Huh? Oh! Right." Alex grabbed the controls and pulled the plane to level. "Anyhow, one day Rob comes sauntering into the local bar with a grin on his face, claims he'd trapped a bird larger than anything he had ever seen. When it flapped its wings, he said, it sounded like a thunderstorm was rolling through."

"The Thunderbird," Stephanie said from the back. "According to Native American tradition, it's a giant bird with no head but a massive beak with rows of pointed teeth."

"Your friends know their stuff," Alex said with a wink to Clivo. "So, Rob comes into the bar, his chest all puffed out like he's the baddest dude on the block, and demands free liquor. Of course, Carl, the bartender, scoffs and says that Rob needs to at least trade something for it besides some story about a make-believe bird, and Rob says that in exchange for liquor, he *won't* destroy the bar. Well, everyone thought that was a weird exchange; didn't seem fair that Rob wanted something for nothing."

"Not fair at all," Hernando agreed.

Alex continued. "So Carl, the bartender, assumed that Rob had maybe been spending too much time alone and had finally lost it, so he pulled out his shotgun and asked Rob to kindly get out of the bar. Well, Rob stood up and pulled out a giant feather and—now, I was there, so I saw this myself—he swiped that feather across the barrel of the shotgun, shearing the darn thing clear off clean as a whistle. Needless to say, Rob drank to his heart's content at the bar that day, with nobody saying a word otherwise."

Amelia looked at Clivo and nodded, her expression telling him everything. The cryptids were definitely evolving better protection mechanisms.

Alex put the goggles back on and folded his hands in his lap. "Before long, Rob was really living high on the hog. He realized that he could 'trade' with everybody in town for food and goods, and what he provided in return was the promise not to destroy their homes with those crazy feathers. One guy stood up to him, old Jim Darling, and said that Rob had to contribute something instead of just taking stuff, and I'm not lying when I say that Rob went ahead and sawed Jim's house right in half. Right in half! After that, nobody dared speak against Rob and just gave him whatever he wanted. Rob quit being a homesteader and became fat and lazy, eating and drinking more than anybody else in town. As long as he had those weapon feathers, he was king."

"So what happened?" Charles asked weakly as he wiped some spittle from his lip with the back of his hand.

"Well, the folks in town decided that enough was enough. Carl mixed some sleeping pills in with Rob's whiskey one day, and while Rob was asleep the townsfolk snuck into his cabin to gather up all the feathers. Now, don't think it didn't occur to all of them what they could do with that kind of power, what they could force others to give them if they wielded those weapons. But one thing stopped them."

"What was that?" Clivo asked, gently putting Alex's hands back on the controls since Alex seemed to have forgotten that he was flying the plane.

"The townsfolk crept into a back room and discovered the Thunderbird, as you called it, all caged up and looking worn and torn. This poor creature was pinned in the cage, its wings clipped so it couldn't cut through the bars, most of its feathers plucked clean off. And the sound coming from it, whew, nobody had heard such a pitiful cry for help in all their lives. The townsfolk looked at each other and realized that by wielding such power, the only thing that came from it was the ability to hurt others."

"With great power comes great responsibility," Amelia quoted.

"Best quote from Spider-Man, ever, dudette," Adam agreed.

"That's right," Alex said. "So the townsfolk made a decision right there and then that the only way to make things right was to return the creature back to where it belonged and destroy every feather they could find. They called in a local Native American tribe, whose members performed a sacred dance around the Thunderbird, asking for its forgiveness and promising it protection. Then they let the bird go, unsure if it would attack them or what. But the bird hopped out of the cage, flapped whatever noble wings it had left, and bowed its head to the folks before taking off into the wilderness."

"That's beautiful," Stephanie said.

"Sure is," Alex agreed. Then he let out a cackling laugh. "And woe be to those who come to Montana in search of the great bird, 'cause they've got a whole Native American tribe and group of townsfolk who will quickly show them the door. That thing will be protected for a good while to come."

Clivo took in the story. In addition to the Wasi in Egypt, there were obviously others in the world who lived in harmony with cryptids and did their best to protect them. Clivo and the Blasters weren't alone in their endeavor, and it made Clivo feel better that maybe there were more good guys in the world than he knew.

"Anyway, you asked me why someone would want to take the creatures," Alex continued. "And there's only one reason why: power. And not the good kind of power, where you help others. The bad kind, where you hold it over people just to make your life easier. That's why you gotta keep the myths a secret. They give folks something to hope for, and they keep the power balance in the world right. Humans aren't fit to be kings, not yet anyway."

"Don't worry, Alex, we don't want to be kings, and if we're ever lucky enough to see a creature, we'll do everything we can to protect it," Clivo assured him.

"Everything," Hernando quietly agreed.

Alex pulled his goggles away from his face and wiped his eyes, a few stray tears running down his face. "You're good kids, very good kids. Now, you may want to strap your seat belts on tight, 'cause I haven't been paying attention and we're about to say hello to another bird."

Clivo cinched his belt just as Alex rolled the plane to the left. Another small plane whizzed by so close to them that Clivo saw the shocked face of the other pilot, who dropped a doughnut onto his shirt as he scrambled to grab the controls.

IX

Six hairy hours later, the plane landed at a small airport south of the city. Everyone climbed out, and Charles dropped to his knees and kissed the ground. "I prayed to so many different gods on that flight, I think I just converted to twenty religions."

Clivo shook Alex's hand. "Thanks, Alex. We'll be back in a few hours."

"No problem, kids. I'll just be doing a few repairs on Bertha here while I wait and then we'll get you back to the mountains safe and sound." He patted the plane, which let out an ominous, creaky groan of protest. "Bertha! Quit being a drama queen!"

They took a taxi van into Boston, the air in the city as hot and humid as it had been in Egypt. Clivo was grateful that the driver had the air conditioning on full blast.

The taxi wound its way downtown between the tall skyscrapers, and eventually it stopped in front of a narrow cobblestone alley lined with buildings that looked like they were from colonial times. The redbrick structures with black shutters were squeezed together without any space between them, and old-timey gas streetlamps flickered on the sidewalks. Clivo felt like the British redcoats were going to come running around a corner at any second.

"Okay, remember, let me do the talking," Amelia said. "The Oracles are tetchy and clam up if you offend them. Agreed, Adam?"

Adam gave her a salute. "Yes, commander, but let the record show that I'm gonna hate every second of this."

"Charles? Do you agree?" Amelia asked.

Charles snorted, but nodded. "That doesn't mean I can't curse them silently in my brain."

"That's good enough for me. Let's go in," Amelia said.

They walked down the deserted cobblestone alley until they were standing in front of a run-down storefront. The door was made of weather-beaten wood, and gold lettering on the fogged-up window read ORACLE BOOKS: RARE COMICS FOR THE DISTINGUISHED READER.

"They're so pretentious," Charles mumbled.

"Charles! Zip it!" Amelia warned.

She pressed the button on an intercom system, and a doorbell that sounded like a laser echoed inside. After a moment, a monotone voice sounded. "Who seeks entry?"

"Hello, Exalted Ones. It's Amelia and the Myth Blasters," Amelia replied.

"Who?"

Adam clenched his teeth. "They *always* pretend not to remember us, and we've been here, like, a million times."

Amelia gestured to Adam to keep quiet and continued speaking. "I've brought an offering to The Ones Who Know All." There was a pause and then a buzzer sounded, unlocking the door. "Come on, guys, we're in."

Clivo followed Amelia through the door and entered a stuffy room covered in the most comic books he had ever seen. Rows of boxes held thousands of comics, each one delicately encased in a plastic sleeve. Several cases stood throughout the room, all heavily padlocked. The room was completely dark save for a few spotlights that shone on what must have been very special comics on display inside the cases. The room smelled like dust and ink, and Clivo's nose itched with a desperate need to sneeze.

Amelia walked to the back of the store, where two people, a guy and a girl, sat behind a counter. Clivo was surprised that they looked to be about his age, as he definitely had been expecting someone older and wiser, perhaps with a long white beard that stretched to the floor. Both kids wore black clothes, fedoras, and dark sunglasses even though the store had such dim lighting. The girl's purple shoulder-length hair was really the only feature that distinguished her from the boy next to her.

"Hello, Oracles," Amelia said, giving them a little bow.

Adam sniffed behind her and she flung her heel back

and kicked him in the shin. He shuffled backward, limping, as Amelia continued.

"I brought you an offering." She laid a paper bag from her satchel on the wooden counter and pushed it forward.

The girl, who, like the boy, had extremely pale skin like a vampire's, stared at Amelia for a long moment before taking the bag and peering inside. "All green M&Ms?"

Amelia nodded. "With one red one. Just as you like."

Clivo felt as if he had entered some kind of twilight zone. He definitely had not pictured anything like this scene.

The girl oracle put the bag under the counter and motioned for Amelia to continue. Amelia cleared her throat. "We're looking for a creature, not human, that might be immortal. What traits must this creature possess that can help lead us to it?"

The girl was about to speak when the boy next to her held up his hand and spoke in the same monotone voice, like a bored emperor addressing his subjects. "Before we answer, I have a question for the one in the back."

Adam looked up from where he had been flipping through a comic and adjusted his glasses. "Don't get started with me, dude."

The boy crossed his arms. "Who's stronger? Martian Manhunter or Superman?"

Adam let out a loud groan, and Amelia spoke to him in a harsh whisper. "You know the answer he's looking for! Just give it to him!"

Charles walked over to Adam and patted him on the back. "Be strong, dude, you can do this. We're working for the greater good here."

Adam answered through clenched teeth, looking as if the words physically pained him. "Martian Manhunter is more powerful than Superman."

The boy oracle slowly rocked back and forth in his chair. "That is the correct answer."

Adam grimaced and mumbled to himself.

"I know that hurt," Charles whispered to Adam. "I'm proud of you, dude."

The girl oracle continued. "Let us look at the immortal traits in the comic mythology, and let that guide you to the creature you seek."

The Oracles stood up and slowly walked around the room, sorting through the boxes and pulling out comics.

Charles held one up and spoke to the Oracles. "Dudes, do you need a copy of *Avengers* with Mister Immortal?"

The boy oracle waved his hand dismissively. "The Oracles require no help."

Charles looked like he was about to angrily say something, so Stephanie put her hand on his arm to keep him calm. "Do your breathing exercises," she whispered.

Charles began breathing heavily through his nose, apparently to calm himself, but all it did was make him look like an angry rabbit.

After gathering several more comics, the Oracles returned

to the counter at the rear of the strange shop. The girl began speaking like she was imparting pearls of great wisdom. "Looking at every immortal superhero won't give you clues about immortality, because their origin stories are all different. The samurai Manji was made immortal by an eight-hundred-year-old nun, Deadpool was cursed by Thanos, and Ultron can simply download his mind into other machines. There's no unifying thread for why they're immortal."

The boy oracle took over, pulling up his pants, which had begun sliding down. "So we need to look at other unifying factors." The boy reverently held up a comic book whose cover showed a woman shooting a bolt of lightning from a broom. "Witches." He held up another comic, delicately stroking the plastic cover. "Vampires."

Adam reached for it excitedly. "Dude! You have the new issue of *Vampire Hunter D*? That's, like, a super limited edition!"

The boy pulled it out of Adam's reach and addressed Stephanie. "Please control your minions."

Stephanie squeezed Adam's shoulder. "Just a few more minutes; you got this."

The boy held up another comic, the cover showing a creature that appeared to be half man, half dragon. "And finally, the shape-shifter."

The girl oracle nodded. "All of these are immortal, and all of them have something in common."

"They're all super cool, that's what," Adam muttered.

The girl oracle stomped her foot, all decorum lost. "Would you just let us finish! Geez! We're doing this totally awesome presentation, and all you do is interrupt! You're so rude!"

The boy oracle agreed. "Yeah, man. It's, like, do you want to know this or not?"

Adam pushed his way to the countertop. "You could do it with a little less pomp and circumstance, you know!"

"Then you figure it out, Skeletor!" the girl shot back. "We're done here! Get out!"

Clivo moved Adam out of the way and faced the Oracles, who were gathering up the comics. "Wait! I'm really sorry. My friends and I are just under a lot of stress right now because we're in a lot of danger."

The Oracles paused and watched him warily.

Clivo stared at the countertop, wondering how much information he should divulge to them. The Blasters were out of clues, and the longer he waited to find the immortal, the more time someone else had to find it. Clivo took a deep breath and made his voice as serious as he could manage. "There's an evil presence in the world, and it's growing day by day. The only way we can stop it is to find this immortal creature, but we don't know what it is. If you help us, you'll be saving the world."

The Oracles shuffled their feet, seeming to like the sound of it. The girl oracle spoke. "So, we'd be like the superheroes we read about?"

"Better," Clivo said, nodding his head slowly. "These characters are myths. You'll go down in history as *actually* saving the world."

The boy scratched his nose. "Like, from really evil stuff? I mean, super evil?"

"The worst," Clivo confirmed.

The Oracles looked at each other, their solemn faces breaking into big grins. The girl jumped up and down. "I told you all this reading would come in handy someday!"

"Yeah, and to think Dad wanted me to take up baseball instead! As if that's going to save the world!" the boy oracle agreed, also jumping up and down.

The girl gathered herself and leaned forward on the countertop. "Okay, so the one thing you need to look for if you want to find this creature is this." She looked down at all the comics, waving her hand over them like she was casting a spell. "They're all eaters of the dead."

Hernando leaned into Amelia, who gently held him upright.

Clivo swallowed. "Eaters of the dead?"

"That's right," the boy said, equally as excited as his sister. "In cryptid mythology, which is your territory, look for an eater of the dead. That'll be your guy."

The girl oracle pulled a comic from a box behind her and put it on the counter. It showed a vampire-like creature with huge wings and ferocious claws, teeth sharp enough to rip through anything. "Witches, vampires, and shape-shifters are the only myths that can be found in every country. They've been around forever, and they're woven into the fabric of world lore. They're more than just stories; they're real. Find the cryptid that combines their qualities, and you've found your immortal."

"One that eats the dead." Clivo swallowed.

The boy oracle gave him a lopsided smile. "Nobody said that saving the world was going to be easy."

The door to the shop slammed open and the lights blazed on, causing everyone to jump and blink at the sudden brightness. A man with a shiny bald head stood with his hands on his hips, looking fuming mad. "Brian and Sarah! This is a shop, and a shop needs to be open! How many times do I have to tell you that if you want to run the place, you have to actually unlock the door?"

Brian and Sarah whipped off their sunglasses and looked ashamedly down at the counter. Sarah brushed her purple hair away from her face. "Sorry, Dad, we were just—"

"Your job here is to sell stuff! Not play make-believe!" their father yelled.

Clivo stepped forward. "It's my fault, sir. I always like mood lighting when I'm making an important purchase." He pointed to the *Vampire Hunter D* comic. "How much for that one?"

Brian, the boy oracle, looked at the comic in surprise. "It's, like, five hundred bucks."

Clivo pulled out his wad of petty cash and handed over some money. "I'll take it. Thank you for all of your help."

The dad's face broke into a shocked smile. "Well, now! Looks like I was mistaken. My apologies! Thanks for coming in, kids! Thank you for your business!"

Sarah glanced at Clivo and mouthed, "Thank you."

Clivo leaned forward and whispered, "Keep what we talked about a secret, please?"

Sarah smirked. "Don't worry. Saving the world *never* involves adults."

The Blasters exited the store, with the dad clapping them on the backs and shaking their hands in thanks on their way out. Once they were outside, Adam exploded in a tirade. "The Martian Manhunter is *so* not stronger than Superman! Superman has heat vision! He just says that to toy with me!"

Clivo handed Adam the vampire comic. "Here, Adam— a gift for playing it cool in there."

Adam held the comic as gently as a newborn baby. "Oh, duuuuuude! Have I ever told you how much I love being on this team with you?"

Clivo turned to Amelia, who was spinning her nose ring in thought. "Did we get what we needed?"

"Oh, yes," she said. "Now we need to find an eater of the dead, and I know just where to look."

Half an hour later, they were standing in front of a massive library that was at least four stories tall and had giant Roman pillars out front.

Stephanie inhaled deeply. "Mmmm, I love the smell of a library on a warm summer afternoon."

Amelia eyed the place hungrily. "This place has a great section on rare world mythology books. I just need half an hour in here, if that's okay?"

"Yeah, totally fine," Clivo said, looking at his watch. "We should get back to the plane soon—I don't want to give Alex a reason to forget about us—but we have a little bit of time."

Clivo glanced around the large grassy area, which was filled with people enjoying the waning afternoon sun. He wasn't sure what was bothering him, but an eerie feeling was making his hair stand on end, as if someone was watching him. He scanned the lawn. People were lounging on benches reading, kids ran around while their parents stared at their phones, and one guy in a mime's outfit was juggling some bowling pins.

It was a very serene, lazy-summer-day kind of scene, but still, something felt off.

Then Clivo saw it. At the far corner of the lawn sat an older teenage boy with spiky red hair. His eyes were definitely trained on Clivo's group, and his face was set in a knowing grin as his fingers viciously pulled the heads off dandelions.

Who was he? Had someone from the evil resistance found them? The kid was young, but Lana from Luxembourg was

Clivo's age and had ended up being a much better fighter than him. Were they suddenly in danger?"

"Clivo?" Stephanie asked, gently tugging on Clivo's sleeve. "You ready to go in?"

"Huh? Yeah, let's just all stay together, okay?" None of the Blasters knew how to fight, so warning them that they were being watched wouldn't do anything except frighten them, and Clivo wanted them focused on the task at hand.

The group walked up some stairs to the second floor and into a large marble foyer with a gold-plated dome roof and tile floor. The happy chattering of Adam and Charles echoed through the cavern.

They headed down a hallway into Bates Hall, the library's main reading room, with its rows of tables illuminated by brass reading lamps. Bookcases nestled between pillars lining each side of the giant room. There were just a few people studying at the tables, and they all shushed Adam and Charles as they walked by.

"Do you think Nosferatu will rise up and kill the head vampire guy?" Charles asked, pointing to the comic book cradled in Adam's arms.

"Dude! He can't be killed! Remember the last edition, where they put a stake through his heart, doused him with holy water, threw garlic at him, and he *still* didn't go down?" That loud exclamation earned Adam another shushing from a nearby table.

Amelia turned to them. "Do you guys think you can behave yourselves while I hop into the rare-book collection?"

Charles groaned and flopped into a wooden chair, its legs making a horrible squeaking sound on the tile floor. "This has just been a 'day of don't' for us."

"Come on, dude, let's crack open this baby," Adam said, sitting next to Charles and pulling the comic book out of its plastic sheath.

Hernando sat down across from them. "I'm going to sit and quietly contemplate life for a bit."

"Clivo, do you want to join us in the rare-book collection?" Stephanie asked, pointing to a room off one end of the hall.

Clivo kept his eyes trained on the entrance to the reading room. "No, you guys go ahead. I'll stay out here."

Everyone went about their respective tasks as Clivo traveled back toward the entryway, keeping his eyes peeled. Within moments he saw the kid with the spiky hair turn the corner. Clivo quickly darted behind a pillar and waited for the kid to walk by, but he never did.

Clivo peered around the corner in confusion and realized the kid had disappeared. "Shoot," he mumbled to himself.

He kept watch until he saw a flash of red. The kid was on the near side of the room, walking stealthily, as if stalking prey.

Clivo ducked and followed as the kid wove his way around the bookcases and big pillars. Chairs squeaked on the tiles, and from his hiding place behind a row of book-shelves, Clivo noticed the other readers leaving the room, obviously annoyed by the occasional loud laughs and snorts coming from Charles and Adam as they read their comic.

The redheaded kid kept moving forward, and it had become obvious that he was heading toward the Blaster boys. Clivo slowly parted two books for a better view as the kid walked past, and he noticed something silver and shiny clutched in the boy's hand. Was it a knife?

The kid eventually stopped behind a bookcase just next to Adam and Charles. He tapped the silver thing on his leg as if he was gearing up to spring.

Clivo sprang first. He jumped forward and pinned the kid's arms behind his back, slamming him chest first onto the table directly in front of Adam and Charles.

Hernando jumped up and promptly tripped on his feet, falling over, as the redheaded kid began to yell, "Excalibur! Excalibur!"

"Is that your safe word?" Clivo yelled, his breath coming in gasps.

Adam tilted his head to look at the kid, whose face was smooshed against the wooden tabletop. "McConaughey?"

"Hey, Adam, whatcha guys up to?" McConaughey asked casually, even though his nose was pressed painfully against the table.

"You know this guy?" Clivo asked, his body still flooded with adrenaline.

"Unfortunately," Charles said, rolling his eyes. "He's a fellow cryptozoologist, from Vermont. We told you about him last summer."

"What are you doing here?" Adam asked, pulling his comic away from McConaughey's face. "You're always all up in our business!"

"My dad is here for work and I just happened to see you guys!" McConaughey said, squirming against Clivo's grip. "Hey, how many times do I have to say my safe word before you'll let me go?"

Clivo grabbed the silver item out of McConaughey's hand and released him, then tossed the object onto the table. "He was stalking you guys and carrying this. I wasn't sure if he was dangerous or not."

Charles scoffed. "Dangerous? As if!" He picked up the metal item. "It's just a flash drive, and a crappy one at that."

"So what are you guys doing here?" McConaughey asked, rubbing his shoulder. "And why are you traveling with a bodyguard?"

"We're researching, as always," Adam said, kicking his feet up on the desk.

"Oh yeah? What are you guys researching?" McConaughey asked excitedly, taking a seat at the table.

Charles snorted. "There's no sitting with us!"

McConaughey stood up with a groan. "Guys, it would be so much more fun if we could just combine forces once in a while! I have stuff to offer, seriously!"

Adam was about to say something when Clivo interrupted. "What can you offer?"

Charles and Adam looked at Clivo in disgust, but the cryptid catcher put his hand up to give McConaughey a chance to speak. Things were picking up speed in their search for the immortal and the other cryptids, and if someone could offer some information, like the Oracles, he was ready to take it. As the Blasters had said, every possible answer, no matter how far out there, needed to be explored.

McConaughey jumped up and down excitedly a few times and blew air through his lips as if preparing to run a race. "Okay, get this. Do you guys know that the cryptids are disappearing? Like, nobody's seen at least a dozen of them for a while!"

Charles snorted, but Clivo encouraged McConaughey to continue. "We know that. Anything else?"

McConaughey seemed crestfallen for a moment, but continued. "Oh, okay. So ANYWAY! Either they're dying off, which would be a massive bummer. OR they're all being corralled together, and that can only mean one thing!"

"What's that?" Clivo asked.

McConaughey put his hands on the table and looked everyone in the eye in turn. "Someone is forming a cryptid army, fellas."

Adam looked as though he was about to say something, but stopped. He dropped his feet off the table and leaned forward. "Go on."

"May I sit?" McConaughey asked.

"You can sit next to me," Hernando said, offering the chair next to him.

"Thanks, Hernando," McConaughey said, eagerly taking a seat. "Okay, so picture this. We don't know what special powers the cryptids have, but they must have something. You don't live to be thousands of years old without learning how to do some pretty cool stuff. If I lived that long I'd absolutely learn how to shoot lasers out of my eyeballs."

"You're losing us," Charles said in a singsong voice.

"Okay, okay, sorry, you know how excited I get about this stuff." McConaughey wiped his hand across his face, which had begun dripping sweat. "Anyway, so if someone could bring a bunch of cryptids together and chain them to, like, a chariot with spiked wheels, that someone could take over the world with an army of feared creatures who shoot lasers or spit acid or whatever cool stuff they've learned how to do!"

Charles groaned. "Dude! This is what you always do! You start with a great idea and then you totally spoil it! What are we supposed to do with that hypothesis?"

McConaughey bounced on his chair a few times as if to calm himself down. "Okay, maybe the chariot thing went too far. But listen, if we can find the enslaved cryptids, then we can stop them from being used for world domination!"

Adam laid his forearms on the table. "Now take this slow . . . How do we find the enslaved cryptids?"

McConaughey plucked the flash drive from Adam's hand. "With this."

"What is it?" Clivo asked, taking a seat next to McConaughey.

"This, my friend, is the next revolution in cryptid finding," McConaughey said, beginning to bounce on his chair again. "Every person emits heat and energy—that's why infrared goggles work in finding people, right? What if it's the same for cryptids? What if they emit some kind of unique electromagnetic signature that can be traced?"

Adam pushed his glasses up on his nose. "You are starting to sound really awesome, so don't ruin it. Go on."

McConaughey tapped the flash drive on the table. "This, gentlemen, holds the basic schematics for a crypto-thermal reader."

"You are sounding even more awesome," Charles agreed, leaning forward as well. "You have our attention. Don't lose it."

"Okay, okay," McConaughey said excitedly, obviously thrilled to be the center of their focus. "So, this device will be able to read a cryptid's electromagnetic emissions. You use the device anywhere in the world, and you can find where the cryptids are hiding."

"How does it work?" Clivo asked, intrigued.

McConaughey ran his hands over his face a couple of times. "Okay, so it's a super-cool pair of goggles that you put on. Big goggles, like a space helmet. Once you put them on, the real world vanishes and all you see is the energy emitted by the cryptids. It's like you've stepped into a totally awesome secret world, the world of myth and legend, instead of just the boring stuff that's all around us."

"Neat," Hernando agreed.

"Thank you, Hernando," McConaughey said, catching his breath after the exciting presentation.

"And you've built this crypto-thermal reader and it works?" Adam asked, his eyebrows raised in challenge.

McConaughey swallowed. "Well, no. I just came up with the idea and designed the goggles. But I figure that if you guys wanted to go in on this with me, I'd give you the design and you can, you know, figure out how it actually works."

Adam was staring off into the distance, and Clivo could actually see the wheels of thought spinning in his eyes. "McConaughey, I never thought I'd say this, but you are a genius," Adam said.

"I am?" McConaughey asked, surprised. "I mean, yeah, I know I am."

Adam leaned over and whispered something to Charles, who nodded. Charles stood up. "Listen, man, your ideas are getting better. Like, *a lot* better. Just do some more research on how this crypto-thermal reader might actually work, and we'll consider bringing you in."

"You will?" McConaughey asked, jumping to his feet. "I

mean, yeah, sure, that'd be great. I'd be happy to share my research. Thanks, guys, thanks a lot!"

Clivo noticed Stephanie and Amelia coming out of the rare-book collection. Time to go. He turned to McConaughey, who shifted his eyes nervously under Clivo's penetrating gaze. "I don't know you, but I'm going to make the assumption that you're one of the good guys. Am I wrong to assume this?"

McConaughey's face melted in disbelief. "Yes, I'm one of the good guys! My mom would *kill* me if I tried to take over the world!"

Clivo smiled. "Then you're already on our team. Just make sure you stay there."

McConaughey waved as the Blasters hurried away. "Bye, guys! Thanks! I'll be in touch!"

"Was that McConaughey?" Stephanie asked as they exited the library. "What's he doing here?"

"He wants us to help him build a cryptid-finding device," Adam said distractedly.

"Do you think it'll work?" Stephanie asked.

"It's actually a solid hypothesis, for once," Adam replied, still staring off into the distance. "If we had more time, we could explore it. But here's the main thing—all of McConaughey's chatter gave me another idea about how to find the cryptids."

"Nice," Amelia said. "And I'm maybe closer to finding

the immortal. I've been working on something for a while and needed to check a source I couldn't find online. This place had exactly what I needed."

"High fives, Blasters!" Charles said. "Let's hope that crazy pilot doesn't crash on the way home, so we can get to work!"

X

They arrived home in one piece on Sunday morning after what turned out to be an overnight flight back home. The trip had been pretty uneventful, save for a few unintentional descents when Alex drifted off now and then, and a tire that popped as they landed, causing the plane to come to a stop on the wheel's rim in a shower of sparks.

But everyone had managed to catch some shuteye on the flight, and when they reached their mountain home they were ready to get back to their research.

"Hernando and Charles, I'll need your help checking this hypothesis I have about how to find the missing cryptids," Adam said, walking up the driveway toward the house. "Amelia and Stephanie, you keep working on who the immortal is."

"Careful of the rope!" Clivo yelled a split second too late.

Adam took one more step, and instantly the rope lasso tightened around his leg with a *snap*, whipping him off the ground and upside down and sending his glasses flying.

"I'm coming, buddy!" Charles yelled, darting forward to

help Adam. But just when he was almost to him, another *snap* sounded and Charles had just a moment to scream in surprise as a punching bag came flying through the air, knocking him on his back with a brutal *thwack*.

Jerry came running out of the house and began slapping his leg and laughing. "Whoa! Sorry, guys, I didn't hear you coming! As you can see, I added a few more traps while you were gone."

"Yeah, we noticed," Clivo said over Adam's overdramatic yelling. "Are we safe to move?"

"Sure, just make sure you skip the third step here," Jerry said.

Clivo slowly lowered Adam to the ground, and Hernando helped Charles to his feet, brushing pine needles out of his puffy hair. Charles was a bit wobbly and had to be supported by Hernando, who struggled to keep him upright.

Adam was not pleased. "Dude! Your traps keep attacking the wrong people!"

"Well, if you'd tell me when you're coming back instead of just taking off without me, I could plan better!" Jerry retorted. "Am I part of this team or what?"

"Yeah, yeah," Adam said, climbing the steps to go inside.

"Watch the third step, man," Jerry reminded him.

Adam stopped. "The third step up or the third step down?"

Jerry screwed up his face and scratched his chin. "Good question. Skip both, just to be safe."

Adam rolled his eyes and used the banister to help him climb over the booby-trapped steps. Everyone else followed, being careful to avoid those steps as well.

They descended to the basement, with the Blasters going to work on their individual tasks while Clivo filled Jerry in on everything.

"So two comic-book nerds and a random guy in the Boston Public Library helped you guys figure stuff out?" Jerry asked.

"Don't ask me how, but it seems like everyone is suddenly onto something," Clivo replied, watching as the Blasters huddled in corners, talking to each other about their discoveries.

Jerry looked down at his hands, which were busy tying a rope into knots. "You guys just took off on me yesterday morning. I showed up and only Pearl was here. I had to pet her cats for an hour before she let me get to work."

"Huh?" Clivo asked, bringing his attention back to Jerry. "Oh, geez, I'm sorry, Coops. It totally slipped my mind to tell you we were going out of town."

"That's the thing," Jerry began. "It never even occurred to you to take me with you. If I'm not part of the team, Wren, then just tell me. But don't ignore me, hoping that I'll go away. Friends don't do that to each other."

Jerry's words shocked Clivo. Clivo didn't feel any of those things, but when he really thought about it, he could totally understand why Jerry thought he did. "Coops, that's not it at all. Having you on the team is the best. Yes, your booby traps have made coming in and out a little unpredictable, but I asked you to design them. I didn't ask you along to Boston because, I don't know, I'm just trying to protect everyone, and the easiest way I can do that is to keep you here. Believe me, I would have left half of the Blasters behind if they had let me; they just make more noise about it than you do."

Jerry eyed Clivo carefully. "Truth?"

Clivo nodded. "Total truth."

"Okay, then I'm going to say this once and only once. By leaving me behind, you're leaving the one person out who can actually protect *you*." Clivo started to say something, but Jerry cut him off. "Listen, Wrenmaster, the evil resistance isn't coming after me, they're coming after *you*. You need protecting, and it's my choice if I want to do it or not. You can't be the only person in danger—others of us need to shoulder the risk. Leaving me behind to keep me safe isn't going to cut it anymore."

In a smooth motion, Jerry slipped the rope around Clivo's wrists and yanked it tight so Clivo's hands were stuck in a rope handcuff. Jerry flashed him a wide smile. "I got skills, man, you know I do. And you need 'em."

Clivo laughed. "Okay, Coops, you're right. As long as you understand the dangers, I won't keep you out of the action anymore. Fair?"

Jerry rubbed his hands together eagerly. "You know I love nothing more than being in the middle of the action!"

Charles suddenly called to them from the middle of the room. "Dudes and dudettes, we've discovered something."

Everyone gathered around Adam's workstation, where he was holding something behind his back. "Okay, McConaughey's idea about all the cryptids having the same electromagnetic energy is an interesting possibility, but super hard to prove. But it did get me thinking about other physical properties the cryptids have in common. Like this." Adam pulled a tranquilizer dart from behind his back.

Clivo furrowed his brow. "But we used that dart earlier to see if the tranquilizer was contaminating the cryptids' blood. And it wasn't."

"Actually, it was," Charles broke in, his rabbit teeth sticking out ominously. "With this."

He held up a glass slide with a black square on it that was no bigger than an ant.

"What is it?" Clivo asked.

"It's a tracking chip," Adam said, taking it from Charles. "Every time you caught a cryptid, you implanted a tracking device in it. Did you know that?"

Clivo shook his head, unsure if this was good news or bad. "I guess Douglas did that so he can track the immortal once I find it."

"Well, someone's been hacking the signal and tracking the other cryptids," Adam said. "Stephanie, any chance *you* could hack into the signal and find out where the cryptids are?"

Stephanie took the glass slide and looked at the tracking device through a magnifying glass. "I think I could. I would just need access to a satellite."

Everyone's eyes swung to Jerry, who immediately began shaking his head. "No and no and, in case you didn't hear me the second time, no and forever no."

"Just hear her out, Coops," Clivo begged.

"Anything regarding my dad's work is off-limits. You know this!" Jerry said. "I gave you access to a SETL satellite once. *Once!* That was the deal, man. You need to find another way."

Clivo put his hands on Jerry's shoulders to calm him down. "Coops, I hate to ask you to stick out your neck again like this, but we need to find these cryptids."

Jerry kept shaking his head. "After getting kicked off the football team *again*, my dad is *this* close to sending me to a military academy. If I mess up one more time, I'll be in basic training by fall."

"Just give her the codes, dude," Adam said, peeling an orange.

"Hey, man, this could get me in real trouble!" Jerry retorted.

Adam flung an orange peel at him. "And Clivo was drugged by a demon chicken! We're all taking risks here!"

Jerry took a step back and looked Clivo up and down. "You were drugged by a demon chicken?"

"Momentarily, but I'm fine," Clivo assured.

"Don't worry, Jerry, I'll protect you," Stephanie said, her hand resting on his arm in reassurance. "I'm good at what I do—*very* good. If you just give me the security codes, I'll hop on and hop off, just like I did before. Nobody will know. We'll just ask those sensitive receivers on the satellite to point in the opposite direction for a while."

"Are you really as good as you say you are?" Jerry asked, looking at Stephanie sideways.

Stephanie cracked her knuckles. "As far as hackers go? I'm pretty darn good."

Jerry blew air through his lips a few times in exasperation before finally saying, "Okay, let's do this before I regret it."

Stephanie sat at her laptop, rolled her wrists around as if she was about to perform a gymnastics routine, and hovered her fingers over the keyboard. "Ready whenever you are."

Jerry glanced at everyone, who had huddled in close. "A little space here, please?"

"Right, sorry, dude," Charles and Adam said in unison while backing away.

Jerry whispered something to Stephanie, who giggled. "Really? That's the password for their computer system?"

Jerry nodded. "Right? My dad chooses it, and he's such a dork."

Stephanie focused on the computer, her hands flying around like hummingbirds. Her blue eyes flashed as number-filled screens popped up in front of her with incredible speed. With the password, she could walk right into the system through the internet. "Now I just need to make it look like the system is offline for a bit so I can hijack its equipment. It's a LEO bird, meaning it's in a low-Earth orbit and takes about ninety minutes to circle the planet. I'm asking it to turn away from outer space and sweep the surface of the Earth for what we're looking for as it makes its orbit. Hopefully Douglas used the same bunch of transponders for each tranquilizer dart, so by tracking this one, I can track them all."

Stephanie typed rapidly, humming to herself quietly. Her pursed lips were the only sign of effort as screen after screen of computer codes scrolled by.

With a final click of her mouse, she sat back and took a sip of water. "That should do it. Now, you all have to leave me be for an hour and a half while the satellite and I get better acquainted."

The impatient gang took a break for a late breakfast, making a mess of Aunt Pearl's kitchen and then cleaning it up again before she'd even surfaced from her bedroom. Clivo assumed it had been a late night of dancing the evening before.

They reconvened at Stephanie's workstation exactly ninety minutes later.

"Okay, this has been going well. I have been plotting some coordinates from the satellite onto a map. We can throw it up on the wall so everyone can have a better view. Adam?"

Adam turned on a digital projector and a map of the world glowed on the wall, a collection of bright dots pinpointing different locations.

Amelia took it from there. She grabbed a yardstick to point at places on the map, like a lecturing professor. "Okay, folks, look alive. These are the locations of all the transponders from Clivo and his dad's tranquilizer darts."

Clivo studied the map. "There's a dot over here by itself. Where's that?"

Stephanie zoomed in from her keyboard. "Loch Ness. That must be Nessie."

"Okay, so she's still in the loch, but we knew that already 'cause of the sightings," Clivo said. "Where was that other single dot?"

Stephanie moved the map to the other dart. "That one is in Russia, where you found the Ugly Merman. Maybe he's okay, too?"

"Maybe," Clivo said, scratching his chin, "but I also used a dart on a black bear who had invaded my camp, so there should be two dots there, not just one."

Stephanie zoomed in on the western United States until they were suddenly looking at a large cluster of dots. She caught her breath sharply. "This is bad, guys. Over a dozen cryptids are all in the same place. Someone *has* been taking them, and they're all gathered together."

Clivo's blood began to boil. As twisted a plot as it would be, he could understand someone taking the immortal; that made sense. But why gather up *all* the cryptids?

He and his dad had fought so hard to keep the other cryptids' whereabouts a secret. Who'd done this, and why?

"Where are they?" Clivo asked, his jaw clenched in anger.

Stephanie zoomed in even closer, her face melting in confusion. "You can see for yourself. They're right here. In Old Colorado City."

"What?" Clivo asked, leaning in closer to the map. He had been prepared to fly across the globe to figure out who'd been doing this. Discovering the cryptids were all in his own backyard made his stomach turn. "Can you get me the exact address?"

She brought up a street-map layer and without much trouble zeroed in on the location. She scribbled down an address and handed it to him. "It looks like it's near the Air Force Academy."

Clivo grabbed the paper and stalked toward the stairs, where Jerry immediately stepped in front of him. "Where do you think you're going, cowboy?"

"Out of my way, Jerry," Clivo said, his face red with anger.

"So you can do what? What are you going to do?" his friend asked.

Clivo stared at Jerry. He had no idea what he was going

to do. He just wanted to rescue the cryptids. "I'm a little short on plans at the moment," Clivo admitted.

"That's what I thought," Jerry said, putting his hand on Clivo's shoulder. "Now, you're a little hot under the collar, so why don't you simmer down, put your feet up for a while, and let your coolheaded friend plan our next move?"

"And what's our next move?" Clivo asked. He was so angry, even his breath felt heated.

Jerry brought his face close to Clivo's and smiled. "Time to do some reconnaissance work, my friend, which your old pal Jerry happens to be very good at."

Clivo shook his head. "Jerry, I know I said you could come, but this is too much. Like, level-ten danger."

Jerry wagged his finger in front of Clivo's face. "We just talked about this. You can't do everything alone, Wrenmaster, no matter how dangerous. I won't let you. And that's the end of that discussion."

Jerry was right. Clivo couldn't do everything alone, especially when he wasn't even sure what lay ahead of him. He wanted to keep Jerry safe, but the reality was, maybe they were more powerful together. Clivo finally nodded. "Looks like it's time to jump into the middle of the action, Coops."

Jerry clapped his hands. "Right where I belong."

XI

By the time the taxi dropped Clivo and Jerry off that
evening, it was fully dark and the air had cooled from the
heat of the day. Gray clouds had rolled in over the mountains, and rumbles of thunder echoed in the distance.

The address led them to a warehouse nestled up against
the mountains on the outskirts of town. A row of lights
blinked in the distance, and a massive military plane landed
on the nearby Air Force Academy's runway with a roar of its
engines. The academy was so close by that Clivo thought
the warehouse was perhaps one of their abandoned buildings. It was redbrick, with towers and turrets reaching to the
sky like on a castle. A bolt of lightning lit up the clouds, illu-
minating gargoyles with evil, grotesque faces and pointy ears.
Clivo half expected an army suited up in chain mail to start
shooting arrows at them from the roof.

"The creep level of this place is totally off the charts,"
Jerry whispered as a crack of thunder made him jump.

Clivo gripped the tranquilizer gun in his hand and stared
at the castle-like structure. It really was ominous-looking,

and it seemed like an appropriate place for something nefarious to happen. "Okay, Coops, this is an exploratory mission only. We're here to see if the cryptids are actually in there, and if they are, we'll come back once we have a plan."

"You got it, Wren," Jerry said, shifting the coil of rope over his shoulder.

They jogged toward the building, Clivo's eyes swinging to the roof to make sure nobody was watching them. He still expected to see a glint of armor from a medieval army, but the flashes of lighting illuminated nothing but the turrets and gargoyles. They circled the castle, looking for windows to peer through or doors that might be easily broken into. No cars were parked outside, which hopefully meant it was deserted, although there was a large helicopter sitting on a landing pad in the back.

"That could be how they transport the cryptids," Clivo whispered. "It looks just like the one I saw in Germany when the Elwetritsch was taken."

Jerry nodded. "Should we sabotage it so it doesn't fly anymore?"

Clivo thought about that. "No, let's keep it exploratory only, remember? Also, we might need it to get the cryptids back home."

Jerry looked at Clivo sideways. "You know how to fly a helicopter?"

"Well, no, but don't you think it's better to have the option of a helicopter than not?"

Jerry shrugged. "Can't argue with that."

They inspected the whole building, but the walls were solid brick and the only door was an arched metal structure with a glowing number pad next to it that must have been the electronic lock.

"Looks like next time we need to bring a catapult or battering ram," Jerry whispered.

Clivo pointed toward the roof. "Do you think we can use your rope to climb up there?"

"Easy," Jerry said, tying the rope into a lasso. He swung it over his head like a professional cowboy and tossed it high, and it easily caught around the head of a particularly nasty-looking gargoyle. Jerry leaned on the rope with all his weight to make sure it would hold, then began to climb.

"Hang on, let me go first," Clivo said. "I want to make sure it's safe up there before you come."

Jerry sighed. "And *I* want to make sure it's safe for *you*, got it?"

Clivo stepped away and let Jerry continue his climb. Clivo knew he had to get used to Jerry wanting to protect him, even though he really didn't like it.

Jerry easily shimmied up the rope and swung his legs over the brick ledge. He ducked down into a crouch and ran along the parapet, jumping around corners with his fists held up, ready to tackle anyone who confronted him.

Clivo watched the display and almost began laughing. Jerry was taking his job as protector a little too seriously.

After an extended sweep of the roof to make sure all was clear, Jerry finally motioned to Clivo that it was safe to climb up.

"Thorough, aren't you?" Clivo whispered as he heaved himself over the ledge.

"Never assume you have the element of surprise," Jerry replied, helping Clivo over. "Come over here. I found something."

They walked around the roof, avoiding the sharp horns of the gargoyles. Set in one of the towers was a metal door with a keyhole.

"Do you know how to pick it?" Clivo asked.

"Does an astronaut float?" Jerry replied.

Jerry pulled two paper clips out of his pocket, straightened them out, and began fiddling with the lock. Within seconds, a click was heard and the door swung open, revealing a stone spiral staircase that descended into darkness.

"Nice job," Clivo whispered.

Jerry blew on his paper clips like a Hollywood gunslinger blows on his trusty Colt revolver and holstered them in his pocket. "My dad has yet to find a lock I can't pick, and trust me, he's tried them all."

Clivo peered through the door. There was no sound coming from the darkness, but there was a very sharp smell. Clivo couldn't quite place what it was, and he had the strange notion that it didn't smell like a thing, it smelled like an emotion: *fear*.

Clivo was about to say something, but Jerry beat him to it. "I'm going down with you, Wren. End of discussion."

"Will you at least let me go first, since I have the tranquilizer gun?" Clivo asked.

"Just this once, but don't think it's going to become a habit," Jerry replied.

Clivo began to slowly creep down the stairs as a light rain started to fall outside. Jerry quietly closed the door behind them so the pitter-patter of raindrops didn't echo down the stone stairwell. As they wound their way downward, Clivo could feel Jerry getting closer and closer behind him. He finally stopped and turned around.

"Do you want a piggyback ride or something?" Clivo whispered.

Jerry backed up in embarrassment. "Sorry, I just have an irrational dislike of spiral staircases. They make me dizzy."

"Okay, put your hand on me if you think you're going to fall over."

Jerry put his hand on Clivo's shoulder and they continued on, the stairs descending farther and farther into an unknown abyss. Clivo was certain that by then, they were deep underground.

After what felt like forever, they finally exited into a large room lit by overhead iron chandeliers that glowed with flickering bulbs made to look like candles. Heavy tapestries covered the high stone walls, and a wide hearth stained with the soot of old fires stood in a corner. The air felt cold, as if no warmth had ever penetrated the place.

"Wren," Jerry whispered as audibly as he dared, "there they are."

Clivo looked to where Jerry was pointing and his heart froze. The other side of the room was filled with cages, all lined up against one another. There were no lights hanging above the steel bars, and at first the cages appeared empty. But as Clivo peered closer, he could see cowering shapes and figures, and the reality of what he was looking at hit him like a brick to the head. The cryptids, at least seventeen of them, were locked in the prison with no food or water in sight. Now Clivo understood what he had smelled—the odor of animals crammed together in their own filth combined with the cold sweat of terror. He tried to identify which cryptid was which, but all he could see were the whites of eyes that stared at him in fear as the creatures tried desperately to squeeze themselves deeper into the corners. These animals were beasts and some were even dangerous, but treating them like this was inhumane. Whoever had put them here was the real animal.

Clivo let out a roar of anguish and ran over, putting his gun on a nearby table without care, and grabbed the bars on one of the cages. He was so angry, he felt like he could snap the bars in half, but the steel was unbending even against his fury. The cryptids cringed in corners and stared at Clivo with human-like sadness. Their fur was disheveled, and in some cases matted with blood.

Clivo spied the Ugly Merman and noticed that its mouth was taped shut, probably so its tongue couldn't attack. It looked so much thinner than when Clivo had caught it. Next he saw the Elwetritsch, its feathers sagging, its poisonous beak wrapped in gauze. In a smaller cage sat an otter that kept trying to shape-shift into the Otterman, but every time his body shivered and expanded, electricity sparked, shocking the otter into recoiling back into its harmless shape.

"What are they doing to you guys in here?" Clivo moaned. He didn't know if he was angry, sad, or in shock. How could someone treat these majestic creatures so terribly?

A familiar voice sounded behind him. "I'd be happy to show you."

Clivo whirled around to find Douglas pointing the tranquilizer gun directly at him. "Douglas!" he said, a growl of anger issuing from his throat—anger at Douglas's betrayal, and anger at what Douglas was doing to the creatures they were supposed to be protecting. He balled up his fists and, without thinking, ran toward the old man.

"Clivo, no!" Jerry screamed.

The tranquilizer dart hit Clivo squarely in the shoulder and his knees instantly went weak. The dart didn't hurt that much, but the drug it injected definitely made his head swim and his body suddenly feel like it was trying to walk through water.

Clivo saw his friend's eyes swing back and forth between Douglas and him, as if he was unsure of what to do. In his blurry mind, Clivo instantly regretted bringing Jerry along. Jerry wasn't used to being attacked, and the first instinct was to freeze. With Clivo's limbs hanging useless at his sides as he struggled to stay upright, he realized there was nothing he could do to help his friend, and Jerry just didn't have enough experience to help *him*.

The situation got even worse as Douglas pulled a gun—a *real* gun—from his waistband and pointed it at Jerry. "Why don't you pretend to be a smart kid and lock yourself in that cage over there?" Douglas growled.

"Jerry, do it," Clivo mumbled as he dropped to his knees and fell onto his side.

Jerry grimaced, realizing there was nothing he could do, and walked into an empty cage. "Betraying Clivo like that is a cold move, man," Jerry said as he shut the door behind him.

"Yeah, yeah, cry me a river, kid," Douglas replied.

As Clivo's eyelids got heavy and he slowly slipped into unconsciousness, he heard the jangle of the Egyptian rattle being shaken over him to protect him. All along, the person he'd needed protection from had been the person he'd trusted the most. Someone he'd considered a friend.

Clivo's mind slowly went black. The last thing he heard was a rumble of thunder as the storm raged somewhere far above.

He woke to the smell of the cigar that was sticking out of Douglas's mouth as the man lounged in a velvet-upholstered chair.

"Oh good, you're awake," Douglas said.

Clivo struggled to sit up, which was hard to do considering that Douglas had tied his hands behind his back and his feet together. Looking around, he found he was locked in one of the empty cages alongside the cryptids.

Jerry ran to the front of his cage. "Wren, you okay?"

"I'm fine, Coops. The demon chicken poison was worse, trust me."

Clivo's brain was slowly coming out of its fog, and the only thing that hurt was his shoulder where the dart had pierced it.

"Hello!" Douglas said, waving his arms around. "Doesn't anybody care that I'm sitting here holding a gun?"

Clivo glared at Douglas with a seething hatred. "You're the last person I care about right now, Mr. Chancery."

"Yeah, no offense, Mr. Chancery, but you're kind of a jerk," Jerry said from his cage.

"Fine by me," Douglas said, heaving himself up and

stretching his back. "Being nice never got anybody anywhere in this world. Now, do you want to see why I gathered all the cryptids together or what?"

"Not really." Clivo shrugged, not wanting to give Douglas even a second of satisfaction, even though he was deeply curious to know what awful fate Douglas had planned for the creatures.

Douglas moaned in exasperation. "Can't you just have a little appreciation for the dramatic at least once?" He extinguished his cigar in an ashtray and walked over to a stainless-steel table that was covered with various bowls and test tubes. "Well, seeing as how you're a very captive audience, I'm going to show you anyway, and I'd *appreciate* it if you feigned interest."

Douglas picked up a pair of heavy rubber gloves and put them on. Clivo exchanged nervous glances with Jerry.

Douglas hobbled over to the cage that held the blue tiger, a massive beast colored a light shade of blue. Douglas reached inside the cage to grab the tiger's collar, but the creature let out a low growl and swiped a giant paw at Douglas's hand. "Hey! Don't be nasty!" Douglas grabbed what looked like a cattle prod and gave the tiger a shock.

"Leave it alone!" Clivo yelled, unable to stomach watching a cryptid being abused.

The tiger let out a roar of pain and cowered on the floor.

"Come on, now, don't make me ask again," Douglas

said, holding out his hand and the cattle prod. The tiger crawled forward, opened its mouth, and from its tongue a drop of pearl-colored saliva fell into Douglas's palm. "See, that wasn't so hard. Okay, kids, prepare to have your minds blown."

Douglas faced a stone wall, wound his arm up like a pitcher, and threw the saliva at the granite. The second the pearl hit, it exploded into a bright light, then settled into a roaring green flame that covered most of the wall. Clivo blinked rapidly from the brightness and heat.

"Hoo-wee!" Douglas cackled with excitement. He faced Clivo and Jerry and spread his arms out wide. "You *have* to be impressed by that."

"So you kidnapped a tiger who spits fire? Congratulations, you must feel pretty proud of yourself," Clivo said.

His eyes were scanning the room, trying to figure out if there was a way out of this mess, but with both Jerry and him in cages and his own arms tied, things weren't looking too good.

"You are really becoming a pain in my rear, you know that?" Douglas complained, sitting back down in the chair with a grunt. "As you probably were beginning to guess, each cryptid is endowed with some pretty spectacular properties. The Honey Island Swamp Monster over there has teeth harder than the strongest substance on earth, the chupacabras can shoot claws that are sharper than obsidian, and that chicken thing there has a poison in its beak that renders a person unconscious as effectively as the best tranquilizer out there."

"Yeah, I've experienced that," Clivo said. "So are you just keeping them around as pets to show off to your friends, or what?"

Douglas rested his forearms on his knees. "Kid, stuff like this can only be used for one thing."

"I'm guessing it's not for world peace," Clivo replied.

Douglas cackled and slapped his hand on his leg as if that was the funniest thing he had ever heard. "Nah, never had much use for world peace—makes things a bit boring, if you ask me. No, kid, this stuff is much better put to use as organic warfare."

"What's that?" Jerry asked, his face pressed against the bars.

"Ah! That got your attention!" Douglas stood up and went to some cupboards, where he poured himself a drink.

Clivo looked at the cavernous underground dungeon and realized that part of it looked like a laboratory, complete with beakers and Bunsen burners. The other half was a dark, cozy living room with a hearth, overstuffed chairs, and thick wooden coffee tables. It was like a mad scientist's lair, and Clivo and Jerry had stumbled directly into it.

Douglas took a hearty swig of his drink and let out an annoying sigh of contentment. "Time for a history lesson, kids. The military has been working on how to use animals for warfare since the Civil War. But really child's-play stuff.

They trained horses not to shy away from cannon blasts, taught dogs to drag wounded soldiers off the battlefield, dumb stuff like that. Then they got a little more sophisticated, such as training dolphins to warn submarines about any underwater mines. But they never really did anything *big*. Until now."

Clivo glanced around him at the cryptids. It was like they knew he was there to rescue them. Their expressions were desperate and pleading, and it killed him that there was nothing he could do to help.

"Hey! I'm talking here!" Douglas said, nudging Clivo with his foot.

"Sorry my attention wandered from your boring presentation," Clivo replied sharply.

"You always were a brat, you know that?" Douglas said. "Anyway, to continue my story, I started out as one of the good guys. I made my millions in the family fracking business and was living a rather boring life of excess when I met your dad."

Clivo's head whipped up at the mention of his dad. He wasn't sure he wanted to hear this story. "What about my dad?"

"We met at church, if you can believe it. Ha! Can you picture me in church now? God would come straight down from heaven and kick me out himself. But your dad and I were both real Goody Two-shoes at the time, trying to find ways to save the world and all that crap. Then, after your dad and I became friends, he confided that he had discovered a way to *really* save the world with this immortal cryptid thing. He just needed some money for those worldwide treks of his. I was hooked. Not only could I save the world, but all I had to do was write a check and someone else did all the heavy lifting. You see, I always was the lazy one."

"So what happened? Why did you stop being one of the good guys?" Jerry asked.

Douglas took another swig of his drink and rocked back and forth in his chair, as if remembering a pleasant memory. "Turning evil is actually quite easy. It's staying good that's hard, and I was never up for a challenge. Things were all fun and exciting at first, while your dad was catching cryptids. He'd come home and show me photos and talk about his adventures. But it got boring after a while! You can only hear about the awe of catching legendary creatures for so long before it becomes as mundane as going to the bathroom. And who knew how long it would take to find the immortal? Time was passing, my money was dwindling, and I was no closer to saving the world. But then something miraculous happened."

"Do tell us about your miracle. I can hardly stand the suspense," Clivo said dryly, although he had to admit that he was curious about his father's history. His father's time as a cryptid catcher was such a mystery to him that he was eager for any information that would shed light on how his father had gotten involved in such an adventure.

"I thought you'd never ask," Douglas said, waving his drink around. "Russell's boring cryptid-catching stories started taking a more exciting turn. He started talking about how each cryptid seemed to have evolved all sorts of neat natural defense mechanisms. Exploding saliva, tranquilizing beaks, shape-shifting abilities. Real blow-your-mind-type stuff. All of a sudden, life was fascinating again, and my wheels started turning. While Russell was looking for the immortal, I could take the stuff from the other cryptids and sell it to the military for a pretty penny. Organic warfare was about to take an incredibly interesting leap."

"And so you changed? Just like that? You went from wanting to protect the world to wanting to destroy it?" Clivo asked.

Douglas finished his drink with a gulp. "Trust me, kid, you just have to care about yourself and ignore the needs of others, which has always been very easy for me. Besides, which is more fun—saving the world, or building a super soldier complete with indestructible armor, shape-shifting abilities, and explosive powers that can wipe out a town with a fling of the wrist? You have to admit that's pretty cool!"

Jerry raised his hand. "I'm more of a 'save the world' type of guy myself. Learning how to fight war better still means you're waging war. And in war, nobody really wins."

Douglas leaned back in his chair with a heavy grunt. "Bah! You kids are such Goody Two-shoes, it makes me sick."

A thought struck Clivo. He looked at Douglas, wanting to ask the question but terrified of the answer.

"How did my father die?"

The words were barely a whisper.

A shadow fell across Douglas's face. "I killed him."

Clivo's chest clenched so tightly he couldn't breathe. His jaw locked together and the next words came out in a choke. "Why? He was your friend."

Douglas waved his hand as if swatting away a fly. "Not after he discovered what I was doing. He had no interest in using the cryptids for organic warfare. He wanted to protect them, which is so *boring*! I knew he had never told you anything because he wanted to wait until you were older, so you could enjoy your frivolous childhood without being burdened with the knowledge of the immortal. So I figured I'd just get him out of the way and start fresh with you. Please tell me you're not completely against turning evil. It really is great fun."

"I'm so sorry, Wren," Jerry said, his hands gripping the bars of his cage.

Clivo was having a hard time catching his breath. His father had been killed by Douglas, a man whom Russell had considered his friend. Clivo couldn't imagine how he'd feel if one his friends betrayed him—the thought was unbearable. His father being murdered was one thing, but being murdered by someone Russell had trusted made it even worse. Someone whom *Clivo* had trusted. He had even been beginning to *like* Douglas. Why hadn't he seen it? He felt so, so stupid.

Clivo was suddenly grateful that he had kept the Blasters a secret. He and Jerry might be trapped with this evil man, but at least Pearl and the Blasters were safe.

Douglas stood up and grabbed the gun that he had left on a table. "So, in case you're interested—and you really should be—here's what's going to happen next—"

He was interrupted by a rather loud banging coming from what must have been the front door.

"What the—?" Douglas's eyes narrowed as he whirled his head toward the sound. He clutched the gun tightly and hobbled to the spiral stairs, gripping his cane in his other hand.

Clivo and Jerry stared at each other, questioning, as Douglas disappeared, followed by the squeaky sound of a door opening. Immediately a cacophony of voices floated down into the dungeon—a mixture of several loud, excited voices interspersed with guttural responses from Douglas.

After a moment there was the sound of the door being slammed shut and locked, followed by a stampede of footsteps coming down the stairs.

Clivo's eyes just about bugged out of his head when he saw Douglas enter the room, the Myth Blasters right behind him, all nervously clutching their laptop computers close to their chests.

Douglas smiled at Clivo with satisfaction. "Well, kid, looks like I now know how you're so good at finding cryptids."

XII

Clivo stared at the Myth Blasters from his cage in shock and panic. *What are they doing here? They should be safe at home with Pearl. Why did they put themselves in danger?*

The Blasters glanced around the room, their eyes lighting up at the sight of the cryptids. Clivo had forgotten that they had never seen one, much less *seventeen*. He wished their first time seeing the magnificent creatures wasn't in the dungeon of an unhinged lunatic who had the beasts bound and caged.

"Mr. Chancery, I don't know who these kids are. You should probably just let them go." Clivo didn't know what to do or say; he just wanted the Myth Blasters out of there.

"That's not what they tell me," Douglas said, waving his gun at them. "They say they know you pretty well, and that without them there's no way you'd ever find a cryptid by yourself."

"Hi, Clivo. Hey, Jerry," Hernando said and waved.

"What's up, dudes!" Adam said, puffing out his chest proudly.

Clivo grunted in frustration. The Blasters obviously weren't picking up on his attempt to get them out of harm's way.

"Guys, what are you doing here?" Clivo finally asked in a strained voice.

Stephanie stepped forward, her eyes darting around nervously. "We do everything as a team, remember?"

"And that includes the dangerous stuff, too, dude," Charles agreed, his buckteeth sticking out in defiance.

Douglas let out a cackle. "Well, well, well, isn't this a nice, cozy reunion!"

Clivo needed to stall so he could think of a way out of this, or they'd all be dead. "Mr. Chancery, I'm warning you. Let them go. You need me to find the cryptids, and I won't help you if you hurt them."

"Hurt them?" Douglas said. "Now why would I do that when they're obviously the brains behind your whole business? I think that keeping them here is a much better idea, don't you?" Douglas leaned over and put his face next to Clivo's, his breath smelling evil. "But if you don't keep catching cryptids for me, then we're going to have a problem. Do we understand each other?"

Clivo was stuck. Douglas now was holding not only Jerry hostage, but the Blasters, too. Everything he cared about was in danger. If he didn't do something soon, his friends would be prisoners and he'd be forced to continue catching cryptids for the purpose of waging war.

Douglas straightened up and motioned to the Blasters with his gun. "Okay, nerd herd, into that cage with you."

Adam looked at Clivo out of the corner of his eye and whispered, "So, dude, we really didn't have much planned because brave rescue attempts aren't really our forte, but if we distract crankydude for a minute, do you have anything up your sleeve?"

Clivo's mind whirled. He was a good fighter, but locked in a cage with his hands and feet bound, he was worthless. "Can you distract him without getting hurt?"

Adam nodded. "Maybe. As we were coming down here on our bikes, we realized we were unarmed, so we came up with a plan in case of trouble."

Douglas waved his hands up and down at Clivo. "Hello! I can hear you!" He turned toward the Blasters, his gun at the ready. "In the cage. Now! And come to think of it, maybe I'll shoot one of you since you obviously aren't taking my threats seriously."

Douglas raised his gun and fired. Hernando jumped in front of Amelia, his laptop held in front of him like a shield. The bullet ricocheted off the computer as Hernando landed on his face with a splat, the destroyed machine clattering across the floor.

"Blasters! Fire!" Adam quickly said. In a surprising move, he flung his laptop toward Douglas like a Frisbee. It just missed the man's head, smashing against the wall instead.

With reluctant grimaces on their faces, the other Blasters flung their precious laptops at their enemy. He dodged all of them except Amelia's, whose machine knocked the gun from his hand before shattering.

"Blasters! Pile on!" shouted Adam.

The Blasters ran and jumped on Douglas, who tried to shake them off as he snarled with anger. He lifted his cane and began swatting at them like a professional swordsman. The cryptids had all moved to the fronts of their cages and were moaning and barking sounds of terror, as if begging for the battle to stop. The wombat-like gunni was running its antlers across the cage bars while moaning pitifully.

"This is as far as our plan goes, Clivo!" Charles yelled over the ruckus, ducking away from a swipe of the cane. "So if you could take over from here, dude, that'd be awesome!"

Clivo, in his cage, turned toward Jerry in his. "You got anything up your sleeve, Coops?"

But Jerry had already pulled out his two lock-picking paper clips. "I'm on it!" He reached around to the front of the cage and grunted as he fiddled with the lock.

The basement lair was filled with ear-piercing noise as the Blasters yelled at Douglas while avoiding his swinging cane that was quickly shattering every lamp and test tube in the dungeon. The cryptids kept up their howls of pleading and the Beast of Bray Road was banging its bear-like body against its cage as if in desperation to escape its prison. The scaly dingonek was gnawing on the bars with its saber-like teeth in an attempt to chew its way out.

Jerry finally unlocked his cage and ran over to open Clivo's as Clivo hopped unsteadily on his tied feet. "Untie me, Coops," Clivo said once Jerry had the door open. He had his eyes trained on Douglas, who had just given Charles a solid whack in the shins with his cane. Clivo wasn't sure what his next move would be. All he knew was that it involved getting his hands on Douglas.

"No way, man," Jerry said, suddenly hoisting Clivo over his shoulder like a sack of potatoes. "I'm getting you and the team out of here before someone gets hurt."

"Let me down, Coops!" Clivo said, squirming in his friend's iron grip. "I'm not letting that spawn of Satan get away!"

Suddenly a shot rang out, and everyone froze, including Douglas, who had his cane raised for another swipe. The cryptids scurried to the corners of their cages where they hunched and trembled.

Clivo's eyes went wide as he saw Hernando huddling in a corner, Douglas's gun shaking in his outstretched hand. The ground was covered in broken glass and dented stainless-steel bowls.

Hernando swallowed and spoke quietly. "I would just like us all to calm down for a minute, please."

"Shoot him, Hernando!" Clivo yelled, tears running

across his forehead since he was still hanging upside down from Jerry's shoulder. "Just shoot him!"

Stephanie gasped. "Clivo! You don't mean that!"

"Yeah, dude, we don't really do that kind of thing," Charles said.

"Not really our bag, you know?" Adam agreed.

"Well, if you're not going to shoot me, can we at least get on with this, please?" Douglas bellowed, his face red and sweaty from the exertion of the fight. He had staggered over to the blue tiger's cage and was leaning against it as he panted for breath.

Jerry turned to face everyone, which was a bummer because then Clivo couldn't see anybody. "I think we need to give Clivo a hall pass for his thoughts. That guy over there killed Clivo's pops, so he's pretty bent out of shape about it. Can't say I blame him."

Now Amelia gasped and whirled on Douglas, who still had his cane of death held in front of him like a broadsword, but his grip looked wobbly. "You *murdered* Russell?"

Douglas gave an evil smirk, but said nothing.

Stephanie ran up to Clivo and grabbed his upside-down face in her hands. "Clivo, I know you're upset, but remember, *Be careful when you fight the monsters, lest you become one.*"

Clivo's face was a mess of snot and tears. "I know, Stephanie. I just want him to pay for what he's done."

"And he will, I promise. Just not that way. Agreed?" Stephanie's face, even upside down, was filled with such compassion that it made Clivo tear up even more.

"Agreed," he choked.

Amelia took the gun from a grateful Hernando and held it expertly toward Douglas. "Here's how this is going to go, you walking piece of contaminated meat."

"Whoa! Solid insult!" Adam cheered.

Amelia continued. "You are going to have a seat in that chair like a good boy while we figure out a way to get these cryptids out of here. Understood?"

Douglas began laughing and pushed himself away from the cage he had been leaning against. "It is just amazing to me what a pain in the rear your entire generation is, you know that?"

Clivo couldn't see what was going on since Jerry was too busy observing the action himself, but he figured it out the second Jerry began to yell, "Watch out! He's going to throw it!"

Jerry turned around and ran, allowing Clivo to see Douglas just as he threw a pearl from the blue tiger onto the ground in front of him. A wall of green flame exploded, throwing the Blasters backward.

"Run!" Clivo yelled as Jerry bounded up the stairs with him.

Clivo was relieved to see all the Blasters scramble to their hands and knees and follow them up the stairs.

Douglas's echoing laugh followed them all the way outside until Charles slammed the front door shut, leaving them alone in the darkness of night.

The gang ran away from the building to where three old bikes and two dusty skateboards sat waiting.

Adam quickly pointed to them. "We figured we'd need some wheels for a quick getaway, and this was all we found in your garage."

Charles grabbed a bike and wobbled as he climbed aboard. "And walking up that hill is super tiring on my legs. Saddle up, everybody!"

Clivo rode on the back of Jerry's bike since he was still weak from the tranquilizer. Hernando sat behind Charles, who complained about the extra weight, and Adam sped in front of them, his arm raised and a yell of triumph warbling from his mouth. Amelia and Stephanie rode the skateboards as they held on to two of the bikes, surfing along with expert balance.

"Hey, Adam," Jerry yelled, "take a left here! We'll go to my place; it's too dangerous back at headquarters now that we know Douglas is cuckoo for Cocoa Puffs."

They finally arrived at Jerry's house, which was in a quaint residential neighborhood.

"You're sure it's okay if we all stay here tonight?" Clivo whispered.

"Totally," Jerry said. "I'll hide you in the basement, and in the morning I'll figure out how to tell Ma and Pops that they need to make a bunch of waffles and put you guys in witness protection."

Clivo turned to the Blasters. "Let's make sure we're quiet as we sneak in."

"No problem, dude," Adam whispered. He took a step forward and something under his foot made a loud *click*, causing him to freeze. "Oh no—"

In a sudden burst, an inflated clown popped up from behind a bush, causing Adam to let out the highest-pitched scream Clivo had ever heard. A bright floodlight popped on and a whooping alarm began sounding. The noise echoed up and down the quiet street.

Jerry winced. "Whoops, I forgot about that."

The front door to Jerry's house was flung open and Mr. and Mrs. Cooper stood in the doorway, both wrapped in bathrobes and looking like someone had just thrown a live rooster in their faces.

"Jerry?" Mrs. Cooper yelled. "For the love of Martians on the moon, what is going on?"

"Sorry, Ma, sorry! I'll turn it off!" Jerry rummaged in the bushes, and a moment later the lights and sound stopped. He turned toward the other houses, where panicked neighbors were spilling out onto their porches. "Sorry, everybody! My apologies! False alarm!"

Jerry ushered everyone inside, where his angry parents

stood with their hands on their hips. "Clivo?" Mrs. Cooper said, her hair wrapped in big curlers that had gone askew. "It's past midnight! What is going on?"

Mr. Cooper adjusted his glasses, which were sitting crookedly on his face. "And who's your crew here? You guys aren't on the run from the law or anything, are you?"

"No, Dad," Jerry said, obviously searching for a proper lie. "It's just, well, there's this thing . . ."

Clivo stepped in. "Remember when I said that our science experiments were having a contamination issue?"

Mr. Cooper scratched his belly. "Yep. Yep, I sure do."

"Well, we've kinda contaminated the whole house," Clivo said with an "oops" face. "I hate to bother you guys, but is there any chance me and my science team could stay here for a few days?"

Charles stepped forward and kissed Mrs. Cooper's hand. "Charles Duncan, at your service. My cohorts are Adam, Hernando, Amelia, and Stephanie, and we formally request the pleasure of staying in your abode. We're clean, don't eat much, and rarely snore."

"But I do have a slight gluten intolerance," Adam added, raising his hand.

Mr. Cooper looked at his wife. "Is that okay with you, Pumpernickel?"

"Well, of course they can stay," Mrs. Cooper said with a wave of her hand. "But, Clivo, what about Aunt Pearl? Where is she staying during the contamination?"

Clivo's eyes shot wide open. He had completely forgotten about Aunt Pearl and the cats, all of whom Douglas could take hostage, or worse.

"Shoot. Um, any chance you have extra room for some cats?" Clivo asked sheepishly.

An hour later, Clivo and Mr. Cooper arrived back at the house with a disheveled Aunt Pearl and two curious cats. The felines instantly jumped on Hercules, who looked as if he knew his peaceful life was about to end in a puff of cat hair.

"Come on, Pearl, let's get you all set up in the guest room," Mrs. Cooper said.

"They really are wonderful kids," Pearl said with a twitch of her nose. "In spite of being teenagers, they haven't burned the house down once."

Mrs. Cooper looked at her in confusion. "But they *did* contaminate the house with some kind of foreign poisonous substance."

Aunt Pearl let that soak in. "I suppose you're right. But it's the first hazardous spill we've had all summer."

The adults led Aunt Pearl to her room. After they left, Clivo turned toward his team. "I want to thank you guys for coming to rescue us. We never would have gotten out of there without you."

"Yeah, we were pretty awesome," Adam said, kissing his nonexistent bicep. "Hey, Amelia, how'd you learn how to handle a gun?"

Amelia blushed. "When I need to rest my brain, I play *Tomb Raider*. I've learned a lot from Lara Croft."

Clivo took a deep breath. "And I want to apologize to you, Hernando, for telling you to shoot Douglas. That was wrong. I just . . . I don't know. I understand what he meant when he said it's easy to turn evil. Thanks for setting me straight."

Hernando gave Clivo a big hug. "As long as you surround yourself with good people, you'll stay good."

Jerry motioned for everybody to follow him to the basement. "Come on, team. I think we should get some sleep so we can figure out in the morning how to wage war on a guy with an arsenal of crypto-weapons."

"Sounds good, dude," Charles said, stretching his arms over his head with a yawn. "I chugged an energy drink before our rescue operation, and I'm totally spiraling into a caffeine crash."

Everyone went to their respective sleeping nooks, with Mrs. Cooper coming down and insisting on kissing everyone goodnight before tucking them in.

Clivo lay down on a blow-up mattress in Jerry's room, the familiar smell of the house giving him comfort. Even though it was close to two A.M., he couldn't sleep, and it wasn't because of Hercules's rattling snores as the basset hound slept at Jerry's feet. His mind was full of so many things, none of which he could sort out. Douglas had murdered Clivo's father, and the cryptids were being used for war—neither of which he had any idea of how to handle. And he still had to find the immortal. All of a sudden, everything seemed dismal and hopeless.

"You awake, Wren?" Jerry asked from his bed.

"Yeah," Clivo said, staring at the ceiling.

Jerry rolled up onto an elbow. "This reminds me of last summer, when you lived here."

"It does," Clivo agreed. "Those were good times. I mean, apart from losing my dad and all."

Jerry picked at a piece of lint on his comforter. "I'm sorry about your dad, Wren. I know you trusted Douglas, and for him to betray your family must really sting."

Clivo rolled onto his side to face Jerry and rested his head on his arm. "I just can't shake the feeling that I should've known. I can't believe I trusted him this whole time, and even vouched for him. I feel like an idiot."

"Don't go there, Wren," Jerry insisted. "If someone's a total jerkbag, that's on them, not you. You're not responsible for Douglas turning into an evil mastermind of epic proportions. Remember, your dad trusted him, too."

"I know, Coops, it's just—" Clivo's voice faltered. "I have so few people left who mean something to me. I know it's stupid, but it just makes me sad that he's no longer one of them."

Jerry got out of bed and picked up Hercules, who snorted awake with a whine of confusion, and placed the dog next to Clivo. "Here. Whenever I'm not feeling so positive, I sleep next to Hercules and it makes me feel better."

"Thanks, Coops." Clivo wrapped his arm around the chubby dog, who instantly snuggled against his shoulder and fell right back to sleep. Clivo had to admit, it did make him feel better.

Jerry yawned and settled back into bed. "You still have a lot of people around you, Wren, remember that. And let's be honest, losing that grumpy grouch probably isn't the worst thing in the world."

Clivo smiled. "You're probably right. Good night, Coops."

"Good night, Wrenmaster."

Clivo eventually fell into a deep sleep cradling Hercules, whose breaths felt like butterfly kisses on his cheek.

Clivo woke early, as the sun began to shine through the window. He walked around to see if anyone else was awake, but the house was silent. Mr. and Mrs. Cooper's bedroom door was closed, but he checked on Aunt Pearl, who was snoring away happily with the cats encircling her head like a fluffy hat.

He quietly walked downstairs and smiled as he saw Amelia and Stephanie asleep on the living room sofas. Mrs. Cooper had even put glasses of milk and plates with a few cookies next to them.

Clivo went into the basement, which was cozy and nicely decorated, save for a bit of Jerry's weight-lifting equipment piled in the corner. Adam, Charles, and Hernando were all sprawled out on the sofa or the floor. Charles was talking in his sleep, his arms flailing as if he was playing a tennis match.

Clivo went back to Jerry's room and lay down, and Hercules once again snuggled against his chin.

He might have lost his mom and dad, but he had found a new family. A family who cared for him and was ready to protect him without a thought for their own safety.

There was a lot to still get done, but Clivo fell back asleep with the comforting feeling that he wasn't alone.

XIII

The next morning, after Mrs. Cooper had fed them a big breakfast of waffles with eggs, bacon, and more waffles, the Blasters gathered in the basement. Everyone was in the same clothes as the night before and nobody knew quite where to sit since they didn't have their workstations.

Eventually they situated themselves on the cushy sofa or chairs, and Amelia took her place at the front. Adam stood in the back, attempting to pump iron with some of Jerry's weights.

"Okay, let's take stock of where we are," Amelia said. "We know where the lost cryptids are and we know that Douglas is the kidnapper. But we've lost our headquarters, our laptops, and any equipment we might need. Other than that, we're in good shape."

"If this is being in good shape, I don't want to know what bad shape is," Jerry replied.

Adam yelled from the back where he was trying to lift what looked to be a rather light dumbbell, "I feel naked without my laptop, dudes, but using them as flying weapons was pretty sweet."

Clivo looked at Stephanie. "Any chance Douglas could hack into one of your laptops and steal your intel?"

"Not a chance," Stephanie said, shaking her head. "If anybody's machine still works, we have a kill switch installed so the hard drive will immediately be erased if someone tries a wrong password three times in a row."

"Great," Amelia said. "Clivo, how do things stand with you?"

Clivo rubbed his forehead with his fingers. "I've lost my tranquilizer gun. But when I went back to the house to get Pearl, I picked up my passport and the blood sampler. They'll come in handy if we ever figure out who the immortal is."

Amelia smiled. "Oh, yeah, we were all kinda distracted with the whole rescue operation, but I've figured it out."

Clivo lifted his head, a bit of hope coming to him. "You have? Amelia, that's amazing!"

"It's just a guess, as the others have been, but at least it's a guess based on clues—the clues the Oracles gave us," Amelia responded. "And it does make perfect sense."

"Who is it?" Clivo asked.

Amelia looked around. "Jerry, do you have a laptop I could use?"

Jerry ran upstairs to grab a computer and returned a moment later, handing it to Amelia. She opened it and began tapping on the keys. "So, the Oracles told us that the immortal must be an eater of the dead."

"Which is so awesome!" Adam said from the back as he struggled to lift the dumbbell with both hands.

Jerry walked over and took the weight easily in one hand. "Why don't you sit down, buddy? You're going to blow a gasket."

Amelia continued. "*Anyway*, we need to find an eater of the dead, which rang a bell for me. In Philippine mythology, there's a being known as the Manananggal, a vampire-like creature with huge bat wings that eats people. It's purely a myth; there've been no actual sightings of it. But I thought I had read something about the word 'manananggal' being applied to other creatures in the Philippines that were also known as eaters of the dead. That's why I needed to go to the library. They have the only known copy of a handwritten account of Philippine mythology written by a Spanish colonist in the seventeenth century. I skimmed it for instances where the word 'manananggal' was used in reference to other beings."

"And you found it?" Clivo asked.

"I did," Amelia said. "I found two other creatures in the Philippines who are often called manananggals. One is the wakwak, which looks similar to the Manananggal; the only difference is that the Manananggal can split itself in half so only the top part of it takes flight to catch its prey."

"Gross," Charles said, "and amazing."

"Agreed," Amelia said. "The other creature is known as the aswang."

Amelia turned the computer screen so everyone could see it. They crowded around and Jerry groaned. "That's not good."

Clivo looked at the drawing on the screen. It was a horrid-looking creature with a human body and face, but with long claws and teeth like a saber-toothed tiger and impossibly long bat wings. Blood dripped from its teeth and claws, and its mouth was open in a terrifying roar.

"Please tell me that's not who you think the immortal is," Clivo said, his stomach flip-flopping at the prospect of having to catch it.

"Unfortunately, yes," Amelia said apologetically. "There haven't been any verified sightings of the wakwak, but there have been plenty of the aswang, and it's known as an 'eater of the dead.' It's also been confused for a vampire, witch, werebeast, and shape-shifter—basically, all of the immortal myths."

Clivo looked at the picture again. "But it looks *human*."

Amelia hesitated, as if she didn't want to say the last part. "It does look human, because that's what it shape-shifts to."

"Whoa, whoa, whoa!" Adam said, jumping up. "We deal with cryptids, which are hidden *animals*, not hidden humans disguised as bats! There's no such thing!"

"But there is," Stephanie said, nervously picking at a fingernail. "When we got back from the library, we checked and double-checked. There have been enough sightings and there's enough data on this thing that it *has* to be real. And keep in mind, humans *are* animals, so it's completely possible that a shape-shifting human is our immortal cryptid."

"And it makes total sense," Amelia added. "What creature could live forever and truly never be discovered unless it's simply an ordinary-looking person or animal who blends in among us? It's been around at least since the fourth century B.C. That's over two thousand four hundred years."

"How do you know that?" Clivo asked, although he wasn't sure he wanted to know the answer.

Amelia hesitated again before saying the next part. "The word 'aswang' comes from the Sanskrit language. It translates to 'demon.'"

Clivo hung his head. Of all the creatures that could possibly be the immortal, why couldn't it be a nice furry koala bear instead of a flesh-eating demon?

Jerry put his hand on Clivo's shoulder. "Remember, you're not alone in this. Not even a demon stands a chance against the Cooper-Wren team."

Clivo tried to smile, but his whole body felt frozen with fear.

"Here's the thing," Amelia said, taking a seat across from Clivo. "The aswang is only dangerous once it's shape-shifted.

When it's in human form, it's harmless, and it has lived for millennia doing its best not to draw attention to itself. Apparently, it lives a rather normal, boring life."

"Boring except that it turns into a vampire witch and eats people," Clivo said dryly.

Amelia nodded. "But only on the full moon."

"Oh, well, that's good," Clivo said. He rubbed his hand across his forehead. "I'm sorry, I don't mean to be sarcastic. It's just that there's really no good news with this thing."

Stephanie's face lit up with reassurance. "But there is! If you can find this aswang when it's in human form, it's not dangerous. And it's not even in hiding! It's just walking around somewhere, going to work."

Charles raised his hand. "But how is Clivo supposed to identify demon dude when it's not a demon?"

"Now, that's the cool thing," Amelia said, raising a finger. "When the aswang is in human form, there's one thing that sets it apart from the rest of us."

"Please tell me it's something obvious that I can see from afar," Clivo said.

Amelia grimaced. "Not exactly. But it is obvious. When you stare into its eyes, your reflection is upside down."

Charles grabbed Adam and pulled him face-to-face, staring intently into his eyes. "Yeah, dude, you gotta be at least this close to see your reflection."

Clivo suddenly felt exhausted, even though he had just woken up. "Okay, so I just have to go to the Philippines, find an immortal human who is harmless until it shape-shifts to a man-eating demon, get close enough to it that I can see my reflection, and then convince it to willingly give me a sample of its blood?"

"It could be worse, dude," Adam encouraged. "I'm not really sure how, though, 'cause this scenario is pretty bad."

"I'll be right by your side, Wren, all the way," Jerry said.

Clivo rubbed his eyes, taking in the information. He didn't like any of it, not one bit.

"Do you need a pep talk, captain?" Hernando finally asked quietly.

Clivo smiled. "I'm okay, Hernando, thanks." He stared at the carpet, his mind a blur. Apart from the immortal cryp-tid, something else had been bothering him. "Listen, guys, you didn't sign up to be in this much danger. Douglas knows your faces, but not your names or where you live. If you want to go back home to Maine where you're safe and forget about all of this, I won't hold it against you."

The Blasters looked at each other in shock, obviously not having expected Clivo to say that.

Adam was the first to speak. "You see, the thing about us Blasters is that once we become a team, we *stay* a team. To the end."

"All the way to the end," Charles agreed.

"Never a question," Amelia said.

"Ever," Stephanie added.

Clivo looked at Hernando. "Hernando?"

"Remember, boss, trying isn't good enough. We don't stop until we win," he replied, his voice sure.

"Coops?" Clivo asked, glancing at his friend.

Jerry blew through his lips. "As if you even have to check with me."

Clivo stood up, renewed energy coming into his bones. "Okay, if that's the way it's going to be, let's do this. Amelia, can you narrow down where the aswang might be, exactly?"

Amelia perked up, her mind going into its thinking mode. "There's over seven thousand islands that make up the Philippines. It'll take me a day or two, but I've got you covered."

"Great. Stephanie, any chance you can find out if my Diamond Card is still working?"

Stephanie cracked her fingers and took over the laptop. After a few clicks, her face fell. "Rats, it looks like Douglas has already canceled it."

"That's okay, I still have some petty cash left," Clivo said. "But after this catch I'll be out of money, so keep your fingers crossed that this is the last one." He looked at the rest of his team. "While I'm gone, can you come up with some ideas for how we deal with Douglas and return the cryptids back to their homes?"

Adam rubbed his hands together excitedly. "Attack plan number two, coming right up!"

Clivo exhaled, feeling like a little bit of the weight of the world had been lifted off his shoulders. "And remember, in the meantime make sure you help Mrs. Cooper with the dishes."

Clivo spent the day in town, looking for supplies that he would need for his trek with Jerry to the Philippines. He wasn't even sure exactly what he should buy, seeing as how he was catching a person and not a wild animal in the rugged wilderness. He couldn't walk through a town with a tranquilizer gun, binoculars, and other catching supplies strapped on without drawing attention to himself. After staying hidden in plain sight for thousands of years, the aswang was probably pretty good at noticing if someone was looking for it. The best thing Clivo could do was blend in as much as possible and not carry anything except the blood sampler. He'd feel naked without his gun, but he had a feeling that this catch was going to come down to brains and not muscle.

Speaking of muscle, he was still uncomfortable with the thought of Jerry joining him. Jerry was strong and most definitely brave, but he didn't know how to fight. Clivo figured it would be nice to have Jerry around for company, but was it worth risking Jerry's safety just to have a buddy there?

For the first time since Clivo discovered his dad was a cryptid catcher, he finally understood the choices his father had made. Clivo had been so angry at his dad for never telling him everything. Sure, his dad had trained him, but he had done it secretly, without telling him why. Clivo hadn't been sure if his father just hadn't trusted him, or if he had been waiting, judging if Clivo was good enough to be a catcher.

But now he understood that his father had wanted to protect him the way that Clivo now wanted to protect Jerry and the Blasters. Not because they weren't good enough, but because they were *too* good. The world needed people like them, good-hearted people who fought for what was right, no matter the risks. The least Clivo could do was limit the amount of danger to them, the way his dad had with him.

Keeping everything a secret had been the only way his dad could make sure Clivo was safe, and he understood that now. His father had trained him well, and Clivo felt ready for the task ahead. But it didn't mean he wasn't scared.

He returned to Jerry's house that afternoon, his arms full of bags of clothes that would help him blend in on his trip. As he entered the house, he was greeted by a lovely, yet shocking sight. Mr. and Mrs. Cooper were in the living room with Aunt Pearl, and loud salsa music was blaring through the speakers. Hercules was in the corner, his usually mournful eyes looking rather contented, with the cats snuggled against his pudgy body.

Mrs. Cooper was laughing hysterically as Pearl twirled her around, teaching her a few dance moves.

"That's it, Dolores!" Aunt Pearl encouraged. "You have to roll your hips! Roll your hips!"

Mr. Cooper clapped his hands in time to the rhythm. "Come on, Pumpernickel! Let out your inner cha-cha!"

Mrs. Cooper squealed with delight as she swiveled her round body in a circle, accidentally knocking over a lamp with her backside. "Hee-hee! I'm moving body parts I didn't even know I had!"

Clivo put down the bags and leaned against the doorway, enjoying the scene and wishing it could go on forever.

Aunt Pearl noticed him. "Hi, sweetie! You wanna learn the rumba?"

"No thanks, Aunt Pearl. I think you ladies should have the dance floor all to yourselves," Clivo replied with a smile.

Aunt Pearl stuck out her tongue and blew a raspberry at him. "Party pooper! Come on, Dolores, let's pick up the tempo a bit!"

Mr. Cooper eyed Clivo. "Ladies, Clivo and I are going to step out onto the porch and enjoy the sunset."

"You boys have fun!" Mrs. Cooper said, laughing hysterically as she almost fell into a potted plant.

Mr. Cooper put his hand on Clivo's shoulder and led him outside, where they sat down on the porch swing. The sun was just dipping below the horizon, flashes of lightning occasionally bursting from a bank of dark clouds hovering above the mountains. Clivo had always loved the summer afternoon thunderstorms that rolled in because they made him feel like something exciting was about to happen. Now, they just felt like an omen of the dangers ahead.

Clivo and Mr. Cooper silently rocked on the swing, the only sounds the chirping of crickets and the occasional scurrying of a raccoon underneath a bush. Eventually, Mr. Cooper cleared his throat. "Now, son, I don't claim to know everything, but being a scientist has given me certain powers of observation, and I can tell that something is amiss with you kids. Something big."

Clivo was about to say something, but Mr. Cooper held his hand up.

"Now, don't worry, I'm not going to ask what it is. I know far better than to pry secrets out of a teenager. The only thing I want to know is—are you okay?"

Clivo almost burst. He wanted nothing more than to tell Mr. Cooper everything, just to have some support. But he and the Blasters had decided to trust no one. They had to keep their circle small, they just had to. Besides, if he told Mr. Cooper everything, there was no way he would let Clivo and Jerry fly to the Philippines to confront the aswang.

Still, Clivo didn't like the feeling of keeping secrets from Mr. Cooper, so he proceeded slowly.

"I'm okay, but I do have some questions. You know, about life," Clivo said.

"I'm happy to lend an ear, son," Mr. Cooper said.

Clivo spoke the next part carefully. "Well, your work at SETL deals with really important secrets, like, major secrets."

Mr. Cooper chuckled. "I guess you could say that. The search for intelligent life in the universe is a tricky one because everyone has their own ideas about what we should do with said life when we find it."

"And are all of those ideas good ones?" Clivo asked.

Mr. Cooper let out a full-blown laugh. "Not at all, son! One guy we interviewed for a position on the team believed that if we found four aliens, it'd be 'nifty' to turn them into a touring barbershop quartet. He said it would be a sensation."

"So, what have you decided to do with the aliens, if you ever find them?" Clivo knew from Jerry that Mr. Cooper had already found at least three UFOs, but he figured it was best not to let on.

"Well, that took a while to figure out," Mr. Cooper said, adjusting the large glasses on his face. "The first thing my team discussed was how much the study of alien life and its spacecraft could help the human race. Imagine how much our technology could advance if we studied a ship that had the ability to travel light-years. Think how much our understanding of the human body could increase if we had an alien life form to dissect. The possibilities for how this information could benefit us are astounding."

"So, is that what you decided to do? Capture aliens and dissect them?" Clivo's belief that Mr. Cooper was one of the good guys had suddenly begun to wane.

Fortunately, Mr. Cooper shook his head emphatically. "No, no. Me and a small group of folks decided that in this grand universe of ours, we didn't want to confine ourselves to just watching out for the human race. We wanted to protect *all* races, even alien ones. We're in this marvelous area of space together—why not make sure it's a good place for everyone?"

"So, what did you do when you found the aliens? I mean, if you ever happened to find one," Clivo corrected himself.

Mr. Cooper looked at the sunset, which was reflected in an orange glow on his glasses. "We'd communicate. We'd figure out a way that we could help if they were in distress. We'd make it known, somehow, that we meant no harm. Hopefully, we'd go from being strangers to being allies." Mr. Cooper let out a little chuckle. "And *then* we'd ask if they'd share how they travel at light-speed, 'cause we are having a heckuva time figuring that out."

Clivo looked up as a flash of lightning lit up the clouds. He'd been wondering what to do if he actually found the aswang. It felt weird to just let an immortal man who could turn into a people-eating bat at the full moon wander the Earth. But he had committed to protecting *all* the cryptids, and that had to stand even if the cryptid was a demon person. "Thanks, Mr. Cooper, that actually helps a lot."

Mr. Cooper looked at him in surprise. "I'm not sure how discussing dealing with alien life could have helped you. Unless we're actually talking about girls in some weird kind of metaphor?"

Clivo laughed. "No, I'm not talking about girls. It's just, life sometimes gets confusing, and knowing what's right and what's wrong can get all jumbled up."

Mr. Cooper put his hand on Clivo's shoulder. "I understand. And all that stuff can be even harder to figure out when you don't have the guidance of your folks around." Mr. Cooper cleared his throat. "Now, I know I'm not your father, but I hope you know that you can always come to me—about anything—and I'll do my best to help you. It doesn't matter what it is, good or bad. I'm always here for you."

Clivo smiled. "Thanks, Mr. Cooper. I know I'll definitely be taking you up on that offer."

Mr. Cooper scratched his belly and wiped a tear from his eye. "Okay, let's get back inside. My eyes have started leaking, and we should probably make sure Mrs. Cooper hasn't destroyed the whole living room with her rolling hips."

XIV

Clivo walked back inside and was instantly accosted
by Jerry. "Wren, come upstairs, I gotta show you something.
And why are you hogging my friends, Dad? We need our
man space!"

"Take all the man space you *boys* need," Mr. Cooper
said, giving Clivo a wink. "I'll be right here if you need me."

"Thanks, Mr. Cooper," Clivo replied.

They ran upstairs to Jerry's room, where his bed was
covered with an assortment of items. "Okay, so I've been
using my own personal genius to put together a few tricks
that will help us catch the bat thing."

"Nice. What are they?" Clivo asked, reaching for what
looked like a metal coil attached to a battery.

"Whoa, not that one!" Jerry said, gently moving the
contraption out of Clivo's reach. "That belongs in the 'Definitely Not a Good Idea' pile." He picked up a can with a
plastic lid. "Here, open this."

Clivo eyed his friend warily as he slowly opened the lid.
A loud springing noise sounded and a green snakelike thing

flew out of the can and straight into Clivo's face, causing him to jump back with a cry of surprise. Jerry laughed hysterically as Clivo shot him a glare. "That's hilarious, really funny. What are you going to do, scare the aswang to death?"

Jerry wiped the tears from the corners of his eyes. "That just never gets old!" He picked up another can and handed it to Clivo. "Open this one."

"Coops—" Clivo protested.

"Last one. Come on!" Jerry pleaded, bouncing up and down.

Clivo held the can a safe distance from his face and slowly opened it. Nothing happened, so he brought the can closer and peered inside. Instantly, the most horrible smell he had ever encountered washed over him, and he was sure he was going to get sick. It smelled like a dirty gym sock stuffed with a very dead hamster tucked into a sweaty armpit. "Geez, Coops! We're trying to catch it, not overwhelm it with grossness!"

Jerry laughed hysterically again and quickly put the lid back on the can. "A stink bomb is the best weapon out there. You don't want to go to war without one of these bad boys in your pocket."

"I'll just have to trust you on that one," Clivo said, waving the lingering stench away from his face.

Jerry picked up a small bag and tossed it to Clivo. "Here, I made a trick pack for you, too."

"A fanny pack?" Clivo asked, clipping the small zippered

bag around his waist. "You couldn't find something better to keep the tricks in? Like a magician's trunk?"

Jerry clipped his pack on, as well. "Trust me, fanny packs are the best for weapon storage. They're discreet, and they can hold a ton of stuff."

Clivo unzipped his pack and pulled out a handful of plastic objects in all different colors. "There's just a bunch of yo-yos in here."

"That's right," Jerry said, picking one out of Clivo's hands and wrapping the string around his finger. "These may seem like innocent toys, but they're extremely versatile. Watch."

Jerry began flinging the yo-yo up and down, making it spin faster and faster. Once it was up to speed, Jerry flung it sideways and knocked a gold trophy off his bookshelf with a thwack. The yo-yo came back to him and he flung it under one leg, knocking a football cleanly off the windowsill. With a final flick of his wrist, he wrapped the yo-yo string around Clivo's ankles and toppled him to the floor.

"Whoa! That is impressive!" Clivo said from where he was lying on his back.

Jerry unwound the string and helped Clivo up. "I figure that with all your martial arts training, picking up the ancient art of yo-yo attack should be a cinch."

Clivo picked up a yo-yo and spent the better part of an hour learning how to use it. Jerry was right—his jujitsu training made picking up the skill easy. Before he knew it, he could fling one of the toys with one hand while wrapping

Jerry's wrists together with another. It had seemed silly at first, but he had to admit, there really was an art to the yo-yo attack.

A knock sounded on the door and Jerry opened it to find Stephanie wringing her hands. "Guys, we have a— Blah! What's that smell?"

Clivo pocketed the yo-yos and pointed his thumb at Jerry. "Jerry's been busy working on his stink bombs."

Stephanie covered her nose with her sleeve. "It's horrible! Perfect, but horrible!"

Jerry gave her a bow. "Thank you, m'lady."

"Anyway, can you guys come downstairs?" Stephanie asked, her voice muffled by her sleeve. "We've got a problem. A big one."

Clivo's heart sank. "I didn't realize it was possible to have more problems."

The three of them ran to the basement, where the rest of the Blasters were huddled around Amelia and the laptop. By the looks on everyone's faces, whatever the problem was, it was really bad. "What's going on?" Clivo asked.

Amelia furiously spun her nose ring between two fingers. "Douglas has logged into every crypto chat room and is posting GPS coordinates for a transponder, claiming that if anyone follows it, they'll find what Nostradamus predicted."

"How do you know it's Douglas?" Clivo asked, his blood beginning to boil at the old man's continuous meddling.

Amelia pointed to the computer. "His screen name is GotchaClivoYouAnnoyingTwit."

"That's Douglas all right," Clivo said, clenching his jaw in anger.

Adam shook his head. "He's gone off his rocker. He's basically telegraphing to everyone in the evil resistance how to find us!"

"Wait, what do you mean 'us'?" Clivo asked. "Where are the coordinates that he's leading everyone to?"

Amelia's face was a mixture of worry and fear. "Right here. To this house."

Clivo didn't waste a second. He grabbed Hernando and frantically began patting him down. "He must have put a tracking device on one of you guys when you jumped him. Hurry! You're all wearing the same clothes as yesterday. Look for something attached to you! He's calling a whole army down on us!"

Everyone began to furiously pat down themselves, checking for some kind of tracking device. Stephanie rummaged through Charles's thick hair while Hernando emptied all his pockets and Adam checked the insides of his socks.

"Nothing, Clivo!" Stephanie said, her voice rising with hysteria. "We can't find anything!"

Clivo forced himself not to panic. He stood with his hands on his hips, slowing his breath and letting his mind remember the events in Douglas's lair. He went through everything—what had happened, anything Clivo might have touched, any contact any of them had had with Douglas . . .

Clivo's blood froze. His hand slowly reached for the spot on his shoulder where Douglas had shot him. He spoke, but his voice sounded faraway. "It's me. He shot me with a tranquilizer dart. There's a tracking device *in me*."

Stephanie's hands flew to her mouth, but she quickly recovered. "Okay, that's okay. Let's think about this. Maybe I can somehow block the transmitter in you from responding to a signal."

"Can we cut it out?" Adam asked. "I'm not trying to go all crazy, but we gotta get that thing out of you and destroy it!"

"Yeah, dude!" Charles agreed. "Wherever you go, the evil resistance will now be able to follow you. And we don't even know what these creeps are capable of. You're in serious danger, man!"

"Which is why I need to get away from you," Clivo said, knowing without a doubt that it was the right choice.

Jerry grabbed Clivo's arm. "This is no time to be alone, Wren."

"Actually, it's the perfect time," Clivo said. "I'm now a target. I can't be anywhere close to any of you." He looked at Jerry. "This isn't what I wanted, but it's the way things are going to go down. I need to leave, immediately."

"And there's no way that's happening, you hear me?" Jerry insisted. "I'm definitely going with you. I'm not letting you face the evil resistance and the aswang all at the same time. Are you kidding me?"

"I'm coming, too," Stephanie said. "I can be a good set of eyes and ears."

"I'm coming too, dude," Adam said. "And count me in for the fighting part. I think."

Charles took a ridiculous fighting stance. "You know how good I am at karate. I'm in."

Hernando shifted from side to side nervously. "I can be eyes and ears. Fighting makes me faint."

Amelia nodded. "I can help look for the aswang. It can't be that hard to pick an immortal human out of a crowd. Speaking of which, I printed out a map of the island that has the most aswang sightings. The guy should be there."

Clivo accepted the paper from Amelia and glanced at the island's name. "Okay, team, if you really want to do this, let's get busy."

Stephanie's face relaxed. "I'm glad you're okay with us coming. I was worried you'd put up a fight to try to protect us or something."

Clivo shook his head and smiled. But then he thought of something and his smile faded. "Wait! None of you have passports. You won't be able to go on an international flight or get through Customs in the Philippines."

One by one, the Blasters pulled passports out of their pockets. Adam smiled. "We got them in order to fly out here. None of us have driver's licenses, so we figured we should have some kind of ID. And we can't always have Serge helping grease the wheels."

"We're a team to the end, remember?" Hernando said.

"Blasters! Prepare!" Adam yelled, raising an arm in the air. "We travel to victory!"

"Give me a minute. I just need to grab my passport and come up with a good reason to tell my parents why I'm going to the other side of the planet for a few days," Jerry said, running upstairs.

Clivo headed out of the basement, too. "I'm going to pack up some stuff. I'll meet you upstairs in half an hour."

Clivo ran up to Jerry's room and threw his clothes and Jerry's fanny pack of tricks into his backpack. He snuck downstairs and noticed Jerry huddling with his parents in the living room, his arms waving around as he came up with a believable lie. Aunt Pearl was in a recliner, her fingers gently stroking her cats.

Clivo hesitated for just a moment before opening the front door and sneaking away into the night alone, the way his father often had when he didn't want Clivo to know that he was disappearing on another trip. The Blasters would be mad, the way that Clivo always had been when his dad snuck away, but they'd be alive, and that was all that mattered.

XV

A little more than twenty-four hours later, a small propeller plane was carrying Clivo over Batan Island in the Philippines. He looked out the window at a tropical island covered in rolling green hills, lighthouses, and white-sand beaches. It looked like paradise.

Clivo smiled to himself. He'd been asking the Blasters all year to send him to a tropical island where he could wait for a cryptid while lounging beneath a palm tree. He supposed it was only fitting that his last catch (hopefully) would be in such a place.

The plane landed with barely a bounce, and he and the few other passengers exited into a warm breeze that smelled deliciously like the salty sea. It was morning, and Clivo closed his eyes and lifted his face to the sun, hoping the light would help him overcome his jet lag.

He kept his eyes closed for just a moment before quickly opening them. His hand reached up to his shoulder where the tranquilizer dart had pierced him, leaving him with no ability to hide. He had to stay alert for anyone tracking him.

Clivo walked through the airport terminal, which was just a small stone building with wooden doors. There weren't that many people around, but he studied each and every one of them, making sure they weren't studying *him*. He had no idea how many people in the evil resistance were spread across the globe, so he decided to act as if *everybody* on this island was part of it. That way he'd never let his guard down.

Clivo walked to town along an empty road, his senses heightened for any sign that someone was watching him. But the place was quiet save for the ruffling of palm fronds in the warm breeze.

The town was small and the architecture was a mash-up of many different styles—Spanish colonial, Japanese, and American. Small homes that looked like slope-roofed pagodas stood next to a magnificent redbrick church. Other buildings were painted in bright pastels. The whole place had a slightly worn feeling about it, like nothing new had been built since the 1950s.

Clivo wished he'd had more time to learn about the history of the area—all he knew was that the island was part of what was known as the Ring of Fire, because of all the earthquakes and volcanic eruptions that took place. That must have been why all of the buildings were so low, Clivo figured—in case an earthquake hit.

Clivo wandered through the town for an hour. He knew where he wanted to stay, but he also wanted to get a feel for the place and make sure nobody was following him as he checked in to the hotel. He didn't need a repeat of Egypt and having someone ransack his room while he was away—not that he had anything of importance to steal. He'd be sure to keep his passport and the blood sampler on him at all times, as well as Jerry's fanny pack of tricks.

Once he was sure he wasn't being followed, Clivo checked in to the hotel and was relieved that everyone spoke English, so at least he didn't stand out too much by not knowing the language.

The two-story hotel was made of stone, and Clivo's room on the top floor had polished wood floors and shutters that overlooked the backyard. It was a very pleasant space, but Clivo didn't intend to spend much time in his room. He had an immortal man to catch.

The thought made him pause. *Was* the aswang a man? For some reason he had pictured the aswang as being someone like Dracula, a distinguished person who walked in the shadows all day and then fed on blood at night. But perhaps it was more like a witch? Clivo reminded himself to remain open to all the possibilities.

He put on a loose-fitting long-sleeved shirt and long pants like the typical dress of the area. If he put on a pair of shorts and a short-sleeved shirt, he knew he'd stick out as a tourist for sure, and perhaps catch the attention of the evil resistance.

Clivo chuckled ruefully to himself, because he supposed

it didn't matter what he wore since he had a tracking chip floating through his blood.

He stepped out of his air-conditioned hotel into the heat and humidity, his eyes flitting up and down the street. He relaxed for a moment, thinking that even if people were following him, they probably wouldn't arrive for a while. With any luck, he'd have a day or so to get to know the town and narrow down who the immortal person walking among them might be.

Feeling alert, he began his exploration. There were corner grocery stores with fresh fruit carts out front, tiny clothing stores with their doors thrown wide open to the air, and a butcher shop that must have sold beef from the cows that grazed in the nearby fields.

Clivo considered what kind of job the aswang might hold. Did an immortal creature need a job? It must, unless it somehow had a stash of riches to last infinite lifetimes. Whoever the aswang was, Clivo thought, it didn't seem to flaunt any wealth—there were no gaudy palaces or fancy cars around.

Clivo spent the day wandering and observing people. He noticed if people looked directly at him, or if they averted their gaze, perhaps to avoid revealing the telltale sign of an upside-down reflection in their eyes. He took note of the people who wore sunglasses possibly for the same reason.

Most of the townspeople were very friendly, greeting

him with nods or smiles as he—obviously a tourist—walked past. He pictured the aswang as shy and reserved, more of an observer of the world than anything. But these were just guesses and, as the Blasters always said, anything is possible until proven otherwise.

Clivo wished for a moment that he hadn't left the Blasters back home. It was so beautiful on this tropical island, and having their company would have made it even better. And he could really have used their help in identifying who the aswang might be. But he reminded himself that this idyllic town was likely about to be invaded by the evil resistance, not to mention, come the full moon, also by a people-eating bat creature. As lonely as Clivo felt halfway across the world by himself, he was glad that everyone he cared about was safe, far away from this place. And from him.

He wandered down a dirt road out of town and to a stone church that stood among the picturesque rolling green hills. He wasn't sure why he was drawn to the church, although pictures of an immortal creature living in a candlelit catacomb did flash through his mind. Maybe it was something about the church being the oldest thing around; the plaque on its thick wall dated it to the seventeenth century.

Clivo poked his head inside and gasped in awe. Rows of dark brown pews sat on a colorfully tiled floor, and a large stained-glass window cast an otherworldly glow over the room. Even though the space was cavernous, it felt welcoming, and its silence was serene.

Clivo noticed a few people quietly sitting in the pews, so out of respect he took a seat in the back, the wooden bench squeaking beneath his weight.

He watched the other people, trying to sense something from them. Was the immortal religious? Having lived for centuries, it must have seen religions come and go, gods rise and fall. What did it believe in, if anything?

Clivo was so lost in thought that it took him a moment to realize that a man had turned around and was staring directly at him. The man was old, although not exactly ancient, and he had a mess of curly white hair that stood out against his dark skin.

Clivo jumped a bit at the man's gaze, not just because it was trained on him, but also because he was wearing dark glasses even though the church was bathed in low light.

Clivo returned the man's stare, not quite sure what to do. Was it possible that he had stumbled upon the aswang as easily as that?

The man slowly stood up, his long black robe reaching to the floor. He was a priest! Of course! It was genius! Nobody would accuse a priest of being a demon! Living inside a church, which was a sacred, protected site, was the perfect hiding place.

Clivo was practically shaking with adrenaline as the man walked up to him. The cryptid catcher was tempted to grab the man and take a blood sample right there, but the other people in the church probably wouldn't take too kindly to their minister being tackled by a tourist. And if he *was* the aswang, what then? Clivo hadn't even made a plan as to what to do if he found the creature. That was supposed to be Douglas's job.

The man approached Clivo with a slow gait, his robe swishing on the mosaic floor. He was so tall that he looked down at Clivo like a leaning tower, his face holding a knowing smile. "Have you found what you are looking for?"

Clivo gulped. Did this man know who he was? "Um, I'm not sure. I think I'm still looking."

The man nodded. "I'm sure you have a lot of questions."

"I do. Wouldn't you?" Clivo asked. He wasn't sure if they were talking about the same thing, but figured he should continue the conversation.

The man chuckled. "I had questions many, many, many years ago, but I've come to accept what is, and, once I did, my life became quite amazing."

Clivo tried to see his reflection in the man's eyes, but they were shrouded by the dark spectacles. "I'd like to learn more, if you don't mind sharing."

The man stopped smiling and he leaned over, whispering in Clivo's ear, his breath smelling like dust. "I'm sure you'd like to learn about the secret, wouldn't you?"

Clivo gulped again. "I would. That's why I'm here."

The man straightened up and patted Clivo on the shoulder. "I thought so. It's always the young ones who are so curious. Death is a fascinating thing to children, but the adults"—again the man leaned over and whispered in Clivo's ear—"they just want to know how to live *forever*."

Clivo clenched the blood sampler in his pocket. He wished the other people would get up and leave so he could wrestle the priest to the floor and get this over with. The full moon was still two days away, but he didn't like being so close to someone who could turn into a flesh-eating demon bat. It was giving him the willies.

The priest straightened and motioned for Clivo to accompany him. Clivo stood up, his legs rubbery with nerves, and followed the man as he headed for a small wooden door at the back of the church.

The priest stopped and turned to stare at Clivo, his eyes still hidden behind his glasses. "Are you sure you want to know all this? Once you understand everything, the world will never be the same for you."

Clivo let out a nervous chuckle. "I'm up for the challenge."

The priest nodded and opened the door. They entered a tiny interior room lit by a small desk lamp. On the opposite wall was an old bookshelf holding leather-bound books. The room smelled like candle wax and parchment, and must have been the priest's office.

The priest walked to a stone wall and began pushing on it. Clivo wasn't sure what the man was doing until a portion of the rock wall opened, a puff of dust filling the room.

A dark chasm opened before them, with a set of

crumbling stone stairs leading downward. A cool breeze that smelled of mold wafted up from the depths.

The priest looked at Clivo, the shade of his glasses somehow going even darker. "Below is the answer to the questions you seek."

Clivo gulped, but nodded for the priest to continue.

The priest grabbed a flashlight from the wall and turned it on. "Follow closely."

They walked down the stairs and into a narrow underground cavern, its walls carved out of bedrock. The smell of damp dirt filled the air.

"Follow me to the end," the priest said, motioning Clivo forward. Clivo hadn't even realized that his feet had quit moving. "You wanted the answers, and I will give you all of them."

Clivo forced his feet to shuffle forward as he pulled the blood sampler from his pocket and gripped it tightly.

The priest held his light aloft, but the glow barely pierced the darkness ahead of him. He spoke in a flat monotone. "These caves were dug in secret, right after the construction of the church. Nobody knew about them. They were kept a mystery. The only people who knew about their existence were the DEAD!"

The priest whirled around, pointing his flashlight at a cavity in the wall where a skeleton lay, its vacant eye sockets staring directly at Clivo.

Clivo screamed in shock, then sprang forward to tackle the priest.

"Now, hold on!" the priest yelled as he dropped the light.

Clivo grabbed the man's arm and stabbed it with the blood sampler, the light on the device springing to life.

"Ow! What the *devil* are you doing?" the priest complained, his spooky demeanor completely gone.

"Just give me a second, please," Clivo said, sweat pouring down his face as he held down the priest with one hand and clutched the blood sampler in the other.

"You knocked me over!" the priest complained again. "Oh, for the love of holy water, I've lost my glasses!"

"I'd appreciate just another moment of patience, please!" Clivo said as the blood slowly crept up into the chamber.

It seemed to take forever until the familiar words lit up the screen: NOT IMMORTAL.

Clivo couldn't believe it; he had been so sure. He grabbed the priest by his collar and held the flashlight up close to his face. "Look into my eyes."

The priest shied away. "What are you going to do, hypnotize me?"

"Just please look into my eyes! Please!"

The priest popped his eyes wide open in an exaggerated manner and stared straight at Clivo, who saw that his reflection appeared right side up. "There! Are you happy?"

Clivo sank back against the dirt wall, disappointed and

exhausted. The priest struggled to his feet after a moment of flailing in the folds of his robe. "You *attacked* me! A priest, of all people! Do you mind telling me what these shenanigans are all about?"

Clivo crawled on his hands and knees, searching for the priest's glasses, which he eventually found underneath a skeleton's leg bone. "I'm really sorry, sir. I thought you were a monster."

"A monster?" the priest exclaimed in disbelief. "Do I look like a monster?"

Clivo looked at the rail-thin man with hollow eyes and cheeks. He kind of did look like a scrawny version of Frankenstein's monster, but Clivo figured it was probably best not to mention that. "No, sir, it's just . . . Well, you were wearing sunglasses inside—" He handed the man the glasses, embarrassed.

"Because I left my regular ones at home!" the priest said indignantly as he put them on.

"—and you kind of freaked me out, bringing me down into this tomb! What did you expect me to do?" Clivo said, doing his best to defend himself.

The priest looked at the ceiling in exasperation. "It's what the kids want! They love coming to see the tombs and happen to enjoy the little show I put on! That's what I figured you were here for! I'll have you know I'm *very* popular."

"I'm sure you are, sir. It's a wonderful show. Just super

scary if you're not really prepared for it," Clivo said sheepishly.

The priest rubbed his arm where a dot of blood had risen from Clivo stabbing him. "What'd you stab me with? It's not a poisonous dart or something, is it?"

"No, sir," Clivo said, holding up the blood sampler, "it's just a device to check to see if someone's a monster or not."

Thankfully, the priest began chuckling instead of asking further questions. "You kids and your imaginations. I had a boy in here last week who made a special potion that he was sure would bring these skeletons to life and cause them to dance around." The priest looked over at the bones, his eyes taking on a faraway look. "But if you've come looking for monsters, you've come to the right place. These islands are old; people have inhabited them for hundreds of thousands of years, and they sure do love their legends. There's a lot of mysticism here, a lot of ghosts—maybe even a few monsters."

"Would you mind telling me about some of them?" Clivo asked, eager to get any information the old priest might have that could make his mission easier.

The priest looked at him with a twinkle in his eye. "That I will not do. But you can read about them on your own in the Quester's Cave."

XVI

Clivo and the priest began making their way out of the tomb, with Clivo feeling much more relaxed even though he was in an old crypt surrounded by skeletons.

"So, whose skeletons are these?" Clivo asked, shying away from a set of dusty bones.

The priest reached over and shook the hand of one of the skeletons, almost causing Clivo to begin dry-heaving. "Oh, these are fake. I thought you might have figured that out from the pirate clothes I dressed them in."

Clivo looked closer at the skeleton next to him and guffawed when he noticed it was wearing an eye patch and had a peg leg. "Yeah, I guess I wasn't paying that much attention, what with the spookiness of this tomb and all."

"It's actually not a tomb, just an old storage space used to keep things cool back before we had refrigerators." The priest paused at the base of the stairs and gave Clivo a wink. "But I prefer to keep it as my year-round haunted house."

They climbed to the top of the stairs, but instead of heading into the office, they veered through a dark wooden door into a candlelit room. A long table ran the length of it, and leather-bound books that looked to be older than the church itself lay on pieces of colorful silk.

"What is this place?" Clivo asked in awe. The air smelled deliciously like candle wax, and the cool air wafting up from the tomb made the temperature pleasant.

"It's the Quester's Cave," the priest said proudly. "These books tell the tales of all the monsters and spirits that roam these islands. After the kids get their little show in the tomb, they're allowed in here. They can research the specter of their choice and someday, if they choose, they go on a quest to find it."

"It looks like I'm in exactly the right place, then," Clivo said, thinking about how much Amelia would love this room where she could spend hours reading all the secrets held in the books' pages.

"All right, then, I'll leave you to it," the priest said. "What's your name, by the way? I'm Father Joseph, and I like to know the names of all the questers who pass through these doors."

Clivo paused. He didn't exactly want Father Joseph to know his real name in case someone from the evil resistance began asking questions, but then he remembered the tracking chip and figured that anyone coming after him wouldn't need to ask any questions to find him. "My name is Clivo, sir."

Father Joseph tilted his head. "Interesting name. Never heard that one before."

Clivo shrugged. "It was supposed to be Clive, after an actor who did a movie about an honorable man saving the world. But the nurse who wrote my name on the birth certificate had sloppy handwriting and it looked like 'Clivo,' so my parents stuck with it."

Father Joseph chuckled. "Life doesn't always turn out the way we expect, does it?"

"You can say that again," Clivo sighed.

Father Joseph patted him on the shoulder. "It's time for me to take the confessions of the parishioners. Please stay as long as you wish."

Father Joseph exited the room, leaving Clivo alone with the tomes in front of him. He took a seat and opened the first book, the parchment pages crackling beneath his fingers.

Clivo intended to quickly find whatever information he could on the aswang, but he was immediately distracted by reading about the other legends of the Philippines. He read about how questers came to Mount Banahaw in hopes of seeing one of the dwarfs who were supposed to live amid the rocks. Many visited the Hinatuan Enchanted River, which was said to have been built by fairies. His personal favorite was Mount Makiling, where a witch named Maria supposedly lived to protect the green forest.

He thought about how much fun he and the Blasters would have running around the islands searching for dwarfs and fairies. That was something they could do together when Clivo wouldn't have to worry about their safety. But that would have to be put aside for another time, *after* they had saved the world.

Clivo forced himself to close the book and reached for another, this one with a terrifying image of a sinewy creature flying through the air on massive wings—the aswang.

Clivo opened it and the spine cracked as if it hadn't been touched in years, as if other questers knew better than to even entertain the idea of searching for such a creature. The parchment was old and faded, but the ink looked fresh, as if the pages had never been exposed to sunlight.

Whereas the other books spent a lot of time explaining the history and stories of local legends with great exuberance, the pages of this book were blank save for a few in the middle. There was hardly any information at all, and what there was seemed to be restrained. The book only mentioned how the aswang shape-shifted at the full moon, how it flew higher than the clouds and was impossible to catch, and how it changed islands every twenty years so nobody would notice that it never aged.

That was some new information to Clivo. He could now narrow his search to people who had moved to the island in the last twenty years, though how he'd figure *that* out was beyond him.

He turned another page and sucked in his breath as he

stared at the illustration of a devil-faced creature. Underneath was an eloquently scrolled caption:

The aswang feeds on the living.
The aswang thrives on death.
If you find it, destroy it.
Demons have no place wandering the earth.

Clivo closed the book and put it delicately back on its cloth, as if just reading the words could somehow anger the aswang. But nothing could get the image of the distorted face with sharp fangs and black eyes out of his head.

Clivo walked back to town, grateful for the sunshine on his face. The chill of the church's tomb combined with the warning from the tome had given him a massive case of the heebie-jeebies.

If you find it, destroy it.

His job was to protect the cryptids, not destroy them. But did that hold true for the cryptid that might just be pure evil—and the immortal?

He shook his head, realizing that before deciding what to do with the aswang, he actually had to catch the thing. A thing of pure evil that didn't belong on the planet. Should be easy enough, Clivo thought, as he sighed in exasperation.

Clivo was so engrossed in his thoughts that he didn't even notice the car barreling toward him.

"Look out!" came a voice to his left.

His eyes shot up just in time to see a Cadillac only feet from hitting him, the driver engrossed in singing loudly along with some song while squeezing his eyes shut.

Clivo leaped out of the way, right into the woman who had shouted the warning to him. She fell backward with a cry of shock, dropping a large plastic bag.

"Oh my gosh! I'm so sorry!" Clivo scrambled to his knees and reached for the woman, who was on her back, rolling from side to side and laughing as if something incredibly funny had just happened.

"Oh, honey!" she said in a thick accent that Clivo couldn't quite place. "The look on your face is so funny! I have never seen anything like it!"

"Can I help you?" Clivo asked, gently assisting the woman to a sitting position. "Are you okay?"

The woman looked at Clivo with the most ancient, wrinkled face he had ever seen. It was like a peach that had been left to dry in the sun. Her eyelids were so heavy that her eyes were mere slits, yet even among the folds and sagging skin, Clivo could somehow detect a smile by a slight lifting at the corners of her dry lips. She wore a simple flowered dress and, oddly, smelled like the sands of Egypt.

"Oh, honey, I am fine," the old woman said. "Believe me, I have been through worse."

"Shoot, you're bleeding," Clivo said, motioning to her hand.

She brought her bleeding thumb to her lips and sucked

on it. After a moment, she proudly presented her thumb to Clivo. "See? No more blood! I am okay, honey."

"Okay, but if you have any broken bones, I don't think a bit of spit will help," Clivo said.

The woman swatted at him playfully. "Oh, you are funny!"

Clivo helped the woman to her feet. She was so stooped over with age that she barely came to his chest. He picked up her bag, which was filled with what looked to be bony slabs of raw meat wrapped in plastic.

"Are you planning a barbecue for the whole town tonight?" Clivo asked.

The woman put her gnarled fingers to her lips and giggled. "No, honey. I am the town butcher. Come. My store is right here."

They walked down the road a few steps and came to a small shop with a painted window that read DAYEA'S DELICIOUS DELICACIES.

"Are you Dayea?" Clivo asked as he opened the door for the old woman, the small brass bell above them dinging with their arrival.

"That is me, honey," Dayea said. She pointed a yellowed fingernail at Clivo. "Your name?"

"My name's Clivo, ma'am."

"Good name. Strong name." Dayea shuffled behind a glass case that was full of ground beef and put on an apron streaked with bloody handprints. "Please empty bag here, honey."

She motioned for Clivo to put the sack down next to a butcher's block, which he did, pulling the wrapped slabs out of the bag one by one. As he laid them down he glanced out the window to where the Cadillac had sped off in a plume of exhaust.

"Thanks for saving me, by the way," Clivo said. "If you hadn't said something, I would've ended up stuck to that car's grille."

"Bah, that man is such a bother," Dayea said, slowly lowering herself onto a chair. "New to town and thinks he owns the place already."

Clivo paused in his task, his hands hovering over the steaks as a thought came to him. "Have you lived here for a while, Dayea?"

"Oh, yes, my home is here, always has been, for a long time." Dayea's shiny eyes were barely visible beneath her fleshy lids.

"So, I guess you know a lot of people in town, being the local butcher and all."

"I do, I do. Nice people, nice town, always has been," Dayea said.

"It's such a pretty place, I can't imagine people ever wanting to leave. I bet a lot of people move here, though," Clivo said, resuming his task of stacking the steaks.

"Yes, yes, a couple of new people. The man who almost ran you over just got here. At the end of the block, the Santos family moved in; nice people. On the other side of town, in the purple house, lives Bathala Bautista. Nice man, but silly name. Name of a god, the one who created man and earth." Dayea let out a cackle. "Silly name."

Clivo quickly crumpled up the empty sack and threw it into a trash can. "Thank you, Dayea. It was really nice meeting you. Can I do anything else to help you before I go?"

Dayea kissed her knobby fingers and patted Clivo's hand. "Sweet boy. Dayea is fine. Come back again, okay?" She stood up with a pained wince and then grabbed a cleaver and began chopping away at the meat.

Clivo exited the butcher shop, almost forgetting to say goodbye to Dayea. He was too focused on finding this man who called himself Bathala.

Clivo strode through town, his eyes still on alert for any sign of the evil resistance. He was also looking for the purple house that Dayea had mentioned.

It was hard to miss, that was for sure. Clivo passed a few homes decorated with pastel paints that seemed out of style compared to the wood and stone buildings around them, but this one was ridiculous. It was an old two-story building with splintered wooden trim, and it was painted the most garish purple Clivo had ever seen. The paint was obviously much newer than the house itself, and the structure stood out like a sore thumb compared to the drab buildings around it.

If this really was where the aswang lived, it was not what Clivo had been expecting. He had assumed that the aswang would work hard to keep its identity a secret, but living in a house painted like a circus tent hardly seemed like a good way to remain hidden. Still, all clues pointed to this man being the aswang. He had moved there recently and just happened to call himself the god of man and earth. It seemed like a no-brainer to Clivo.

There was a tiny grass area across from the house, so Clivo grabbed a cold fruit juice from a small market, took a seat beneath a coconut tree, and waited for the man to emerge. Clivo had to chuckle to himself. He had finally done it—he had finally managed to end up sitting in the shade of a tropical tree enjoying a nice drink while waiting for his catch. He allowed himself a moment of relaxed pause before reminding himself that he still had a bat demon to contend with.

Clivo waited for hours for Bathala to emerge from his home. With all the dangers around him, he welcomed the silence and solitude, the moment to just sit in the sun and relax. That was something he hadn't been able to do since learning about the immortal. But there was nothing to do now but sit and wait, and with any luck, this would all be over soon.

As the sun was beginning to set and Clivo's stomach started rumbling with hunger, the door to the purple house opened and Bathala emerged. The guy looked nothing like someone who shared a name with anything supernatural. Clivo had been expecting someone regal who carried himself with great poise, but this man was more glitz and glamour. He was middle-aged, with bronzed skin that complemented his luscious mane of obviously dyed golden-blond hair. He was wearing a bright blue three-piece suit with an orange handkerchief tucked in his pocket, and carried a silver cane that he twirled between his fingers as he lifted his face to the sky, joyfully sniffing the evening air.

Bathala began to whistle and sauntered down the steps like a man without a care in the world. Clivo stood up and followed at a safe distance. The streets were busy with people mingling in the refreshing breeze, so he figured it was better to track the man and wait for a better opportunity to confront him, when there weren't so many people around.

Bathala strutted along, greeting everyone with a friendly wave and a smile, as if he was the mayor of the town. After a couple of blocks he entered a small wooden building with plucky guitar music floating through the open windows. Clivo peeked inside and saw it was a small bar that was quickly filling up with people. Bathala was greeted with a cheer from those who were already there.

Bathala took a seat at a barstool and ordered a drink, cheerfully patting the back of the man next to him.

Clivo figured he had a bit of time before the god of man left, so he grabbed a sandwich from a nearby store and waited across the street, enjoying the cool air of evening. The streets were festive, with people milling about and laughing. All in all it was a pleasant scene, save for the demon bat across the street, who was currently enjoying a fruity cocktail sipped through a straw.

Clivo waited and waited as the noise from the bar got louder and louder. The music's tempo got faster and the laughter more exuberant as the moon climbed higher in the night sky. Clivo was patient; he was used to doing a lot of waiting during his cryptid catching trips, and waiting in tropical weather was much better than in a cold wilderness where bears could happen upon him at any moment.

After a few hours, Bathala came stumbling out of the bar, his arms wrapped around two equally unsteady men, all three of them singing loudly as they wove their way down the street. Clivo followed, hoping the other men would veer away. Bathala seemed so drunk that Clivo thought he could probably walk right up and take his blood sample without the creature even noticing.

Unfortunately, the men walked Bathala directly to his doorstep and waved as he climbed the stairs, his hand clutching the banister for support. With a final bow of flourish to his friends, Bathala entered his home and slammed the heavy door soundly behind him.

The men continued on their way, and once they were a safe distance away Clivo bolted up the stairs. The door was firmly locked, and so were the wooden window shutters. He peered through the slats and noticed Bathala facedown on a red velvet sofa, already snoring heavily, his tongue lolling out of his mouth like a happy dog's. For a man who might have been alive for a few thousand years, he certainly didn't carry himself with an air of wisdom and strength.

Clivo figured that not even pounding on the door would wake the man from his slumber, and he certainly didn't want to draw attention to himself. He needed a plan, one that he could put in place the next day.

He headed back to his hotel eager for a good night's rest, hoping that he would be able to fall asleep even with the evil resistance breathing down his neck.

After shoving as much furniture in front of his door as possible to block any intruders, Clivo fell into a fitful sleep, with images of demon armies bursting through his door filling his dreams.

XVII

The next day, the evil resistance arrived.

It was just one man, but by the looks of him, one was enough. Clivo knew he was part of the evil resistance, because why else would an incredibly nasty-looking man dressed in black leather strut through town carrying a military-style duffel bag?

Clivo watched him from behind the coconut tree, where he was again waiting for Bathala to emerge from his house. He still didn't have a plan for how to get a sample of Bathala's blood without causing a commotion, but he was hoping that something brilliant would come to him.

Now, however, he was more focused on the muscular man stalking through town, and he wasn't the only one— every Filipino turned their head to gawk at the man as he walked by, the spurs on his cowboy boots clinking. He wasn't subtle, that was for sure.

The man must have felt Clivo's eyes on him, because he stopped and slowly turned, his face lined with the deep wrinkles of someone who had spent way too many hours in the sun.

Clivo jumped as the man stared at him, but the man didn't seem in a rush to come after him. Instead, the man gave a crooked smile, raised his thumb and forefinger into the shape of a gun, and mimed shooting at Clivo. Then he lowered his hand, nodded, and turned and stalked away.

Clivo was utterly confused. The man obviously knew who he was, so why hadn't he come after him? Why hadn't he tried to capture Clivo and torture him for information?

Maybe, Clivo thought, *the man knows something that I don't.*

The next thing Clivo did was dangerous and perhaps incredibly stupid, but he was burning with curiosity. He ran after the man, skidding to a stop behind him and tugging on the man's sleeve. "Excuse me," Clivo said.

The man, who towered over Clivo, turned his head toward him, but didn't say anything.

"Um, I assume you're part of the evil resistance?"

The man turned all the way around, his dusty leather clothes crackling as he moved. The guy looked like he had just finished a motorcycle ride across a desert of some apocalyptic wasteland. "They call me The Ender." His voice was so deep and gravelly it was almost a whisper.

"Who calls you that?" Clivo asked, fascinated by the man in front of him.

"The ones you call the evil resistance. I'm the guy they

232

call when it's time to end something." A breeze blew through his burnished red hair, making him look like some kind of ancient Viking warrior. Everything about this guy was like he had just stepped out of an action movie, but one Clivo would rather be watching instead of participating in.

"I see, that's why you're called The Ender. Makes sense." Clivo let out a nervous chuckle.

The Ender stared at him, his jaw set in a tight line behind his unshaven face.

"So, any chance you'd tell me who the members of the evil resistance are?"

The man snarled, "A group of world leaders whose souls are shriveled from holding power. Just turn on your TV, you can pick 'em out."

Clivo thought about Lana and Thomas and how they had been working for the grand duchy of Luxembourg. What other world leaders were involved in the search for the immortal? Clivo remembered an old quote, *Power tends to corrupt, and absolute power corrupts absolutely.*" He cleared his throat. "So, um, I'm the guy you probably followed here— Clivo. Clivo Wren?" The Ender just stared at him as if that was of no consequence to him, so Clivo continued, "So, I guess we're both here to find the same thing. Any information you'd care to share?"

The Ender took off his sunglasses, revealing one gray eye and one empty eye socket, the eyelid sewn closed to cover the space where an eye should have been. He leaned over and put his face right in front of Clivo's, his breath smelling pleasantly of oranges. "I'm here to end the search for the immortal. It'd be a shame to have to end you in the process."

Clivo shuddered and did his best not to gag at the sight of the man's stitched-shut eyelid. *Shouldn't he be wearing a patch or something?* "Any chance I could persuade you to come to the side of the good guys? We're not evil, and we do great things for other people, which can feel pretty good. No offense, but it seems like you could use some softening up."

The Ender cracked a smile and put his sunglasses back on. As he straightened up he gave Clivo a solid shove, throwing him onto his butt on the dirt road. "Leave the important stuff to the adults, kid. And stay out of my way, or I *will* end you."

Clivo watched the man strut away like a cowboy ending an Old West standoff. Clivo grumbled and wiped the dirt off his hands. The guy had never even caught a cryptid, but he came in there like he owned the place? At least it seemed like he was going to stay out of Clivo's way . . . until the time came when they were going after the same thing.

Clivo walked back to Bathala's house and waited. Hours passed, but there was no sign of Bathala or The Ender. Did he have the right person? If The Ender wasn't torturing Clivo for information, it must mean that he didn't need Clivo's help to find the aswang. But maybe the aswang wasn't the immortal, and The Ender was going after another creature? Clivo doubted it. The Myth Blasters were better at their research than anybody else. He had to be on the right track.

Clivo sat under his coconut tree all day, sipping fresh squeezed juices and waiting for Bathala to exit. He still didn't have much of a plan, but he knew without a doubt that today was the day he would check Bathala's blood, even if he had to tackle the man in broad daylight. With The Ender in town, it was time for Clivo to end this, too.

As the sun slipped into late afternoon, Bathala emerged from his house, this time dressed in a bright yellow suit with a polka-dot handkerchief tucked in the breast pocket. As he had the day before, he twirled the cane in his fingers, happily sniffed the tropical air, and did his stroll to the bar, where he was once again greeted with delighted hellos.

Clivo got his sandwich and retook his perch on the opposite side of the road. Didn't a man who had lived for thousands of years pick up any other hobbies besides going to the bar?

Clivo waited, watching up and down the street for any sign of The Ender. After a few hours, as the sun was just about to set, The Ender arrived, once again strutting down the street dramatically, dust practically billowing behind him.

He noticed Clivo, but just kept on walking, not once glancing at the bar where Bathala sat.

Clivo stood up and approached a bald Filipino man who was walking by. "Excuse me, sir, what's in that direction?" he asked, indicating where The Ender had gone.

The man looked where he was pointing and spoke, revealing one gold front tooth. "An archaeological excavation site of an ancient village. But go in the morning. We have curfew tonight."

The man hurried away, leaving Clivo to wonder what the curfew was for. He was about to ask someone else when Bathala exited the bar, though it was much earlier than the night before. He was steadier on his feet this time, and he began walking back to his home alone just as the sun set behind the palm trees.

Clivo fell into step behind him. He wasn't worried about being noticed, because the streets were bustling with people seemingly all rushing to get home as the sky darkened. The slamming of window shutters followed Clivo as he walked down the street.

Bathala finally got to the steps of his home and took out his house keys. Just as he unlocked the door, Clivo sprang, running up the stairs behind him with his arms held wide. "My friend! Hello!" he shouted.

Bathala whipped around to look at Clivo, first in happy surprise, and then with wary confusion. His mouth opened to say something as Clivo wrapped his arm around the man's shoulder and flung him inside.

"Mercy!" the man squealed in a high, lilting voice.

The man flew across the room and landed on a sofa as Clivo slammed and locked the door behind them. Clivo turned, crouched in a fighting stance, just in case the guy went all bat crazy on him.

The man did go crazy, but not by turning into a bat. He began screaming like a frightened girl and throwing everything within his reach at Clivo. First he tossed his cane, then a lampshade, and finally a wooden carving of an elephant.

"Thief! Marauder! Cretin! Bandit! Plunderer!" Bathala yelled, punctuating each word with another thrown object.

Clivo's forearms were getting bruised from deflecting all the objects. "Stop it! I just need to stab you for a second!"

That was obviously the wrong thing to say, as Bathala's eyes went wide with fright and he began running around the house, tossing his exquisite furniture behind him as he went. "Murder most foul! Butchery! Bloodshed!"

Bathala ran into the kitchen, but Clivo entered through another hallway and jumped in front of the man, who let out another squeal. Clivo pointed his finger at him. "Are you the aswang?"

This stopped the man cold in his tracks. He put his hand on his chest in shock and said, "Me? Do I look like a flying werewolf to you?"

"Then you won't mind if I do this." Clivo jumped forward and stabbed the man's hand with the blood sampler.

The man recoiled with a scream and slumped against a wall, cupping his hand in agony. "Argh! I've been pierced!"

Clivo held his breath as he watched Bathala's blood travel up the chamber. "Come on, come on."

The sampler beeped and the all-too-familiar words flashed on the screen: NOT IMMORTAL.

Clivo roared in frustration and looked around the brightly tiled kitchen for something to throw, finally settling on a checked dish towel that he hurled harmlessly against the wall.

"Mercy!" Bathala said, his hand once again flying to his chest.

Clivo took a deep breath to calm himself, then helped Bathala to his feet. Clivo grabbed the dish towel he had just thrown and placed it gently over the small pinprick on Bathala's hand. "I'm really sorry. I've been on a long journey searching for something, and I thought you were it."

Bathala seemed to relax a little. "I must say, I've never been mistaken for a legendary creature before, although I'm rather flattered by the notion. What put such a silly idea in your head?"

Clivo scrubbed his hands through his hair, "It's a long story, but calling yourself the god of man and earth was one tip."

Bathala let out a surprised laugh. "My parents always did have a sense of humor about them, my name included. I never thought I was actually at risk of being mistaken for a god, however."

"You're not going to call the police on me, are you?" Clivo asked, wincing.

Bathala looked out the window at the quickly approaching night. "I suppose I should, seeing as how you broke into my house and stabbed me and all. But curfew is coming and not even the police dare go out at night. Speaking of which, you should probably hurry up and get out of here or you'll have to spend the night. No offense, but I don't think I could sleep with you around."

"Understood, and again, I'm really sorry."

Bathala brushed it off. "It's okay, my young warrior. This night always puts people on edge."

Bathala walked Clivo to the front door. "By the way, what's the curfew for?" Clivo asked, getting ready to open the door and leave.

Bathala looked confused by Clivo's not knowing. "It's the full moon. We all stay inside for safety because the aswang flies tonight. If you're looking for the aswang, you should be out *there*."

Clivo looked through a shutter at the full moon just as an inhuman cry pierced the air.

"Shoot," Clivo said. With jet lag and the time change, Clivo suddenly realized he had gotten the day of the full moon wrong. He'd thought it was tomorrow, not tonight.

Obviously The Ender knew it was the full moon, though, and knew where to find the aswang. That's why he hadn't bothered to ask Clivo any questions—he'd known the answers already.

"There she goes," Bathala said reverently as another cry pierced the air. "It's too late now. Best you spend the night here, or it'll tear you to shreds and not think twice."

Clivo ignored him. He flung the door open and ran down the stairs, Bathala's cries of warning echoing behind him, and headed in the direction The Ender had gone in earlier. As he ran, a swoosh of air sounded behind him and he turned to see a creature with giant wings shooting up from somewhere in the town and flying toward the moon, its powerful wings pushing it upward with ease.

Suddenly something hit the creature, crumpling a wing and sending it hurtling to the ground.

Shock went through Clivo as he realized The Ender must have shot the aswang. If he didn't do something, and fast, the evil resistance would take possession of the immortal and all would be lost. It really would be the end.

Clivo ran down a hill, jumping over the low stone ruins of the ancient village and avoiding the open pits of archaeological digs. In the moonlight he saw the hulking shape of The Ender wrestling with the fallen beast, who was wrapped in a net.

Clivo hurried toward the struggling creature. It was much larger than Clivo had been expecting—taller than The Ender but much thinner, and it was definitely frightening. It had the sinewy body of a starved person, and bony toes and fingers that ended in claws. The most disturbing thing about it was its face, almost human but with batlike sharp teeth and pointed ears.

It was shrieking and hissing at The Ender, who was doing his best to secure the creature in the net.

"Let it go!" Clivo warned.

The Ender barely glanced over at him, his focus all on the beast that was fighting him. "Get out of here, kid. This is ending here and now. If you want to live, you'd better walk away."

The Ender jerked on the net, and a scream of pain came from the aswang. Clivo gritted his teeth in anger and ran at The Ender, attempting to rip his hands off the net, which was twisted around the creature. The Ender heaved one of his large hands away and slapped Clivo across the face with the back of it.

The blow sent Clivo flying to the ground, with a feeling like having been whacked in the cheek by a bowling ball.

The Ender growled at him, "You get close to me again and the next punch will put you down for good, you hear me?"

Clivo put his palm to his cheek, half expecting to discover his face caved in from the force of the hit. Fortunately it was the usual shape, but he could already feel his eye swelling shut. He was going to be left with one heckuva bruise. His eyes stung from the pain and he let the tears flow down his cheeks. He didn't care that the cruel man in front of him could see him crying. He was scared, in an enormous amount of pain, and worried that he was about to lose the immortal to this giant jerk.

Clivo dropped his hand and it landed on the fanny pack tied around his waist. Jerry's trick bag! He had completely forgotten about it this whole time! There was no way that he could defeat The Ender in a fight—the guy was just way too strong, not to mention that he seemed perfectly fine with hitting a kid—but maybe Clivo could take him down with one of Jerry's gizmos.

Clivo opened the zipper and dug around in the pack. The aswang continued to scream and The Ender held on to the net with one hand as his other one reached for a holstered gun.

Clivo paused. "You can't kill it, it's immortal."

The Ender didn't even glance at him. "You're such a child. It won't die from old age or disease, but getting injured is another matter. A vampire dies from being beheaded, and I'm sure a well-placed bullet will do the same to this thing."

"But, you *can't*!" Clivo pleaded. "You can't just kill something that's been around for thousands of years!"

"Oh yeah?" The Ender said, his dark eyes locking with Clivo's. "Watch me."

The Ender raised the gun just as Clivo pulled his hand from the fanny pack and flung the yo-yo at the man, wrapping the string around the gun. Clivo yanked on his end and ripped the gun from The Ender's hand, the force of his pull flinging the gun into the darkness.

The Ender looked at him in disgust. "Did you really just take my gun with a yo-yo?"

"I did," Clivo said, standing up even though he was still a bit wobbly from the blow to the cheek. "And now I'm going to punch you with one."

Clivo yanked out another yo-yo and flung it at The Ender's stupid face. It got him right in the forehead and he dropped the net, both of his hands clutching his face with a grunt of pain. Clivo pulled out another yo-yo and flung it toward the man, too, the string wrapping around him and pinning his arms to his body. Clivo pulled out yet another yo-yo and tossed it around the man's legs, where it cinched them together tight, and with a final flourish Clivo took his two last yo-yos and whipped them at The Ender's kneecaps, both of them making sickening cracking sounds as they found their marks. The Ender let out a cry of pain and dropped to the ground, helplessly wiggling around like a pig in a blanket.

"What is it with you and the yo-yos?" the man groaned as a painful-looking purple goose egg began to emerge from his forehead.

Clivo grabbed The Ender's feet and dragged him away from the aswang to a deep archaeological pit, and, with a firm shove of his foot, he pushed The Ender into the hole, where he landed with a thud.

"There's nowhere to run, boy," The Ender said as he struggled against his bonds. "It's a small island, and I'll find you. And then I'm going to end you."

"Me and my yo-yos of death will be waiting," Clivo said. He was tempted to spit at the nasty captive, just to punctuate his triumph over him, but decided that that was taking things a bit too far.

Clivo ran back over to the aswang and saw that its damaged wing was dripping blood on the dirt. It had quit struggling and was looking at Clivo questioningly.

"I don't know if you can understand me, but I'm not going to hurt you. I'm here to protect you," Clivo said quickly, panting in his panic to get the creature out of there before The Ender broke free of the yo-yo strings and crawled up from the dirt prison. "But I need to keep you in the net for now, at least until you turn back into human form and we can have a nice talk about how I'd appreciate it if you didn't eat me."

The aswang tilted its head, its face suddenly morphing and changing features. Clivo rocked back in shock as the creature shrank and shape-shifted into its human form. The groaning of bones as they shrank and contracted made Clivo wince, but he watched in fascination as the being changed back to its human self.

Clivo took in a sharp breath of recognition as a weary

yet smiling face looked up at him through the net and a kind voice greeted him. "Hi, honey."

"Dayea?" Clivo asked, amazed at seeing the ancient woman from the butcher shop. He looked behind himself to make sure The Ender was still in his hole and hadn't seen the human identity of the aswang.

Dayea held out a thin, wrinkly arm that was streaming blood. "Sweet boy, help me home?"

Clivo was so shocked that he had just been standing there, frozen. He sprang into action. "Oh, my gosh, of course! I'm so sorry."

Clivo gently untangled the frail woman from the net, his mind still reeling from the discovery that just a moment before she had been a feared beast that could easily have torn him apart in a heartbeat. He took off his shirt and wrapped it around her, leading her back to town.

Nobody was roaming the streets due to the curfew, which was a good thing, seeing as how a shirtless boy leading a half-naked woman through town would hardly go unnoticed.

They arrived at Dayea's butcher shop, and the place was a mess. Raw meat was scattered everywhere and chewed-on bones were discarded on the floor. Above them, a skylight was open to the stars—Dayea must have escaped through it after making her transformation.

Clivo looked at the carnage around him. "Do you own a butcher shop 'cause it's easier to eat when you morph?"

Dayea smiled and nodded. "I enjoy eating live cows more, but it upsets the villagers. This way I can stay safe better."

She hobbled to a back room and returned dressed in a long nightgown and carrying a first-aid kit. Clivo sat with her and cleaned the wound where The Ender had shot her. Fortunately, the bullet had just grazed her arm, and while it must have stung something fierce, it wasn't that bad of a wound.

Clivo focused on her injury, but his mind was spinning with so many questions that he didn't even know where to begin. Fortunately, Dayea spoke first. "Why does that man want to hurt me, honey? You know?"

Clivo dabbed at her injury with a cotton ball. "There are a lot of people who want to take on your special powers for themselves. And most of them are not very good people. There's actually been quite a race going on to find you."

Dayea's brow furrowed, wrinkling her face even more, if that was possible. "But I cannot turn anyone else into shape-shifters. I have tried. Be less lonely, you know?"

Clivo shook his head. "It's not your shape-shifting abilities they want, it's your blood—so that they can become immortal."

"Immortal?" Dayea asked, obviously surprised. "Am I immortal?"

Now Clivo was surprised. He stopped tending to her wound and studied her face. "I think you are. I mean, there's one cryptid in the world that is immortal, and I was really hoping it was you."

Dayea thought about it. "I have been alive thousands of years, but look at me. I age. In a few thousand more years, I will be dust."

Clivo looked at Dayea. She certainly looked ancient. If anyone appeared to be thousands of years old, it was her. A worry began to creep into his stomach, so he pulled out the blood sampler. "I can find out if you're immortal, if you don't mind?"

Dayea stared into the distance, her eyes looking like her brain was processing the meaning of being immortal. This close to her, Clivo caught a glimpse of his reflection in her narrow eyes and saw that it was upside down.

Finally, she nodded in agreement.

Clivo scooped up some of her blood that had dripped on the floor with the needle and waited as the device did its work. It was a familiar feeling at this point—the beating of Clivo's heart in excitement at the thought that the immortal had been found.

The screen lit up, and what it said was so disappointing and confusing that Clivo simply went numb.

NOT IMMORTAL.

Dayea looked down at the screen and a happy smile crept onto her face. "That is okay, honey. Dayea is tired, I do not need to live forever. Too hard living in a time when people are scared of her. Too hard making a living when one is thousands of years old. I am ready for rest."

"I'm glad," Clivo said distractedly. He was very close to losing hope, a feeling that he had never had before. The dangers of the catches were wearing on him, with both the cryptids and the people chasing after him. The Blasters had used every clue they had, and still they couldn't find the immortal. Now that they were out of clues, the only thing left to do was to catch the remaining creatures one by one and hope they stumbled across the immortal. But they knew of thousands of cryptids, and there were surely more that had evaded documentation. He could spend several life-times catching them and never find the right one. Clivo had never felt so tired in his life.

Dayea patted him on the cheek. "I am sorry your jour-ney does not end with me, honey. You are a good boy."

"It's okay," Clivo said, managing a smile. He pulled himself together and began bandaging her arm. "I just wish I knew where to look next. You haven't by chance come across any immortal beings in your incredibly long time on Earth, have you?"

Dayea thought about it and sighed. "No, honey. I am the oldest thing I know. Lonely life. Very lonely. Glad not to be immortal."

"Were you born as a shape-shifter, or did something happen to you?" Clivo asked, trying to distract himself from the crushing disappointment that Dayea was not the immortal.

Dayea nodded. "Born like this, honey. Very scary for my parents the first time I turned. I ate the family dog, poor little thing. But my family loved me, and the other villagers learned not to be afraid. I am no vampire, I do not hunt people. I was seen as special, as touched by the heavens with important gift. But after Mommy and Papi died, people cast me out. My differences no longer were special; they were seen as a curse. That was three thousand years ago. Long time to not have people like you."

Clivo finished dressing the wound and sat back on his heels. He had to get out of there, and fast—he didn't want to be around when The Ender broke free. But he also didn't feel like he could leave Dayea. He hated the idea of her working hard every day, without friends or family for comfort. She was thousands of years old and she was right, it was time for her to rest. Besides, his duty was not just to find the immortal, but to also protect the other cryptids, even if one was a three-thousand-year-old woman who could turn into a bat.

Clivo rocked forward and cupped her hands in his. "Dayea, I'd like to bring you home with me and take care of you, if that's something you'd be okay with?"

Her fleshy eyelids lifted in surprise. "Why would you want to do that, honey?"

"Because that's what I do. I protect special things that others are trying to hurt. Besides, you've been working for thousands of years. Aren't you ready to retire?" Clivo nudged her with his elbow and shot her a dimpled smile.

Dayea let out a laugh through her toothless gums. "Okay, honey. Where do we go?"

Clivo stood up, getting ready to leave. "America. Have you ever been there?"

Dayea accepted his hand to help her up. "One time, long ago, before the white men arrived. But Dayea did not like the taste of buffalo, so I left."

"Do you have a passport?" Clivo asked, peering out the curtained window to make sure The Ender wasn't stalking the streets.

"Oh, sure, honey. In case I need to leave in an emergency."

"I guess with the curfew, the airport won't be open until morning?"

"No, honey," Dayea said. Then she giggled. "One time, before the curfew, Dayea almost flew into a propeller. Not sure who was more scared—me or the pilot!"

Clivo racked his brain for a way to get them out of there. It was a small enough town that, come sunrise, there'd be no place to hide from The Ender. "Any chance you have a boat stashed somewhere so we could travel to the next island with an airport?"

Miraculously, Dayea nodded. "Always, honey. Again, in case of an emergency."

"Awesome! Quickly pack whatever you need and we'll get out of here," Clivo said. He looked at her with a final thought. "Oh, and I hope you don't eat cats."

XVIII

The next evening, Clivo stood on Jerry's doorstep with Dayea, ringing the bell. The door was flung open and Jerry stood there in his football helmet and pads, a golf club raised over his shoulder as if to strike them.

"Whoa! It's me, Coops!" Clivo said, standing protectively in front of Dayea.

"I know it's you!" Jerry yelled. "And I'm going to give you a good club to the head for running off on me like that! I was supposed to help you!"

Clivo was about to respond when Charles, Adam, and Hernando came running out. Adam grabbed Clivo's wrist and slapped a handcuff on it. Clivo pulled back his arm in confusion, but discovered that Adam's wrist was in the other bracelet. "Um, am I under arrest?"

Adam raised his arm and shook it angrily, the chain between their wrists rattling. "As a matter of fact, you are! Until you learn not to go running off like a dog with its tail on fire!"

Amelia came out the door just then. "Yeah, Clivo. You

don't have to keep falling on your sword, like, *all* the time. We are here to help, you know."

Finally, Stephanie came running out and tried to give Clivo a hug, which was awkward with one of his arms attached to Adam. As she pulled away, she looked at Clivo's face and gasped at the sight of his eye, which was swollen shut and horribly bruised by The Ender's blow. "Oh my gosh, Clivo! Are you okay? *This* is why we don't want you running off on your own anymore! It's getting too dangerous."

Amelia peered more closely at Clivo's black eye. "Geez. I guess that answers the question of whether the evil resistance found you or not."

Charles stood on tiptoe to peer over Clivo's shoulder. "Who's the grandma, dude?"

Clivo stepped aside to reveal Dayea, who was standing there in a flowery dress, her wrinkled face set in its usual joyful smile. "Guys, this is the aswang, also known as Dayea."

"Hello," Dayea said with a happy wave.

Stephanie's hand flew to her mouth, "Is it . . . Is she . . . the *immortal*?"

Clivo quickly shook his head. "No, she's not, but I wanted to bring her home anyway. Our job is to protect all of the cryptids, and even though it's kind of weird that one of them is a human who occasionally turns into a flesh-eating bat, she still deserves our protection."

The Blasters crowded around Dayea and introduced

themselves. Stephanie gave her a hug and let out a giggle. "I like your name, Dayea. It's very appropriate."

"What does it mean?" Charles asked. He was watching Dayea warily, as if he thought she was about to sprout wings and fly off.

"Goddess of secrets," Stephanie said.

"It's a nice name," Hernando said quietly, gently shaking Dayea's hand.

Adam grudgingly leaned way over to embrace the tiny Dayea. "No offense, but I was kinda hoping for someone more muscular than you."

"Don't worry, when she shape-shifts you'll be impressed, I promise you," Clivo said.

"I'll be my own judge of being impressed, thank you very much," Adam replied.

Clivo pulled helplessly on his handcuffed wrist. "Anyway, guys, I wasn't going to stay. I need to keep moving and not draw the evil resistance to your doorstep with this stupid chip I have implanted in me. I just wanted to drop Dayea off to see if you could keep her safe until I figure out what's next."

"And we've made it very clear," Amelia said, stepping forward, "that you're not going anywhere without us."

"You guys have no idea of the kind of evil people who are tracking me!" Clivo exclaimed. "The guy who punched me calls himself The Ender, and I have no doubt he would happily end any of our lives to get what he wants. Trust me, I need to get away from you!"

A throat cleared behind them and Clivo spun around to find Mr. Cooper standing in the doorway, with Mrs. Cooper and Aunt Pearl huddled behind him. "All right, kids. We've been happy to play dumb about what's been going on with you, but enough is enough. Time to give us some explanations."

Jerry sighed in exasperation. "What do we need to explain to you, Pops?"

Mr. Cooper raised his eyebrows. "Well, you could start by explaining why there's a very old woman standing on my doorstep, and end with where Clivo has been for the past three days and why it looks like someone has been using his face as a punching bag."

Jerry stomped his foot. "Gaw! You guys are always up in my business! Can't a guy fill his house with strangers and not be hassled about it all the time?"

Clivo put his hand on Jerry's arm to calm him down. "It's okay, Coops. I think it's time to tell Aunt Pearl and your folks what's been going on." He gathered the Blasters in a circle and spoke softly. "You're right, things are getting too dangerous. I think we need to tell them everything in case the evil resistance shows up, so they can at least protect themselves."

The Blasters all glanced at each other, and Amelia

finally nodded. "Who knows how long we'll be searching for the immortal. It would be easier if we didn't have to sneak around to do it."

Stephanie put her arm around Dayea. "Having a few more people around to protect the cryptids wouldn't hurt, either. Besides, maybe Mr. Cooper will give me more access to the SETL satellites."

"We had agreed to trust no one," Adam pointed out. "If we're going to make an exception for these parental units, can you guys vouch for them?"

Clivo nodded. "I can vouch for Aunt Pearl. She's definitely one of the good guys."

Jerry agreed. "My dad's pretty dorky, but he and my mom are solid and will probably be pretty proud of me for trying to save the world."

"But we need to talk about this somewhere else," Clivo reminded them. "Unless you want the evil resistance running up these steps soon."

Jerry scratched his head. "Actually, my dad could take us to SETL. There's a basement there with solid steel walls. That way nobody can use radar or heat-sensing cameras to see inside. I doubt even your tracking chip will be able to get a signal through those walls."

"What do you keep down there that's so secret?" Adam asked.

"Duh! The aliens!" Jerry replied in a hushed whisper.

"What else would the Search for Extraterrestrial Life Institute keep in their basement except extraterrestrial life?"

Charles started breathing heavily and pounded his chest with a fist. "I'm so excited about seeing an alien, I think I just developed asthma."

"Calm down, guys, there's no aliens down there right now. If there were, my dad would never take us. But it's empty, so we should be good," Jerry said.

Stephanie pointed at Dayea, who was swaying back and forth, her eyes slowly closing. "She's about to fall asleep. Can we leave her here so she can rest?"

Clivo approached Dayea, dragging Adam with him since they were still chained together. "Dayea?"

Dayea snapped her eyes open and smiled. "Yes, honey?"

"Is it okay if I leave you here for a bit? I promise you'll be safe, and I'll be back really soon," Clivo asked quietly.

"Fine by me, honey. Could use a rest. Dayea is always really tired after her full-moon fun."

Clivo lowered his voice even more so nobody but Dayea could hear him. "You sure there's no chance you'll . . . you know . . . *change* while I'm gone? I don't think Jerry would like it very much if you ate his dog."

Dayea put her hand to her mouth and giggled. "No need to worry, honey. The full moon is long gone. I will not change again for another 29.53 days."

Clivo turned to Mrs. Cooper and Aunt Pearl, Adam

swinging around with him. "Aunt Pearl, is it okay if I leave Dayea here with you and Mrs. Cooper? We'll tell Mr. Cooper everything, but we need to go to the safety of SETL's basement to do so."

"SETL's basement? Why?" Mr. Cooper asked, his eyebrows lifting high over his glasses.

Clivo wasn't really sure how to break the news. Fortunately, Adam stepped in and said, "Dude here was implanted with a tracking device, and unless we block the signal there's going to be a whole bunch of malicious malcontents storming your house with nothing less than murderous murder on their agenda."

Pearl gasped. "Clivo! What are malicious malcontents and why on earth are you involved with them? All my fears of teenagers doing bad things are coming true!"

"It's okay, Aunt Pearl, I'll explain everything later. But I promise you that we're the good guys!" Clivo said, trying to calm Aunt Pearl down.

"But you've been *handcuffed*!" Aunt Pearl exclaimed.

Mrs. Cooper stepped forward and took Dayea by the arm. "Come along, dear. Let's get you all set up for some rest." She shot Jerry a look. "And I expect a full report on what is going on around here when you return."

Aunt Pearl nervously followed them into the house. "I suppose I can teach Dayea some dance moves while we wait for everyone to return and explain this murderous murder!"

* * *

Half an hour later, Clivo, the Blasters, and Mr. Cooper were standing in the basement of the SETL Institute. Well, Mr. Cooper was standing; the Blasters were all running around the room like a herd of cats on catnip.

The basement looked like a nicer, less ominous place to hold creatures than Douglas's dungeon of horrors. It was a brightly lit laboratory, with examining tables lined up in the middle and small Plexiglas-fronted rooms filled with pillows and comforters. It held all the things necessary to examine aliens, like cameras and microscopes, but felt welcoming and nonthreatening. There was even a cozy kitchen in the corner with a plate of brownies sitting on the counter.

"This place is amazing!" Charles said, trying to open a locked filing cabinet. "So alien feet have really walked on these floors?"

Mr. Cooper waved a finger at him. "Please don't touch that! There's top secret stuff in there!"

Adam guffawed. "Cooperdude, top secret only works for military stuff!" Adam peered closely at a framed photo on a desk that showed Mr. Cooper with his arm wrapped around a small, smiling green creature with one eye who was eating what appeared to be some amber cup squash. "OHMYGOSHISTHATANALIEN?"

Mr. Cooper ran over and clutched the photo to his

chest. "I have taken you to a very sacred space within the SETL Institute because you need my help. But I am not telling you anything about the aliens we have found. Drat! I mean the aliens we are *looking* for! We have not found any aliens! Got it? No aliens!"

Hernando pointed at the photo. "But that sure looked like—"

"Nothing! You've seen NOTHING!" Mr. Cooper exclaimed.

Stephanie smiled at Mr. Cooper. "It's okay, sir. Once we tell you what we've been doing and why we're in so much danger, I think you'll see that we're super good at keeping secrets."

Amelia pulled up a rolling chair. "Why don't you sit down, Mr. Cooper? We're about to share some things that might be rather shocking."

Mr. Cooper stood up straighter, the picture frame still clasped to his chest. "I will have you know that I have a Ph.D. in space microbiology with an emphasis on alien organisms. The things I have seen floating through our universe make me immune to shock."

Jerry patted his dad on the shoulder. "Clivo was recently drugged by a demon chicken, and the old lady he brought to our house turns into a bat every full moon."

Mr. Cooper blinked at his son a few times, then slowly lowered himself onto the chair. "You're right. I'm shocked. I believe I'll take a seat for this."

They all pulled up chairs and sat in a circle.

Clivo gathered his thoughts, trying to decide where to begin. He glanced at the beaded bracelet around his wrist, which his father had given him. "Well, Mr. Cooper, I guess I should start by telling you about what my dad *really* did for a living."

Clivo talked for the better part of an hour. He started at the beginning, when Douglas Chancery had first knocked on his door and told him that Russell was a cryptid catcher. He talked about finding the Blasters and how they had become a team. He talked about his catches, with occasional blurt-ins from Adam and Charles, who insisted upon mentioning their roles in everything. He mentioned Dayea and why it had been so important to him to bring her with him from the Philippines so he could protect her from the evil resistance, who probably thought she was the immortal.

Finally, Clivo talked about discovering that Douglas had killed his father and was now holding a bunch of cryptids captive to be used for organic warfare. His voice caught as he said this last bit, feelings of anger, sadness, and betrayal flooding him.

Mr. Cooper sat silently as he listened to Clivo's story, his face rapt. The only sound he made was an angry grunt when Clivo mentioned the imprisoned cryptids.

Clivo finished his story and took a deep breath. "So, that's where we're at, Mr. Cooper. We have no idea who the immortal is, Douglas has the cryptids, and now every evil person out there can find me thanks to this chip in my body. I guess you could say I've run out of places to hide."

Mr. Cooper stood up from his chair and wandered around the room in thought, one hand scratching his chin. He looked at the photograph that he had had clutched to his chest the whole time and let out a sigh. "I always thought your father was a good man, Clivo. I just didn't realize how good he was."

"Thank you, sir," Clivo said, his throat getting tight.

Mr. Cooper wandered around the room in silence for a few more minutes, occasionally letting out a grunt or nodding to himself. Finally, he approached Jerry and laid his hand on his shoulder. "I'm proud of you, son. Honestly, there have been a few times when I've thought you might have ended up on the side of evil, and it's wonderful to hear you've chosen to walk on the side of good."

"Thanks, Pops," Jerry replied. "You taught me well."

Mr. Cooper looked at the photo in his hand again, and with a nod he handed it to Adam, who grabbed it with a gasp. "Pass the photo around, Adam. We've had four aliens of three different species crash-land here on Earth. We patched them up and got them on their way again."

"Why are you telling us this, sir?" Amelia asked.

Mr. Cooper nodded. "You trusted me with your secrets, so I'm trusting you with mine."

He wandered over to a cupboard and pulled out something that looked like a metal gun. "Now, let's deal with one thing at a time, shall we? Clivo, we implant tracking chips in our little green friends so we know where their homes are. Those chips are much more powerful than what you've probably got, as they're designed to reach deep into the galaxy. If you let me put this chip in you, its stronger signal will scramble the other one and make it impossible for people to locate you."

"Will it hurt?" Clivo asked, not liking the look of the gun in Mr. Cooper's hand.

Mr. Cooper shook his head. "It's smaller than a sewing needle. You'll barely feel a prick." Clivo held out his arm and Mr. Cooper pressed the gun against his skin and fired. There was barely any pain, and only a tiny drop of blood came up from where the chip had been implanted. Mr. Cooper gave him a wink. "I forgot to mention that now I'll know where you are at all times. None of this disappearing to wander around the world alone again, okay, son?"

Clivo rubbed his arm. "After everything I've been through, it will actually be a relief to know that someone will be able to keep track of me."

Adam passed the photo he had been fawning over to Charles and raised his hand. "Okay, now that we know the evil resistance won't be up in our grille anytime soon, can we move on to the next crisis?"

"I'm not really sure how to help you figure out who the immortal is. That's territory for you smart kids," Mr. Cooper said, pushing his glasses higher up on his nose. "But what I *can* help with is getting those cryptids out of that dungeon."

Stephanie looked at him. "So you agree that it's wrong they're imprisoned?"

Mr. Cooper sputtered, "Wrong? It's terrible! The first directive of SETL is to make contact and build relationships with alien species, which are also considered cryptids, by the way. Not to throw them in cages and use them for *war*! It's absurd!"

Jerry stood up. "But, Pops, how are we going to rescue them? Douglas has guns—like, *a lot* of them!"

"Guns?" Mr. Cooper said, looking up with worry. "That makes a rescue mission a little more problematic. I'll have to call George in, that's for sure. He's trained in tai chi, so maybe he can help. And Sandra does yoga, so maybe she's a good fighter. Jeffrey is useless, as he's been dealing with gout."

Mr. Cooper again began wandering aimlessly around the room, muttering to himself. The Blasters gathered together, and Adam talked quickly in a hushed voice. "Is Cooperdude seriously calling in other nerds for this rescue operation?"

"No offense to your dad, Jerry, but I don't think a bunch of astrophysicists with no muscle tone are the guys for this," Charles added. "Besides, we agreed to tell your dad about the cryptids, not the whole SETL world."

"Yeah! Let them stick to finding their own aliens!" Adam exclaimed.

"Their own ones," Hernando agreed.

Adam narrowed his eyes. "Sorry, dude, but we need to blow off your dad and go it alone on this one."

"Well, hang on, let's give my dad the benefit of the doubt here." Jerry looked at his dad. "Hey, Pops, any chance you'll keep your guys out of the rescue mission and let us handle it?"

Mr. Cooper shook his head. "Absolutely not. You kids need to let the adults take over from here. I'm taking you home while George, Sandra, and I sort out this hullabaloo."

Jerry turned back to the Blasters and shrugged. "I tried. Okay, guys, let me grab some telephone cord and then I'll ambush him, okay?"

"You're going to *tie up your dad*?" Clivo asked incredulously.

Jerry shrugged again. "I've done a lot of things to torture my pops over the years. Tying him up at work is probably the least obnoxious thing I've done."

"Do you need our help?" Amelia asked, nervously chewing her lip.

"Nah, I'll take the heat. I always do," Jerry replied.

Mr. Cooper continued to wander aimlessly as Jerry snuck around the room, removing the cords from the telephones. When he had a handful of them, he turned to his dad. "Hey, Pops, we just need to discuss one other thing. Do you mind sitting down for a second?"

"Huh?" Mr. Cooper asked, stopping his wandering.

"Just have a seat, Pops. I have an idea for how we can rescue the cryptids," Jerry said, kicking a chair forward, his hands fiddling with the telephone cords hidden behind his back.

Mr. Cooper absentmindedly took a seat and continued his rambling. "I don't need your help, Jer. I think me and the other astrophysicists should be able to face our fears of confrontation and take down whatever ne'er-do-well is messing with our delicate relationship with the magnificent cryptids, and— Hang on now! What's this?"

Jerry had swung the joined telephone cords over his father like a lasso and pulled them tight. He was now busy tying Mr. Cooper's hands behind his back. "Sorry, Pops. It's actually *we* who don't need *your* help. And trust me, I'm doing this for your safety. It's best that we take it from here."

Mr. Cooper craned his neck to bellow at Jerry behind him, "Jerry! I want you to consider your next actions very, very carefully!"

Jerry came around to face his father and sighed. "You're right, Pops. I should definitely gag you, too, in case someone comes in to check the equipment. Clivo? Hand me that duct tape."

"Clivo! Don't you dare help him with this!" Mr. Cooper said.

Clivo winced as he handed Jerry the duct tape. "I'm super sorry, Mr. Cooper. But Jerry's right, we're doing this to protect you."

Mr. Cooper shot Jerry a warning glare. "Jerry Cooper, if you even *think* about leaving me here and racing off—bumplingargh!"

Jerry finished securing a piece of duct tape over Mr. Cooper's mouth. "I know you're probably going to send me off to that military academy for doing this, Pops. But please know that everything I'm doing right now is for all the right reasons. And someday, maybe years from now, you'll get over your anger at me and be able to see that."

"Harumphgurplunk!" Mr. Cooper loudly mumbled through the tape.

"Thanks, Pops, I knew you'd understand." Jerry faced the rest of the group. "Well, guys, if Douglas doesn't kill me, my dad sure will, so let's make this count!"

XIX

A short time later, the group was huddled in bushes next to Douglas's castle of horrors.

"Okay, boss, what's the plan?" Charles whispered to Clivo.

Clivo stared at the brick building, his mind whirling. What he wanted to do was storm the building and take down Douglas himself, but he knew there was no way the Blasters would let him go it alone. But he wasn't sure how to bring everyone inside *and* keep them safe *and* confront Douglas. They didn't even have any weapons to fight Douglas with— as if anything they could get would hold up against Douglas and his cane of death.

"Jerry, any chance you have something in your bag of tricks that can be used for storming the castle?" Clivo asked hopefully.

"I'm so glad you asked," Jerry said, his white teeth flashing in the moonlight as he smiled.

He unzipped his fanny pack and pulled out a bottle of dish soap, holding it forth triumphantly.

Adam scoffed, "We want to defeat Douglas, not give him a bath."

"I think it's genius," Amelia said.

"Me, too," Stephanie agreed.

"I'm lost," Charles said. "What's so exciting about dish soap?"

Jerry pocketed the soap. "We don't need to go after Douglas, Douglas just has to come after *us*. And once he does, he'll slip on the soap and we can pounce."

"Very simple and elegant," Hernando said.

Adam reached out and gave Jerry a fist bump. "I didn't think it was possible, dude, but you have become an indispensable part of our team."

"Thanks, guys," Jerry said excitedly. "I've actually been meaning to talk to you all about how I'd like to electrify your whole basement in case of intruders."

Clivo patted Jerry on the shoulder. "Let's tackle one challenge at a time, okay?" He looked again at the castle, doing his best to form a plan. "Jerry, do you think the rope we used to climb up to the roof is still there?"

"Only one way to find out," Jerry said.

Without another word, Jerry took off running toward the castle.

"Jerry!" Clivo said as loudly as he dared.

Stephanie put her hand on his arm. "Let him go, Clivo. You can't be the only one taking risks, remember?"

Clivo waited anxiously as Jerry ran behind the castle,

then popped his head around the corner a moment later and gave a thumbs-up.

"Okay, guys, we're going to quickly climb the rope to the roof and break in from there. Ready?" Clivo asked.

"Born ready," Adam said.

Clivo and the Blasters ran to join Jerry behind the castle. The waning moon was rising high in the sky and lit them more than Clivo was comfortable with, but at this point they didn't have a whole lot of options.

Clivo and Jerry quickly scurried up the rope, followed by Stephanie and Amelia. Adam grunted so loudly as he slowly hoisted himself up the rope that Amelia had to shush him. Hernando fared a bit better with the physical exertion, but Charles was so hopeless in his climbing that Clivo and Jerry finally had to pull the rope up with Charles clinging to it for dear life.

"Thanks, dudes. I've always had a weak hand grip," Charles whispered.

Clivo headed to the door they had used earlier, but discovered that the lock Jerry had picked had been welded shut. "Shoot. I guess we should have checked that before having all of you guys climb up here," he whispered.

"What's wrong with using the front door?" Stephanie whispered back.

"It has some sort of keypad on it, and I have no idea what the code is," Clivo replied.

Charles stuck his face between them. "Sounds like you need a code breaker like myself."

"You think you can figure out the code?" Clivo asked. He had pretty much ceased being constantly amazed by how smart the Blasters were, but cracking a coded keypad would definitely re-amaze him.

"Maybe I already have," Charles whispered before sneezing and furiously wiping his nose.

"But you haven't even seen it! How could you have figured it out?" Clivo asked, his amazement meter kicking into high gear.

Now it was Adam's turn to stick his head into the circle. "Are we going to spend all night interrogating his genius, or shall we just let him get to work?"

Jerry and Clivo climbed back down the rope, followed by the others. Adam once again grunted in agony the whole way, and Jerry had to climb back up and tie the rope around Charles's waist to lower him because Charles claimed he had lost the use of his hands after the exertion of the first climb.

They snuck around to the front of the building and stared at the keypad. It was standard, with large green glowing numbers and LOCK and UNLOCK buttons. As he examined the device, Charles wrinkled his nose, which made him look like a rabbit sniffing a morsel.

"Yep, the code is definitely zero-seven-one-three," he finally said. He reached out to press the buttons, but his finger buckled with weakness when he touched the keypad. "Darn it! That rope climb sucked all the strength out of my digits. Stephanie, can you help me with your powerful hacker hands?"

Stephanie stepped forward and pressed zero-seven-one-three on the keypad, followed by the UNLOCK button. Instantly, the sound of a bolt clicking back was heard, followed by the large steel door slightly opening.

"My MAN!" Jerry whispered, giving Charles a pat on the back. "I may be good at pranks, but that was some magic stuff right there."

"Okay, can you just tell me, quickly, how you did that?" Clivo asked.

Charles reached up with a finger and picked his nose. "Simple psychology and observation. Most people use their birthdays for codes. I happened to notice that Douglas wears a ruby ring, which is July's birthstone, and he has a rabbit's foot dangling from his key chain, which means he's superstitious—and was probably born on the thirteenth. Seventh month, thirteenth day. Zero-seven-one-three."

"It is wizardly," Hernando said quietly.

"Now, come on, guys, let's go!" Charles whispered, reaching for the door.

Clivo grabbed his shoulder. "Hang on. How about you let the people who have feeling in their arms storm the castle?"

Charles stepped aside and saluted. "After you, brave soldiers!"

Clivo slowly opened the door into the dark stone foyer. A candle chandelier danced with light overhead, and a sour smell of cold sweat hit him squarely in the nose. He turned and put a finger to his lips to make sure the others stayed quiet, then listened intently. Sure enough, he heard the low moans and growls of the captured cryptids.

Clivo was relieved. He had worried that Douglas might move the cryptids during Clivo's time in the Philippines— or do something worse. Douglas was probably counting on being able to track Clivo's movements with the tracking signal so he could properly prepare for an ambush.

Well, get ready, Douglas, Clivo thought. *The ambush is coming.*

Clivo crept down the staircase, with Jerry walking next to him with the bottle of soap clasped in one hand. The Blasters crowded in close behind, letting out an occasional mumble when someone stepped on another's foot.

Their plan was simple. Throw down some soap, get Douglas's attention, run when he started shooting at them (which he most definitely would), then return and tie Douglas up once he slipped on the soap, which would (hopefully) have knocked the gun from his hand. As for what to do with the cryptids, Clivo hadn't gotten that far.

He was almost to the bottom of the stairs when he saw Douglas, his back to them, leaning over a desk.

Clivo froze and nodded to Jerry, who unscrewed the cap on the bottle of soap and quietly dumped a bunch of it on the lowest two steps. Clivo looked at the Blasters behind them and mouthed that they should get ready to run. They all nodded in confirmation, but Clivo could see the fear in their eyes as they huddled together.

All of a sudden, it seemed like such a dumb plan. There was no need for everyone to be there, in danger. They were about to *dare* someone to shoot at them. Clivo could have done that by himself, without putting everyone else at risk.

Besides, something didn't seem right. Why was Douglas just casually going about his business when he knew Clivo would be coming back for him? Why hadn't he moved the cryptids? Everything seemed too . . . normal.

He was about to call the whole thing off in favor of returning after he could make a better plan and face Douglas alone when Jerry suddenly shouted, "Hey! Evildoer! You want us? Come and get us!"

Clivo gritted his teeth with frustration that he hadn't been able to stop Jerry from shouting in time. He watched as Douglas slowly straightened up, seemingly unsurprised by the group's sudden reappearance.

Douglas stood with his back to them, not saying a word and not turning around.

"Clivo, what's he doing?" Stephanie asked.

"I don't know, but I want you all out of here. NOW!" Clivo responded.

But it was too late. Douglas whirled around, a gas mask covering his face and the tatzelwurm, a snakelike cryptid with only two legs in the front and a cat's face, held in front of him.

Douglas squeezed the tatzelwurm with both hands as Clivo turned and began pushing his friends up the stairs. But they were too slow. A purple cloud that smelled like freshly baked bread spewed from the cryptid's open jaws and surrounded them.

Clivo held his breath and frantically pushed on his friends to keep them moving, but one by one they began to fall backward like dominoes as the fumes overtook them.

Hernando fell against Clivo, causing Clivo to stumble back onto the soap-covered step. He clawed at the air as his feet flew out from under him, sending him crashing to the hard stone floor and knocking the wind out of him.

Clivo writhed on the ground, his body begging for air but his mind doing everything it could to keep him from taking a breath of the tainted air. Finally, his diaphragm released and he involuntarily sucked in a lungful of the poisonous fumes. As Clivo's vision began to go dark, he glanced at his friends, all lying unconscious on the floor; for all he could tell, they were dead already. Then his mom's Egyptian rattle sounded somewhere off in the distance, and Clivo's heart burned with the sadness that, as hard as he had tried, he had been unable to protect everybody from the storm of evil.

He reached a hand out to his friends, his vision waning. "I'm so sorry."

XX

Clivo woke up as he heard shouting and the scrape of metal on stone.

"Careful! Don't drop it, you idiot!" Douglas yelled.

"Don't call me an idiot, you old cartoon!"

"Yeah, do you want our help or not?"

Clivo recognized the other voices from somewhere, but it was hard to place them because his head was swimming with different sensations. Part of his brain was trying to drag him back into unconsciousness, while the other part was dragging him out of it.

"Help?" Douglas laughed. "Let's be very clear. I called you in to do you a *favor*. You're the only other ones in the stupid evil resistance who know I'm selling these monsters for organic warfare, and I'm willing to cut you in on the deal. And you're the dumbest of the bunch, so don't think I can't find someone else who'd be happy to be here without giving me any lip!"

"You Americans are so rude!" a female's voice said.

Clivo slowly opened his eyes, but the world swam before

him, so he immediately shut them. After a deep breath he opened them again and moved his head ever so slightly so he could see the rest of his gang. They were all still on the floor, with nobody moving or uttering any sounds.

Why was he the only one coming to? He became keenly aware of his hand burning uncomfortably and realized that that was where the demon chicken Elwetritsch had pecked him with its poisonous beak. Maybe the poison was still in his system and was somehow acting as an antidote to the tatzelwurm's smog of death? It sure felt like many different things were at war inside his head.

Moving as little as possible, Clivo turned his head to see who was talking, and his mind clicked into sharp focus. Pushing a cage that contained the Beast of Bray Road, apparently unaffected by the tatzelwurm's poison, were none other than Lana and Thomas. The previous summer, Clivo had been duped by these Luxembourgers into helping them find the immortal so they could use it for their own evil purposes. Fortunately, the Luxembourgers really *were* pretty dumb, and the vicious Otterman they were sure was the immortal had turned out to be a harmless creature that loved chocolate.

Clivo had defeated Lana and Thomas in the Alaskan wilderness, and Douglas had said they would be banned from the United States for a while—apparently, yet another lie Douglas had told.

"All right, you incompetents, let's load the cage onto the

elevator and take it to the copter," Douglas said, motioning with his hand.

"What about Clivo and his nerds?" Thomas asked.

Clivo shut his eyes as the three of them glanced his way.

"I'll take care of them," Douglas spat.

Clivo tried to tense his muscles, preparing to jump up to defend his friends, but he couldn't even feel his limbs, much less get them to respond to him.

"Hang on now, chief, we only agreed to work with you if there was no bloodshed! We want riches and world domination, but we're not murderers!" Thomas wailed in his obnoxious voice.

Douglas looked at him with exasperation. "The last time I saw you, I believe you were shooting at Clivo, now weren't you?"

Lana stepped forward. "Only because he wasn't being cooperative. But killing someone who's just lying there seems so *gauche*."

"You two are already becoming a pain in my rear, you know that?" Douglas groaned. "Fine, they'll be out for days anyway. By that time we'll be safely ensconced in our new fortress that not even he and his dork army could find. It's a shame. He was worth a lot to me, and his dad, too. It just goes to show you, being good never did anyone any good in this world. Now, come on, I'm getting peckish."

The three of them pushed the cage into an elevator and closed the door.

Clivo had to move fast, which was impossible due to the lack of control he had over his body. At least he knew his friends were just unconscious and would be okay, though not for a while. Finally, Clivo was alone in doing what he needed to do—but it was right when he most needed the help. Still, he was not going to fail.

How he was going to do that lying down, he had no idea.

He took another deep breath and focused his fuzzy mind to move his toes; thankfully, they wiggled a bit. After a few minutes of feeling like he was pulling himself out of wet concrete, he was able to rise to his hands and knees. The spot where the Elwetritsch had bitten him was red and swollen, with black lines tracing across his hand like a spiderweb. He had never been so glad to have been bitten by a demon chicken, that was for sure.

Clivo was so busy dealing with his wet towel of a body that at first he didn't notice how silent the dungeon had become. It had been full of chirps, roars, and guttural moans as the Luxembourgers loaded the Beast of Bray Road into the elevator, but now all was quiet.

He lifted his head, panting with the exertion, and saw something wondrous. All of the cryptids were pressed against the bars of their cages, watching Clivo with looks of concern. They all had chains and bandages on them to prevent them from using their special powers, and that stirred Clivo's anger even more.

"Hi, guys," Clivo said, his voice weak. "You remember

me, right? And you know I'm on your side? I'll get you out of here, I promise. I'm just not really sure how to do that yet."

Clivo looked each cryptid in the eye and spoke to it the way he had seen the Wasi speak to the Salawa. He used all the languages he knew, soothing them with his voice. He lifted his arm, which felt as heavy as a dumbbell, and motioned in swooping loops, as if casting a spell. He tried to extend the parts of him that were good and true and feed them into the eyes of the creatures so they would understand that he was on their side.

The exertion was finally too much for him and he dropped his arm, sweat pouring off his face.

Just as he was about to give up any hope, an amazing thing happened. One by one, the cryptids began to kneel, their majestic bodies bending toward Clivo, their eyes telling him that they understood. They were on the same team.

Clivo smiled in amazement. "Wow. Okay, guys, let's do this."

A few minutes later, Clivo came stumbling out of the elevator and onto the roof and was instantly hit by dirt and gravel that were kicked up by the rotating blades of a helicopter. He shielded his eyes with one arm and held on to the doorway to steady himself.

Lana and Thomas were fumbling with a cable that

would connect the cage to the helicopter while Douglas pointed and yelled about their incompetence.

Clivo brought his fingers to his lips and let out a loud whistle, causing the three of them to whirl around in shock.

Thomas's face broke into a wide grin and he held his arms out wide. "Hey, chief! Nice to see you again! How've things been?"

Lana, wearing her usual bloodred lipstick, rolled her eyes. "Now's not the time, Thomas."

Clivo steeled his jaw and spoke as loudly as he could over the whirring of the helicopter blades. "Release the cryptid. Now."

"Or else what?" Douglas spat. "Whatcha gonna do, kid? Swat at us? Look at you, you can barely stand up."

Clivo gripped the doorway to steady himself. He would *not* kneel in front of these people, even though his legs felt like wet noodles. "I'm a fair person, so I'll give you one more chance. Release the cryptid, or I can't be responsible for what will happen next."

"Ha!" Douglas let out a cackle and then immediately went into a coughing fit. "I gotta hand it to you, kid," he said after a moment, "you certainly have some courage. It makes you stupid, but you got it nonetheless."

Lana stepped forward. "Clivo, just go back inside and let us do what we came here to do."

"Yeah, chief. We've really put up a case against killing

you, but if you become uncooperative again, we're kinda gonna have to." Thomas gave a "what can you do" shrug of his shoulders.

Clivo stood up as straight as he could, shaking with the exertion. "Let the record show that I gave you fair warning."

"For what, kid? You got an army hiding behind you?" Douglas asked, casually lighting up a cigar.

"Actually," Clivo said with a grin, "I do."

He motioned behind him and spoke a few quiet words. Stalking out from the darkness of the elevator came the chupacabra, the Ugly Merman, and the blue tiger. They stood next to Clivo, their throats emitting low growls of contempt.

After the cryptids had shown they understood that Clivo was on their side, Clivo had quickly unwrapped the chupacabra's claws, and the creature had instantly sliced through its cage and freed itself. At first Clivo had backed away, wondering if he was about to be attacked. Instead the cryptid stood by him, watching for a signal of what to do next.

At first Clivo had wanted to release all the cryptids, but he was worried about gathering them all back up again. So he pointed to the cages of the blue tiger and the Ugly Merman, the other cryptids whose special powers Clivo knew might be helpful in defeating Douglas. He wasn't sure what most of the other cryptids could do and figured it was best to leave them out of it, in case one of them happened to spontaneously burst into rainbows or something else rather harmless.

The cigar fell out of Douglas's open mouth and sparks and ashes flew up as it hit the ground.

Thomas's eyes bugged out of his head. "You can control the cryptids? That's so cool, mate!"

"Now's not the time, Thomas!" Lana growled.

The Beast of Bray Road let out a roar, followed by the other cryptids.

"Like I said," Clivo said, "release the cryptid."

Douglas sighed. "Kid, you have officially become a massive pain in my backside."

Douglas dropped his cane and in one swift motion pulled out a gun and fired right at Clivo. But one of the chupacabra's paws darted out even faster and knocked the bullet away with a claw, a spark shooting into the air.

Immediately, the Ugly Merman unrolled its tongue and pulled the cage holding the Beast of Bray Road away from the helicopter. And then the blue tiger spat out a pearl that exploded on the ground in front of them, protecting Clivo and his team in a semicircle of blue fire that was whipped into a frenzy by the swirling helicopter blades.

"Oh my GOSH! That was so cool!" Thomas said, jumping up and down with glee.

Lana swatted his arm. "He's just defeated us again, you clod!"

Douglas stared at Clivo through the flames, the flickering light casting a devilish glow upon his face. "If you think this is over, kid, you're wrong. Dead wrong. There are a lot more of us in the evil resistance than you've even imagined. And we're coming for you. And *them*." He pointed a gnarly finger at the three cryptids, who all hissed or croaked back in defiance.

Clivo returned Douglas's steely gaze. "If you come, we'll rise up again."

Douglas deepened his glare and muttered, "Stupid child." He hoisted himself into the helicopter and was followed by Lana and Thomas. "We could have been something great, kid, you and me. You chose the wrong side."

Clivo glanced at the cryptids next to him, all prepared to defend themselves—and him. "Actually, you antiquated jerk, I'm happy with the side I'm on."

With a final menacing glare, Douglas revved the motor and the helicopter lifted up and away, disappearing into the night sky as Thomas waved a final goodbye.

XXI

Alex had his head turned around for so long that Clivo finally had to tap him on the shoulder. "Eyes on the road, please."

"Huh?" Alex turned, his eyes as wide as a pair of full moons.

Clivo pointed forward, gently reminding him that he was flying an airplane. "We're beginning to go into a bit of a nosedive."

"Oh! Yes, yes. Gotta focus. Have some very precious cargo back there. Very precious indeed." Alex righted the plane, but kept stealing glances behind himself and occasionally letting out a little giggle of joy. "I never thought I'd see it. Such a wonder!"

"Yeah, it's something special, isn't it?" Clivo turned around to look at the Otterman strapped into a seat behind them, its head bowed because of the airplane's low ceiling. The creature was purring while it happily munched on a chocolate bar.

Stephanie and Amelia sat next to the beast, going over

their maps of where the best place to drop it off would be. Amelia leaned forward. "Alex, I think the airport in Sitka would be the most remote place to drop off Otty. Don't you think?"

"Absolutely, absolutely," Alex said, stealing another glance behind him. "That's right around where the most sightings of the beast—excuse me—of *Otty* occurred before it disappeared."

"And it seems like there should be plenty of sea otters around, so Otty won't be lonely there," Stephanie said, gently stroking the Otterman's hand.

The beast let out a little roar of delight and took another bite of its chocolate bar.

Clivo swiveled his head around. "How do you think the others are doing?"

Amelia let out a laugh. "Adam was pestering the Honey Island Swamp Monster so much that I bet it's already wrapped him up again in those ropes of sticky boogers it emits from its nostrils."

"Yeah, we probably shouldn't give those guys the tatzelwurm to take back home," Stephanie said. "One poke from Charles and they'd be unconscious for a week again."

"It would serve them right." Amelia sniffed. "It's not the cryptids' job to show people their special powers. The boys need to leave them in peace."

"Although the gunni slime was pretty neat," Stephanie said with a laugh.

"It was," Amelia added, also laughing.

Alex shook his head. "You kids have certainly been on some adventure, haven't you?"

Clivo didn't even need to think about his response. "Yes, we definitely have."

After Douglas and the Luxembourgers had fled, Clivo called Mrs. Cooper from the dungeon and asked her to please untie Mr. Cooper and come help them. Mr. and Mrs. Cooper had been so busy making sure that Jerry and the Blasters (all of whom stayed unconscious for the next few days) were okay that they barely noticed the room full of legendary creatures. The same could not be said for Aunt Pearl, however, who had hidden in a corner and let out a little panicked squeal anytime a creature came close to her. She was finally calmed down by the blue tiger, which curled up at her feet and let her scratch it behind the ears. Dayea simply walked around the room cheerfully saying hello to every cryptid, finally meeting creatures like herself for the first time.

"Thanks for helping us return the cryptids to their homes, Alex. I'm really sorry I can't pay you," Clivo said.

Alex swung his head around from staring at the Otter-man. "Pay me? Nonsense. There's no greater payment than to be of service to others." Alex let out another chortle of disbelief. "And seeing that these legends are real and well cared for by you kids has made me rich beyond my wildest dreams."

"And I'm sure I don't have to tell you how important it is that you keep it a secret that these creatures are real. Not everyone wants to make sure they're well cared for. We're kind of a minority in that department," Clivo said.

Alex quit laughing and looked at Clivo earnestly. "The world needs its mysteries, Clivo, like I've always told you. And you won't catch me spoiling that." Otty reached forward to offer Alex some of its chocolate, sending Alex into a fresh round of giggles. "Although I am certainly honored that you let me in on the secret. Honored indeed. It's a secret I'll keep in my heart forever."

"Thanks, Alex, I knew we could count on you," Clivo said, twisting in his seat so he could pat Otty's furry hand. "With all the bad guys out there, we've realized that we need to bring more good guys onto our team."

A high-pitched voice squeaked way in the back: "Count me in on that, too, Mr. Wren! I'm one of the good guys!" Serge said.

Amelia looked behind her. "You are indeed, Serge, and we're so grateful."

"Definitely," Stephanie added. "There's no way we could have snuck Otty through the airport without your help."

"Anytime, you guys. We'll get the rest of the folks home safely, too!" Serge said.

Clivo leaned back in his seat, and for the first time in a while took in a long breath of relaxation as Alex flew their plane through the clouds toward Alaska. The evil resistance was still out there, but the good-guy numbers were growing.

Two weeks later, after all the cryptids were back in their proper homes, Clivo was sitting in the Coopers' living room with Dayea. Everyone else had gone to bed exhausted, still with so many questions. Clivo and Pearl had to find a new place to live where Douglas couldn't find them, as well as figure out how to keep Dayea hidden on every full moon. They also had to decide how to keep searching for the immortal with no money and with the Blasters heading back east because school would be starting soon. So many questions, and no easy answers. But for the moment, everything was calm and Clivo was enjoying a nice talk with Dayea, who sipped steaming ginger tea from a mug.

"Dayea, do you know anything about the Lost Prophecies of Nostradamus?" Clivo asked as he chewed on a moist chocolate brownie.

Dayea let out a laugh. "Nostradamus? He was always such a funny fellow."

Clivo practically dropped his brownie. "You *knew* Nostradamus?"

"Oh, sure," Dayea said, taking a sip of her drink. "Went to him when he was a doctor in France, as I had the sniffles. Became friends and drank tea together. He loved his prophecies! What is this one, honey?"

Clivo didn't even have to think about what the prophecy said; he had memorized it word for word long before. "All creatures, one blood. Some remain hidden, others come fore. In one who is hidden, the blood is gone, replaced by the spring of life. A silver lightning drop of eternity."

Dayea thought for a moment, then nodded. "That is a good one! I'm glad he cannot hear me say that, though! Nostradamus always had a very big ego. Nice man, but so pompous!"

"It is a good prophecy," Clivo agreed as the picture of Dayea hanging out with Nostradamus threatened to make his head explode. "I just wish we could find the immortal."

"How do you know it is not found already?" Dayea asked as she rocked back and forth in her chair.

Clivo paused with the brownie halfway to his mouth. "Well, if someone had already found the immortal, I'm sure the whole world would have heard about it by now."

"Why, honey?" Dayea asked. "If you found it, you would not do that."

"Yeah, but I'm one of the good guys. One of the few."

"Really?" Dayea asked with a twinkle in her eye. "I have lived for long time, honey, and there are a lot more kind people than nasty people. Buckets more."

Clivo thought about that. "But, I don't understand, you said living this long has been lonely. I thought that meant you didn't have any friends."

Dayea waved dismissively. "Oh, Dayea has had lots of

friends! Always! People in every century were so nice. Of course, they get scared when I eat a whole cow at the full moon. But otherwise people are very sweet to me, like you! I get lonely because I outlive everybody. Life gets very sad when you are always saying goodbye."

Clivo put down the brownie and wiped his hands on a napkin, his mind whirling with fresh possibilities. "So, you really think it's possible someone has already found the immortal and is protecting it, the way I would?"

"Very possible," Dayea said with a sip of her tea. "You are a wonderful person, honey, but you are not the only wonderful person on the planet."

"You know, Dayea, I think you're right," Clivo said, staring off into the distance as a new world opened up to him. His mind a million miles away, he stood and began walking to his room.

"Where are you going, honey?" Dayea asked.

Clivo turned around. "I'm not supposed to go anywhere by myself, but it'll be faster this way. When the others ask about me, please tell them I'll be back soon and make sure they know that I won't be alone on this quest."

"Who are you going to be with?" Dayea asked.

Clivo smiled. "The other good guys."

It took Clivo a few days to get back to Egypt. Alex had talked a fellow pilot into letting Clivo hitch a ride to Israel on her cargo jet, but from there he got stuck. He couldn't enter Egypt directly because his passport was on the "Do Not Enter" list, thanks to Tim and the Wasi, so he had to figure out another way to get into the country.

He had planned to simply walk across the border, as one can do across state lines in America. Unfortunately, he soon discovered that the border between Israel and Egypt was secured by a concrete wall topped with barbed wire. A wall that Clivo was now staring at in frustration.

He sat on a sandy hill eyeing the guard towers and security cameras that kept watch on the wall. The morning air was relatively cool, which he was grateful for since he was wearing appropriate clothing for the area that included long pants and a shirt. But he knew from his time in the desert that once the sun was high in the sky, it was going to be a scorcher.

Clivo scanned the wall that stretched for miles in either direction and grunted. He wasn't sure if the barrier was meant to keep people in or out, but either way, getting to Egypt seemed impossible. He had come so far in his quest to protect the world from the evil resistance only to be stopped, quite literally, by a wall.

"If you're thinking of climbing it, don't bother. It's electric and will light you up like a firecracker," a voice said behind him.

Clivo whirled around to face a red-haired man with light brown freckles across his nose. The man was casually chewing on what looked like a soda straw that should have been recycled ages ago.

"Sorry, I didn't hear you," Clivo said, quickly scanning the man to see if he was holding any weapons or seemed ready to attack. He knew the tracking chip in him shouldn't be working anymore, but still, it never hurt to be on guard for the evil resistance.

"You didn't hear me because I'm The Sneaker," the man said, gesturing to himself.

Clivo tilted his head. "You mean like the tennis shoe?"

The man had to think about that for a moment before blurting out, "No! Not like the tennis shoe! Like a spy! You know, who sneaks around quietly so people don't hear him!"

"Oh right, sorry," Clivo said, rubbing his eyes. "I'm kind of jet-lagged and not really thinking straight right now. And you startled me, too, so there's that."

The man gestured to himself again. "Because I'm The Sneaker."

"Right," Clivo said, looking around to see if there were any more Sneakers sneaking about. "So, um, can I ask why you snuck up on me?"

The man pulled the straw from his mouth and pointed toward the wall. "The only people who come here and stare longingly at that wall are people who are desperate to be on the other side of it."

Clivo kept his mouth shut. He still didn't know who this

"Sneaker" was or what he wanted. Clivo had been attacked one too many times to trust anybody the first time he met them.

The Sneaker continued, "No response, huh? You're a man who keeps his secrets. I can respect that. But if you need to get on the other side of that wall, I know someone who can help."

"You do?" Clivo asked. "That'd be amazing. Who?"

Once again, the man gestured to himself with a sweep of his arm. "That would be me. Name's Gideon."

"I guess your name isn't something you keep secret?" Clivo replied.

Gideon dropped his head forward with a sigh. "Shoot. I always do that." He rummaged in his back pocket and pulled out a small pad of paper and a pencil and muttered to himself while writing. "'Don't tell people your name while in spy mode.'"

"You're keeping notes?" Clivo asked.

Gideon shook the pad of paper in Clivo's face. "Of course! How else am I to learn from my mistakes?" He pocketed the pad and pencil, then smoothed his hair. "Okay then, as I was saying, I'm the local Sneaker and I can get you across that border."

"How?" Clivo asked.

"Easy," Gideon said, putting the straw back in his mouth. "With my camel."

Clivo glanced behind Gideon, but all he saw was an old tan Toyota pickup truck. "I don't see any camels."

Gideon smiled at him mischievously. "Exactly. I call my truck my camel. It's a code word."

"I see. Very sneaky," Clivo replied. "So, can you get me across and maybe drive me to Naqada?"

"Getting across is easy. As I mentioned, I'm a Sneaker. And my brother is a border guard, so he'll just wave me across 'cause he owes me a favor. But getting to Naqada will cost you. That's a good two-day drive."

Clivo dug into his wallet and pulled out his remaining petty cash. "I can give you five hundred dollars?"

Gideon chewed on his straw. "That's almost two thousand shekels. Not a good price, but not a bad one. Why do you need to get to Naqada?"

Clivo shrugged. "I'd prefer not to say, if that's okay with you."

"Wow. You're really good at keeping secrets," Gideon said, obviously impressed.

"Yeah, I've kinda had a lot of practice."

Gideon motioned for Clivo to follow him to the truck. "Well, it's a long drive. Maybe you can give me some pointers on how you do your secret keeping."

Clivo walked beside him, a spring in his step now that he was on his way again. He was so close to the end of his quest he could feel it. "You mean besides simply not saying them out loud?"

Gideon stopped and pulled out his pad and paper again, making a note. "I like that solution. Not too hard to remember, either." Gideon pocketed the pad and pencil. "Okay, Keeper of Secrets, time for The Sneaker to deliver you to your destination."

*　*　*

The next day, Clivo was finally standing in the ruined city where he had first seen the Salawa. It was nighttime, and the moon was just peeking out from behind some hazy clouds. The air was humid and the sand still held the heat of the day.

Clivo put down his backpack and softly called for the beast. He knelt down and whispered words in Arabic, holding his hand out in a welcoming gesture. Calling a cryptid shouldn't be so easy, but he was hoping the Salawa might recognize him from his previous visit. The Salawa seemed like a curious creature that was comfortable around humans, as evidenced by its interaction with the Wasi.

Clivo had waited patiently for almost an hour, jumping at every shift in the shadows, when the Salawa suddenly peeked around a crumbled mud-brick wall, its long snout sniffing the air. Its black eyes fell on Clivo and flashed recognition.

"There you are," Clivo whispered in Arabic. "Come. I won't hurt you."

The creature hesitated, walking toward him and then back a couple of times before finally approaching and sitting back on its haunches. It looked up at Clivo with the saddest puppy-dog eyes, as if desperately searching for a moment of connection and kindness.

Clivo stroked the creature's head with one hand and slowly pulled the blood sampler from his backpack with the other. In one smooth motion, he gently pierced the Salawa's skin and quickly rubbed it. The beast shied away for a moment, but then settled down for more petting.

This time, Clivo didn't have to wait for the blood sampler to give him an answer. He could clearly see in the moonlight that the blood traveling up the chamber was silver. It was merely a formality when the sampler finally blinked IMMORTAL.

Clivo had barely a moment to process his feelings of relief, joy, and fear at being so close to something so powerful when a foot scraped on the sand behind him. Clivo shot his hands over his head, the blood sampler dropping forgotten into his backpack.

"Before you kill me, I have something to show you," Clivo said as quickly as possible.

"You were warned never to come back here, Clivo," Tim's familiar voice said from behind him.

Clivo slowly stood up and turned, his arms still held up, to find Tim's sword pointed menacingly at his throat. "Well, you kinda lied to me, which is super rude, FYI, so I had to come back."

Tim's eyes flicked to the Salawa, which was sitting comfortably at Clivo's feet. "I didn't lie to you. Salawa, *tati*!"

"Uh, yeah, you pretty much did. *Albaqa'*, Salawa," Clivo replied. The Salawa looked back and forth between Clivo and Tim, but ultimately decided to stay by Clivo. "See, you promised that the vial of blood I took was the Salawa's blood, when obviously it wasn't."

Tim smiled, though his eyes kept darting to the beast at Clivo's feet. "If I remember correctly, I told you it was the blood of the beast. I never said it was the blood of the Salawa."

"So whose blood was it?" Clivo asked, grateful that Tim was giving him time to talk before running at him with the sword.

Tim smiled more broadly. "Mine. I am quite a beast, wouldn't you say?" Tim's face dropped and his eyes narrowed. "So you see, my persistent American, I did not lie to you. But you have disregarded my warning about staying away from this place, which means I obviously haven't been firm enough in my request."

Tim tightened his grip on the sword and the Salawa let out a little whine. Clivo dropped his arms and motioned to his backpack. "Hang on! Please, just let me show you one thing. I really think you'll want to see this."

"Make no mistake, Clivo, this will be the last request I shall grant you. Then prepare yourself for death."

"Okay, that's really ominous, but I don't think you'll want to kill me after this." Clivo slowly reached into his backpack with one hand and pulled out a thin photo album. He opened it up and held it so Tim could see the photos.

With each passing page, Tim's eyes got wider and wider, his mouth repeatedly opening as if to ask a question and then snapping shut again. When they reached the end of the album, Tim whispered, "I . . . I don't understand."

Clivo flipped back to the front of the photo album,

which had pictures of Douglas's underground lair with the cryptids wandering around, freed from their cages. "This is where someone from the evil resistance was holding a bunch of cryptids." Clivo pointed to a photo of the Ugly Merman back near its river in Russia, its long tongue giving Clivo's cheek a lick goodbye. "That's the Ugly Merman after I returned it to its home. Same with the tatzelwurm, the chupacabra, the Otterman, and all the others."

Tim lowered his sword and stared more closely at the Otterman's photo. "Is it eating *chocolate*?"

Clivo laughed. "It is. It loves it, particularly if it has peanuts in it." He handed the album to Tim so he could turn the pages himself.

"Extraordinary," Tim said quietly, his eyes darting in awe from photo to photo. "Who's that?"

Clivo looked at the photo Tim was indicating, one of Dayea holding her belly and laughing hysterically as Aunt Pearl pointed to her during one of their daily salsa dancing lessons. "That's the aswang."

"The aswang?" Tim asked with a guffaw. "She looks harmless!"

"She does, but during the full moon she turns into a very impressive monster bat, trust me."

"Just incredible," Tim said, his eyes soaking up the rest of the pictures.

Clivo pointed to a group photo of the Blasters with Jerry and Clivo on either side. Everyone was smiling and some were punching their fists in the air in celebration after the last cryptid had been returned home. It was one of Clivo's favorite photos, save for the fact that Adam was ripping his shirt in two like the Hulk. "And this is my team. We've been working together on a very important mission."

"And what is that mission?" Tim asked. He whistled and the Salawa finally came and sat by him. Still brandishing his sword, Tim moved between Clivo and the beast.

"To keep the immortal's identity a secret," Clivo said pointedly, nodding at the Salawa. "You know it's the immortal; that's why you protect it so fiercely. But if that blood I took really was *your* blood, then you haven't used the gift on yourself, which is really cool."

Tim eyed Clivo for a long moment, as if unsure how much information to divulge. Finally he spoke, though he did not lower his sword. "My people discovered the immortal three hundred years ago. One man took the gift of everlasting life for himself before the community could decide what to do with the Salawa. Immediately he turned into a tyrant, stealing lands and riches to create a kingdom all for himself. Our people discovered very quickly that it is better to believe in gods than to try and become them."

"Someone used the blood to turn themselves immortal?" Clivo asked incredulously. "Where is that person now?"

Tim shrugged. "Who knows. My people rose up against him and banished him from this place. He may be immortal, but he still has the human desire to be loved, so the greatest punishment we could hand down was to strip him of his friends, family, and home. His need for ultimate power left him ultimately and completely alone. One legend says that he fled to Paris, where he sat for ages on a bench with his hand outstretched as if begging for friendship. He waited for something that would replace his lost family for so long that he eventually became a statue. But nobody knows for sure. As long as he isn't trying to take over the world, the Wasi leave him be." Tim tilted his head. "Is this what you and your team desire? The gift of the eternal?"

Clivo shook his head. "Not at all. That's why I showed you those pictures. So you'd see that we want to protect the cryptids, the immortal *and* the mortal ones. But the evil resistance is growing and they'll keep searching for the immortal, and someday you might need our help."

Tim laughed. "*Your* help? You're a child."

Clivo raised a finger. "I'm a teenager, and the last time we fought it wasn't me who ended up tied to a pillar all night." Tim glared at Clivo, so Clivo quickly continued. "I know you said that we come from different worlds, so we could never work together. And I used to think that, too. This whole time I thought that I would be the one to protect the immortal. But you're already doing that, and really well, too. But I've discovered that I'm much stronger when I have people helping me. People I trust. So I've come all this way again to ask you . . . Can we be part of your team?"

Tim finally lowered his sword and his eyes took on a

faraway look, as if calling up a memory. "Many years ago, a man passed through here looking for the Salawa. He pretended to be an archaeologist, but from the questions he asked, we knew immediately that he was searching for something more. At first we were going to scare him and then fight him if necessary. But there was something different about him. He spoke reverently about myth and legend and the importance of keeping mystery alive. He also spoke about his son, about how much he wanted to protect him, but feared he couldn't with all the evil in the world." Tim turned his eyes to Clivo. "We told the man a story that the Salawa could be found many miles away from here and sent him on his way. But before he left, I gave him an Egyptian rattle to shake over his son to protect him from the god of storms."

Clivo's throat was so tight he could barely speak. He pictured his mom passing the rattle over him every night to shroud him in safety. "I think you met my dad. He's gone now—the evil resistance killed him—but he was a good person."

Tim nodded. "I know this to be true." Tim sighed and looked at the Salawa, whose tongue lolled out of its mouth before it gave a happy bark. "It seems as though fate keeps bringing me back to you. The Wasi do things alone, we always have, but perhaps you are right. Perhaps it is time for us to band together. No matter how many are in this evil resistance, they will never outnumber the righteous."

Clivo smiled and held out his hand. "Teammates, then?"

Tim stared off into the desert, as if he was searching for a deeper wisdom to guide him. The moonlight bounced off his dark eyes. Finally, he grabbed Clivo's hand in a firm grip. "Better than that—friends." Tim suddenly pulled Clivo close and spoke directly in his face. "But the Salawa stays here."

Clivo nodded his head fervently. "Believe me, if anyone should be protecting the immortal, it's you. Honestly, I don't think I could handle the stress."

Tim eyed Clivo for a moment longer, then clapped him on the shoulder. "Good. I'm glad that as friends, we are in agreement on this."

Clivo looked at the sand and kicked a pebble with his foot. "As friends, any chance you could fly me back home? I kinda spent all my money on a truck ride across the border to get here."

Tim laughed and put his arm around Clivo's shoulder, leading him toward the village, the Salawa happily trotting behind them. "I was wondering how you got around our passport check! Come, let's drink tea together to seal the alliance between the Wasi and the children."

"We're teenagers," Clivo corrected. "And we're determined to save the world."

Epilogue

Mr. Cooper stood in front of a steel door that looked strong enough to withstand a missile. He peered into a small scanner that ran a laser up and down his eye, pressed his thumb against a digital reader, and spoke a few words into a tiny microphone.

"I hate banjos."

The combination of Mr. Cooper's eye and fingerprint scans along with voice recognition did the trick, and the sounds of sliding locks suddenly echoed up and down the long, dimly lit hallway. The massive door swung open, revealing a vast underground warehouse carved into the bedrock.

The room was at least as big as a football field, and filled with rows of stacked boxes and crates that stretched into the darkness. Bare lightbulbs hung from the high ceiling, and the place smelled like damp earth.

"All right, kids, welcome to Thunderdome," Mr. Cooper chuckled.

Clivo, Jerry, and the Blasters walked into the enormous room, taking in everything.

"What's kept in here, Mr. Cooper?" Stephanie asked, running her finger along a crate stamped with the words METEOR WITH ALIEN FOSSIL.

"A lot of secrets from space, that's what," Mr. Cooper said, leading them through a maze of crates that were stacked high overhead.

"I love space secrets!" Charles said, punching his fist in the air.

Adam raised his hand in a question. "Like what? The bodies of aliens you've dissected over the years?"

Mr. Cooper chuckled. "We don't dissect aliens, Adam. As I told you, we've found four actual aliens after they crash-landed on Earth. We got them up and going as soon as possible by repairing their spacecraft."

A loud thud sounded behind everyone, and they all turned to see Hernando picking himself up off the floor. "Apologies. The thought of seeing an alien made me swoon."

"So, if aliens aren't in the boxes, what is?" Amelia asked.

Mr. Cooper pushed his glasses up his nose. "A lot of it is space junk that comes through our atmosphere. Although it's not *junk* junk—it's parts of alien spacecraft that have floated around and found their way to our planet. We need to keep them a secret because if people knew how many UFOs are floating near us—and I mean close—there'd be quite the little freak-out."

"Is that all? Alien space junk?" Clivo asked.

"Oh, there's some other stuff here, too," Mr. Cooper

said, eyeing Clivo sideways, as if wondering how much he should share. "We keep things here for other people who find earthbound treasures that are best kept secret."

"Like what?" Charles asked, pushing forward so he was walking in step with Mr. Cooper.

"Now, that, I can't tell you, 'cause those are other people's secrets," Mr. Cooper said with a wink. "Just as I won't tell anybody else what secret you're storing here."

"Is there anything dangerous in here, Pops?" Jerry asked as he passed a crate that read DR. JONES—ARK—DO NOT PUT IN MUSEUM!

Mr. Cooper looked around the warehouse, his eyes taking on a faraway look. "Oh, yes. Dangerous stuff, wondrous stuff. Magical stuff that we don't quite know what to do with yet." He pointed to a closed box that Clivo was holding. "Much like you have there."

Clivo looked at the box. "Yeah, I can't believe I forgot about the blood sampler in my backpack. Good thing it wasn't confiscated at the airport, or our alliance with the Wasi would have been off to a very poor start."

"Totally," Adam snorted. "Speaking of which, I can't wait to have our first Skype meeting with them to mobilize our forces."

Amelia raised her hand. "And we still need to discuss bringing in everyone else, too, like the Oracles and even McConaughey."

Charles moaned. "McConaughey, too?"

Stephanie chuckled. "Yes, Charles, even McConaughey. We don't need to tell them everything about the immortal, but the more people we have with eyes on the evil resistance, and Douglas, the easier it will be to track them."

Charles shook his head. "It's a whole new world."

"I like this new world of togetherness," Hernando said softly.

They rounded another corner and Mr. Cooper stopped in front of a crate with a sideways 8 engraved on it. "Here you go. I had a little something carved on the box so you'll always know which one is yours."

"The infinity symbol," Stephanie said with a smile. "Very clever, Mr. Cooper."

Mr. Cooper opened the wooden crate's front, and inside was a small safe. "One by one, you kids step up and let it scan your eye and thumbprint, then say your magic words into this microphone here. Make sure you remember the words, because they'll be your pass code. The only way this safe can ever be opened again is if four of you are here and repeat the process. It's the best method I know of to keep your secret safe. The majority of you have to agree to open the safe again—no one of you can do it alone."

One by one, they stepped forward for their scan and said their words into the microphone.

"Coops, over and out," Jerry said.

"This is Hernando, thank you," Hernando said quietly.

"Yeti master," Charles said.

"Can't hack this," Stephanie said.

"Blasters forever," Amelia said.

"This is Adam Lowitzki, servant to none, master of my own destiny, king of many kingdoms."

Amelia rolled her eyes. "Are you sure you're going to remember that, Adam?"

"I say it to myself every morning in the mirror," Adam said with a nod. "I'll remember it."

Stephanie looked at Clivo, her blue eyes sparkling. "It's your turn, Clivo. Let's finish this."

Clivo stepped forward and put the sampler in the safe, the silver blood that could grant eternal life still floating in the chamber. He pulled the Egyptian rattle his mom had shaken over him to protect him from the god of storms from his back pocket and put it on one side of the box, and on the other he laid the beaded bracelet he wore to remind himself of his father.

He scanned his eye and thumbprint, then leaned into the microphone and said the words that felt right to him.

"Believe in the myth and the magic."

Acknowledgments

First and foremost, I'd like to thank you, lovely reader, for reading this book. Because perhaps that means you also read the first book, *The Cryptid Catcher*, and liked it enough to want to continue with this story, and that makes me so happy.

I'd really like to thank the teachers and librarians I've had the pleasure of corresponding with who are so passionate about getting books into the hands of kids. Namely, Jarrett Lerner and the folks at Nerd Camp and MG Book Village, and all the champions of literacy who belong to #BookExpedition, #BookOdyssey, #BookPosse, #BookExcursion, #BookVoyage, #BookTrek, and #Collabookation. Thank you so much for all you do.

Thank you to all my friends who have been so supportive of me on this journey. I was trying to thank you all by name, but I just knew I'd forget at least one of you, and that would haunt me. I don't like the term "you know who you are," but my friends really do know who they are. At least, I try to make sure they do, and you guys all make my life so rich and crazy and delicious, and I thank you.

This book was written during my dreamy month-long writing residency provided by Aspen Words and the Catto Shaw Foundation. Thank you to Isa, Daniel, Fiona, and Duncan for welcoming me to your incredible artist's retreat. And thank you to the ladies at Aspen Words—Caroline, Marie, Jamie, Nicole, and Adrienne—for being so amazing and taking me out hiking so I didn't turn into a statue at my writing desk.

To Mark, my sweetie. You kept me giggling by peering over my shoulder to see what I was writing about you. Our story has gone through many genres, and I look forward to many more years of eating your homemade pizza while planning our next sandwich. Love you.

As always, thank you to Mom, Wayne, Joel, and Papa, who are the most loving family I could hope for. And to my Auntie Zaiga: I hope you're having a wonderful adventure beyond the clouds. I miss you.

Thank you to Loren Coleman for his expert knowledge on all things cryptid and for re-launching the Junior Cryptozoologist Club through the International Cryptozoology Museum. And thank you to Kirsten Cappy and Curious City for all of your creative marketing ideas that are always out of this world. I flail my muppet arms in your direction!

To my agent, Jason Anthony, who was the only agent to respond to my query letter for what would become *The*

Cryptid Catcher. Success comes down to hard work and luck, and, boy, were you my luck.

Huge thanks to the magicians at FSG BYR and Macmillan Children's Publishing Group who continue to amaze me with their talents—including editorial staffers Wes Adams and Melissa Warten, copyeditor Nancy Elgin, designer Aimee Fleck, illustrator Lisa K. Weber, production manager Celeste Cass, and publicist Madison Furr.

And, of course, to Richard.

Hi Everyone!

Clivo Wren here! Well, we found the immortal, but we're not out of trouble yet! This is just the beginning of our work. The evil resistance is still out there and the cryptids are in more danger than ever. Not only do the Myth Blasters need help keeping their eye on what cranky Douglas and his minions are up to, but I need help traveling the world making sure the cryptids are safe. And maybe rescuing them if Douglas gets his grubby hands on any and throws them in cages again.

Do you want to help us? If so, are you a catcher or a blaster? Be sure to check out LijaFisher.com for information on how to keep joining us on our adventures to save the world! And remember to keep the secret of the immortal safe—because the world needs its myths and its magic!

Clivo Wren